The Hounds of Love

BELLE HENDERSON

Dear Reader
Enjoy!,
Love
Belle
x

Tamarillas Press

Cover photograph:
Design: © Canva
Copyright © Belle Henderson

ISBN: 978-1-913807-13-9

Dedication

Jamie, thank you for believing in me and supporting me as always. Love you x

Special thanks to my Mum, Dad, Sister, Auntie and best friend Kate for all you continued support and encouragement.

Karen and John, our dear dog friends. Thank you so much for looking after our very energetic puppy every Monday so that I could concentrate on writing this book. I hope she hasn't aged you too much.

And finally for Oreo, my sweet beagle puppy and my muse; who's kleptomaniac and mischievous ways have given me much inspiration.

Other books by Belle Henderson
Romantic Comedy

You Grow Girl

Not The Plus One

What's Eating Felicity Frost?

Livin' La Vida Lockdown

We can Work it out

Chapter 1

Amber

Almost forty, that's supposed to be fab, isn't it? I mean, I'm not doing too badly but I'm not too sure I'm feeling fabulous, more like exhausted and a tad on the frumpy side.

Yes, I'm doing just fine, sort of.

'Careful, Sofia, you'll look like a drowned rat by the time we get to school,' I say to my daughter, as we try to dodge puddles from the overnight downpour. I miss one and the bottom of my trousers soak up the water and weigh my legs down, mimicking my heavy mood. I sigh; not much longer to go, soon the school runs will be over for a little while and then we can have a well-deserved break.

A break from all the bullshit.

'Mummy, is it nearly Christmas yet?' Sofia asks as I grab her arm to stop her from stepping in a puddle the size of a small swimming pool.

'Not yet, sweetie, but soon,' I answer, then gently tap my finger on the end of her cute, cold little button nose. 'Just a couple more weeks, then Rudolph the red-nosed reindeer will be dragging Santa through the skies to deliver those well-deserved presents. Christmas will be here before you know it, I promise.' I grin, feeling slightly more cheerful for the Christmas festivities. My stomach even rumbles at the thought of the Christmas cake I've been making for months. Good Lord I'm going to demolish that thing and enjoy every single bite.

'It's Rhubarb the red nosed reindeer, not Rudolph,' she squawks, and I don't correct her, it's too bloody cute that she still thinks this. 'Mummy, Mia said her mummy told her that Santa isn't real and that other mummies and daddies don't tell the truth.' She screws her face up and looks up at me, searching my face for an answer. Shit, this is exactly the bullshit I mean. Who does Jayne think she is? She can destroy it for her own child but not mine. I'll be having a little word in her ear when the bell goes this morning.

Bloody busybody Jayne.

'Oh dear, that's very sad for Mia, of course he's real. Who eats the carrots and the mince pies you leave out every year? You've got to believe in the magic if you want it to happen remember.'

Sofia smiles and nods, seemingly satisfied with my answer, for now. Phew, looks like I got away with that one. Five is too young to destroy the magic, Christ, I'm sure I was about ten before I stopped believing, maybe even older. When did people start telling five-year-olds that Santa isn't real? Is that a thing now, or just a Jayne thing?

Speak of the devil, Jayne, aka the Christmas destroyer herself makes a beeline for us as we arrive at the school gates.

'Oh, hiiii, Sofia, wow you look pretty today, mummy must have spent ages on your hair,' Jayne, the alpha mum, comments as she hangs on the word hair. My attempts to sneak past her have failed again. She's chatting to two other mums who nod in agreement as they stand huddled together in the chilly, December air. All three study my daughter's red pleated Dutch plaits that sit perfectly underneath her pink fluffy earmuffs. They do look good but it feels like a passive aggressive dig from Jayne.

'No, not really, I used to be a hair dresser so it takes me no time at all.' I smile back at them but Jayne doesn't look at me, instead she continues to talk to my daughter.

'Oh, no way, really? My Mia desperately needs her hair cutting, does your mummy still do hairdressing? School mum mate's rates and all that?' She laughs and her mum mates nod along with her, each one of them studying my child as Sofia looks a bit uncomfortable under their gaze. I try to time the school drop off so we avoid Jayne and her gang but sometimes it's not possible. She appears to have a sixth sense for me. And, she is most definitely not my mate.

'No, I don't do that anymore I'm afraid, sorry.'

'Not a problem, it's probably been a while though hasn't it, maybe out of practice?' Jayne slowly moves her fingers in a scissor like motion as she gazes upwards and stares intensely at me. I can't help but think that she's inwardly cutting my face up. 'Not having to work, alright for some isn't it,' she continues, speaking more to her friends than to me but she's still snipping.

Just humour her. I smile and nod as Jayne starts to show off to her mates about her latest purchases. She's dressed like she's about to go to a gym class, her perfect figure filling out the *TikTok* bum lifting leggings just beautifully. I only know they're off *TikTok* because my friend Stella told me, I don't really do social media. Stella also told me that Jayne works part time in a care home.

We did laugh a bit that she cleans up shit for a living but then we felt awful for the old people that she supposedly cares for. I wouldn't want her looking after me when I'm old. I'd be constantly watching my back, paranoid that she'd be poisoning my tea or something.

'Have you got Sofia's outfit yet for the school nativity play? Trust Mia to get the main part, she's such a show off, aren't you, Mia? What part did you get Sofia?' Jayne strokes her daughter's hair as if she's her little show dog before Mia bats her off and runs away to go and play with another kid at the school playpark. Sofia sees her chance to escape and runs after her. That's my girl.

'She's the donkey,' I reply, giving a little shrug and a smile. Being a donkey is absolutely nothing to be ashamed of.

'Oh, so funny,' Jayne says, with a swish of her bouncy brown hair. 'Mia would absolutely hate playing a sad old donkey, so pleased that she got the part of Mary, I've bought this beautiful dress from Next and shoes to match. I mean, what would you even wear for a donkey?'

'Yeah, well Sofia's not fussed. She's more into her art, very talented.' Oh no she made me do it. I hate how she makes me behave. I will not get into a pissing contest about my child.

I will not.

'Oh really? Mia's amazing at art too, a bit of an all-rounder is our Mia. She's had her work published in many a children's magazine. I have her latest piece framed above the fire place at home.'

'That's amazing.'

'I know, it is, isn't it? Anyway I was going to ask if you had seen my latest message in the school mums' chat group…' Jayne's face falls from smug to annoyed as my friend Stella appears. They don't get on, mainly because

Stella doesn't buy into her bragging. I'm grateful that I don't have to get into talks about the school mums' chat group because quite frankly I can't keep up with it all. Once, I didn't check it for two days and there were over 80 messages about school dinners, so I mainly remain silent now and scan for anything important or rely on Stella to filter it and tell me the important stuff.

'Alright my lovely, wow it's so cold ladies. My nips are so hard they'd cut glass right now.' Stella, who's wearing baggy shorts in winter, rubs her hands together then winks as the other women giggle, apart from Jayne who just purses her lips.

'Go on then, Badger, go off and play, you've got two minutes before school starts so make the most of it.'

Badger doesn't have to be asked twice and proceeds to race off towards the other children, tumbling into Sofia who screeches rather dramatically then jumps up and down when she sees who it is.

'Badgerrrrrrr. Don't be such a lump!' Stella yells after him.

Jayne gasps in horror and looks at the other mums for approval.

'You shouldn't call children lumps, it will mess with his body image in later life, causing anxiety and quite probably depression.'

'Oh, is that right, Jayne? Full of wisdom this one, ain't she? Have you got a degree in psychology or summat?' Stella points her thumb to Jayne who shakes her head disapprovingly. The other mums, including me, giggle.

'How's Tamsin?' I ask Stella, as Jayne moves out of earshot and gathers the other women around her for a bitch, probably about me and Stella.

'Yeah, she's alright, bit up and down you know, as expected.' Stella smiles but I can see the pain in her eyes.

Badger is Stella's child, real name Ben. They call him Badger, mainly because he's always badgering them. I think it's funny but some people don't, mainly Jayne. Stella's partner Tamsin also has a child but she recently lost custody of her to the dad so now she is only seeing her once a fortnight. To say they are heartbroken is an understatement.

'Okay, well send her my love.'

'I will, thanks.'

'Be good to catch up with you soon, we could do dinner if you like?' I suggest.

'Sounds great, but let's do it at your palace.' Stella pulls a face.' My place is a bit shabby for the likes of Prince Filipe.'

'Oh behave, he's fine! He won't judge.'

'Yeah, I know, but be good to get Tamsin out the house if she's feeling up to it, I'll get a baby sitter for Badger boy but bring the Pudding, if that's alright?' Pudding is Stella's dog and a beagle like my Olive. She hates the sound of humans sneezing but loves their food more than his own.

'Absolutely, Olive loves her.' Stella and I bonded over our love of dogs when we took them to school on the first day and both got reprimanded for bringing them onto school grounds. We might have even got away with it if the dogs had been quiet but they were far from well behaved. Pudding managed to steal my handbag when I placed it on the ground. Whilst Stella unsuccessfully tried to wrestle it off her, Pudding slipped her harness and ran off scoffing a packet of my ginger biscuits. Meanwhile Olive, my dog, tried desperately to chase after her, barking at the top of her lungs whilst pulling my shoulder out of its socket. The headteacher looked on in horror but eventually saw the funny side when she realised that no-one was hurt or upset but she made it very clear.

No dogs allowed.

Stella and I went for a walk afterwards with the hounds and also found out that neither of us work as we both have other halves with very demanding, well-paid careers. Lucky us. The rest, as they say is history. Our bond has strengthened since we discovered that we share a passionate dislike for Jayne. I've only known Stella since Sofia started school this year but I feel like we've been friends for years. She's jolly, caring and a good mum. Everyone loves her.

The bell rings and we send the kids into school before we part ways for our Monday routine. I scan the playground for Jayne then sigh as I see her too far off in the distance to catch up with. I'll speak to her before the holidays are up, although I'm not quite sure what I'll say yet. *Oi Jayne, don't tell your child to tell my child that Santa isn't real, alright?* Maybe not. I'll have to think about that one.

So now it's back to the usual Monday morning slog, I hope this week hurries up. Friday is my favourite day of the week. I work so hard cleaning, sorting the house and meal prepping during the rest of the week that I can afford to take a few hours for me on a Friday. I wasn't much of a cook when I met my husband Filipe but now, I'm confident I could give Nigella Lawson a run for her money any day. Filipe has high standards and I appreciate that. He keeps me on my toes but I must admit, it can be extremely exhausting and lonely. Men like Filipe just don't understand the work that goes into keeping a home, especially to the level he expects. There are meals to make and he likes everything cooked from scratch, constant cleaning and tidying to be done, beds to be made and let's not forget the incessant DIY and house admin that never ends. Yes, I really do, do it all.

Usually, Stella and I grab a coffee or walk the dogs but this Friday I'll be going shopping for a dress for my fortieth which is looming. I'm quite excited about dressing up for once, it's not often I get to do that. I don't know what Filipe has planned but I hope, no I'm sure, that it will be something wonderful.

Chapter 2

Delilah

'Dylan, I'm off out now!'

'Okay Dee, have fun and don't be too late.' Dylan, my brother, pushes his glasses down to the end of his nose. He only ever does this to show me he's being serious and he means business. Serious lecture, big older brother business. It's weird having him home, weird but also strangely comforting.

'I won't, but remember I'm twenty-one so I'm very much an adult,' I sing, to lighten the mood before giving him the finger as he does the same back then gives me side eye. 'Please don't wait up for me.'

'I can't make any promises,' he says, flicking through the television channels, not looking at me.

'Dylan, I can look after myself.'

'I know, but you're my baby sister and it's a big bad world out there.'

'Oh, please, I'll be fine, stuff doesn't happen like that in Coolsbay,' I say motioning to the TV where there's a sombre murder documentary playing in the background. I count in my head, the new calming technique that

Dylan has taught me. One, two, three, four, five, six. I hope I don't get to number thirteen, that number is a bad omen, in more ways than one for me. No. Stuff like that doesn't happen in Coolsbay. You'll be fine. Calm down. Practice your breathing. 'Shitsticks, you've made me feel a bit nervous now. It's already dark and I'm on my own.'

'Sorry, I didn't mean to scare you, I'm just being realistic. There are psychos everywhere, Dee.' He picks up the remote to turn the TV over for the forty-seventh time, before deciding on another murder documentary about Fred and Rosemary West. I don't know why he just doesn't use catch up, he's so old school sometimes. Mum and Dad are out tonight so he makes the most of the channel hopping and the gruesome programmes that they don't normally like to have on. I said he really needs to get a TV of his own or reclaim back some of his stuff from his soon to be ex-wife. Yeah, that's why he's back home, she left him. It's both weird and nice having him home, we've never actually lived together before. Because of the huge age gap between us, I was still a baby when he moved out.

'Looks like you need to cut down on the murder programmes. I think you might be low-key paranoid and it doesn't really go with the meditating and mindfulness that you're so keen to teach me.'

'I can be more than one thing and I'm high-keyed paranoid if you must know. Anyway, you introduced me to these gruesome programmes so I'm holding you responsible for me being a neurotic brother,' he says, before breaking out into a song. Something about there being a lot of bad everywhere and how it's a wild world. He's right, I did introduce him to them but I don't think it's good for my soul and heart rate to watch them anymore.

I act out holding a pretend gun to my head and shoot it three times, dancing dramatically to my death. Dylan laughs then holds his heart like it's breaking then, as if by a miracle, I come back to life, leaping and twirling all over the living room. Dylan kicks off his slippers, gets up and plods about trying to dance beside me, resembling some sort of slightly aging superman. For a moment, we're consumed in our odd sister/brother dance, his fear and my desire for freedom encapsulated in our strange family performance that we never got to do as kids as he was too old. Then, Dylan stumbles over the tv remote and trips over his feet.

'You literally have no grace,' I laugh, as I gather my things and get ready to leave. He also has no fashion sense, but I keep that to myself as I don't want to upset him. Since coming back home all I've seen him in is dark blue or black, probably to match his current mood. Dylan jumps up and points his toes, pretending his fall was all part of the act.

'Nope, not like you. Heard from that audition yet?'

Upon leaving dance school, my desire to dance has dried up; I just don't see the point anymore after being rejected so many times. The fear I get from auditioning is kind of starting to outweigh the happiness I get from dancing.

'No, not heard from them yet.' I shrug and he gets the hint not to probe further.

'Bye sis, have fun,' he continues, as he reaches down to get the remote. 'Oh, and Dee,'

'Yes?'

'Wear a coat, it's freezing out there, don't forget your pepper spray and don't be too late.' He slumps back down in his chair and I give him the thumbs up before closing the living room door. He's half joking about the pepper spray. I palmed him off with a mini can of fake tan as I know pepper spray isn't legal and I'm also not a freak who would carry that around, he's also given me a pen knife which could come in handy for other stuff, like if I was ever left stranded out in the wild and had to fend for myself. I could kill wild deer for food or something.

Or maybe not.

He's very protective of me, his baby sister. Dylan is almost twenty years older than me, my middle brother Ian, is almost fifteen years older and all I remember about Ian being home is that he was a dick to my parents. He still is, some things never change.

'Bye, see you later,' I say as I close the door, behind me. Being at dance school in a big city, I got used to the independence and the fun of living with people my own age. I did miss my creature comforts though and of course mum's cooking. It is nice to be back in Coolsbay though, and for purely selfish reasons I'm glad Dylan is home too, but sometimes it is a bit like having two dads.

They both want a say in my life.

Chapter 3

Amber

Filipe came home from work and suggested I go shopping for a dress this evening. The shops are open much later than usual as it's nearing Christmas. I quickly hid the piles of clean washing I was supposed to put away in the cupboard or he may have changed his mind. I'll do that tomorrow. Shopping will cheer me up and hopefully help me come to terms with the fact that I'm turning forty, imminently.

Urgh.

I'll probably fit in some Christmas shopping too, kill two birds with one stone. I pad down to the high street and after a mooch around the old toy shop, buying countless things for Sofia, I enter the only decent clothes shop in Coolsbay. If nothing looks good here then I'll have to order a few things online, try them on, then send anything back I don't like but I really do hate doing that. Despite the cold weather, I start to feel a bit sweaty as I approach Emmanuel's and spy the shop window with all the beautiful, velvet and shimmery dresses on wafer thin mannequins.

What if everything looks truly bloody horrible?

The door dings as I enter, and the shop assistant looks

up and smiles from the counter. I give a quick smile back then avert eye contact before sidling over to the women's event wear.

'Are you okay there? Need any help?' the shop assistant, who is now beside me, asks.

'I think I'm okay at the moment thanks, just looking for a dress for my fortieth.' I smile, getting used to how that number feels in my mouth.

'Wow, you don't look almost forty.'

'That's very kind of you, thank you.'

'Well, I'm here if you need any advice, I love helping people dress for an occasion so just let me know.'

'Thank you, I will.' Not. I'm perfectly capable of choosing myself. She pads back to the counter and I sift through the dresses making a mental note of *no* to anything that shows too much arm. I'm self-conscious about my arms and don't like to get them out if I can help it. It all really stems from a photo shoot I had with my sister in my early twenties. We were thrilled with our makeovers and had such a laugh posing for photos but then after hours of waiting we were ushered into a room to view them and every single one of them had been *Photoshopped*, mainly our arms. Yes, our arms were thinned to half the size and they had removed my sister's mole from her top lip which she actually loved as she said it made her feel like Cindy Crawford. When my sister complained, they showed us the unedited version and we were both horrified, not wanting to pay for our real arms, as they looked monumental in comparison but also, not wanting to purchase the fake, slim ones either as we felt we were just lying to ourselves. So, in the end, we bought nothing. Needless to say, the photography company weren't very happy. We'd only paid pennies for the photo shoot, it was one of those deal things where you were expected to spend at least a hundred quid on photos so when we didn't buy a single photo, they were less than impressed. That's what happens when you edit a person's character without their permission.

I find a couple of dresses that I like in numerous sizes then retreat to the changing room. As I strip off and begin to stuff my body into the overly ambitious smallest size dress, I hear the woman in the changing room next door, huffing and puffing.

'This is a joke, an absolute joke,' she grumps, as I try to breath and move as quietly as possible as I carry on stuffing. 'Fucking ridiculous,' she continues. The dress makes it up to my thighs then I give up before deciding I might rip it if I take it any further.

Best to stop now.

'Umm are you okay in there, ladies?' The shop assistant calls from behind the curtains.

'Not really, your mirrors are awful,' the other customer replies bluntly. She's not wrong there, the garish lighting isn't exactly flattering but equally, I hate all those fake slimming mirrors that lie in shops and then you get home and reality stares back at you in your own mirror. It's a trick. A mean trick.

'Oh, I'm so sorry,' the shop assistant says.

'Shows every lump and bump, look,' I slowly peak through the edge to see Stephanie emerge from her changing room in a gorgeous red velvet dress. Stephanie is Filipe's PA and she's about a size ten at the most with absolutely no lumps and bumps. Hmm, maybe the mirrors are bad? Stepping back and avoiding my own eye contact with the mirror, I pull on another dress which thankfully reaches past my thighs this time, I shimmy it up over my body and begin to slip my arms through the arm holes.

'We have another mirror just here if you'd like to take a look, the lighting isn't quite as harsh. I think you look stunning in that dress; the colour really suits you.'

'Yeah, you're right, sorry I was a bit snappy, just a bit stressed right now. One of those days, you know.'

'Of course, going anywhere nice?' the shop assistant asks. Stephanie does look stunning; I take another peak at her then look in the mirror at my own reflection. The too tight sleeves still halfway up my arms.

I want to cry.

I want to *Photoshop* my arms.

'Not really, but it's an occasion I need to dress well for,' she replies, cryptically. 'I'll take it.'

'Fabulous.'

'Good, can I give that to you now? I've got to hurry and get dressed. I'm meant to be working tonight.'

I smile to myself, so it's not only me, skiving off of Filipe's jobs.

'Of course, I'll take it to the till and get it ready for you. Are you okay in there, madam?' The shop assistant asks, as I finally manage to pull the sleeves up onto my shoulders. Once the dress is on it actually flatters my arms a treat, providing suction to slim them down.

Perfect.

'Yes, thank you,' I sing, trying to disguise my voice. I like Stephanie but it's awkward with her looking lovely in her new dress and me feeling not so lovely. I don't want her to know I'm here.

'Okay, let me know if you need anything,'

'Will do,' I trill again.

Moments later I hear Stephanie swish out of the changing room and march over to the counter, making demands at the shop assistant again. I reach around to the back of the dress to do up the zip with both hands, it's so tight, but it is holding everything in nicely. Everything stuffed into the right place. The thick green taffeta material hugs my hips and thighs tightly. I'll have to wear suitable underwear not my old maternity bra and giant comfy knickers and I'll probably not be able to move much in it, but who cares, it's for one night.

It's for my special night out with Filipe.

For my fortieth.

I tug on the zip and it moves just a millimetre, giving me hope. The till beeps which means Stephanie must be paying for her dress now. I tug a little more and it gives me a few inches up and over the bum. Right, last big bit, breath in and pull.

PULL PULL PULL.

Why won't you do up.

PULL.

WOAH.

The dress zips up so quickly at the end of the zip that it completely takes me by surprise. I lunge forward to steady myself but the dress won't let me move my leg that far.

Instead, I lose my footing.

NO NO NO. I fall face down through the curtain onto the shop floor. That wouldn't be so bad, except that I hear an almighty rip come from the dress as I try to stand up and scuttle back under the curtain.

I've ripped it.

My arse has ripped it.

Big grey knickers on display.

Arse in the air.

I plonk back down on my backside to hide the rip. Legs out straight in case I rip it further with any more movement.

'Oh my God.' Stephanie's hand shoots up to her

mouth as she sees me.

The assistant comes rushing over. I hang my head in shame, feeling like an exposed, beached mermaid-whale hybrid.

'Are you okay, madam?'

'Yes yes, so sorry.' I wave pathetically.

'Here.' She lifts up the curtain to cover my modesty as I slide back into the changing room. A beached sea creature, barely able to move.

'I guess I'll be buying this dress regardless,' I say sadly, once we're both in the changing room. I see myself in the mirror, red faced and wanting to cry even more.

'No, no, it was an accident. I'm sure we can fix that. let me see.' I roll over onto my stomach so she can see the damage. 'It's on the seam. Let me finish dealing with this customer and I'll come straight back and help you.'

'Are you sure?'

'Certain,' she smiles, helping me up. I stand up very slowly, conscious that it would be very easy to rip the dress even more. When I'm stable she lets herself out of the changing room, tugging the curtain tightly closed behind her.

In the changing room, I slowly peel myself out of the dress so as not to do any more damage. I half expect Stephanie to come running over to see if I'm alright. She doesn't, but she *was* in a rush. I hope she doesn't tell Filipe; mind you, I bet she's thinking the same about me.

The lovely shop assistant comes back and helps me pick a dress that is in the right size and also the right style for my body shape. She says some of the dresses do tend to come up a size smaller than standard sizes. I'm not sure if she is saying this to make me feel better but either way and after the horrid ordeal, I leave the shop much happier. I'm now the proud owner of a gorgeous new velvet navy dress that both my arms and arse fit into nicely. It even looks okay in the changing room mirror, but it looks fabulous in the one outside the changing room with the less garish lighting. The lovely shop assistant also convinced me to buy some underwear to wear underneath it, it's gorgeous navy-blue silk.

Filipe is going to love it.

Chapter 4

Delilah

I walk into the pub to the loud excited buzzing atmosphere of Christmas music and chatter. The Christmas decorations sparkle and shine as they glimmer brightly in the light. They've already been up for weeks and some of them look like they were dug up from the eighties. I know this because Mum and Dad threw away a load of tacky decorations the other day and were reminiscing about the era when my brothers were born, dad calls it Pre-Delilah.

The Mermaid's Lair has a faint smell of body odour to it and as usual there are the questionable locals propping up the bar. When Sky was barely a teen her parents built her a shed out the back of the pub so she could have her mates over; it started off as a den with a TV. Over time it has turned into a little lounge/bar type area. We often meet here because it is the only place where Sky can smoke indoors. Her parents own the pub, it's been in the family for generations, they almost lost it a few years ago but then the whole community pulled together to raise funds to keep it open. It's a landmark, a little piece of old age Coolsbay and the shed is our hidden gem.

'Hey, she made it,' Sky calls out when she sees me. She throws her arms up in the air in excitement. She's dressed up as a Christmas angel and has pulled out all the stops. Full fairy makeup, wings, glitter and a halo which looks like it could have been fashioned out of an old coat hanger but it still manages to look really cute. Her dog, Luna is sitting next to her in an almost identical outfit. I laugh as the grumpy looking grey pug looks up at me as if to say, don't ask, before letting out a huge snort. Sky is so creative, I guess all three of us are. I'm a dancer although not working as one at the moment, Sky is a makeup artist and Molly, my other close friend, landed on her feet as a social media manager. She's very smart and probably makes more money than Sky and I combined.

'Sorry, Dylan delayed me with his safety talk,' I say, as I rub Luna's head. Luna snorts and her tongue flops out as she rolls onto her back, happy to have someone else to fuss over her but on her terms only.

'Where's Molly?' I ask, rubbing Luna's belly.

'She's just in the loo. I've got something to tell you guys. I'm so excited about it, a new chapter in my life.' She rubs her hands together and grins as her eyes widen with excitement.

'What?'

'Let's wait for Molly first.'

I watch Sky tap her toes on the floor as she lights a cigarette then blows smoke out through her nose. The smoke wafts around the shed and my eyes fall to the maroon velvet curtains that block out the rest of the world. We did most of our growing up here in this cosy, slightly musty smelling shed. As cringe as it sounds, I even lost my virginity in here. Josh and I needed somewhere to go and this was the only private place where we wouldn't get disturbed. It was Sky's idea. She even made it all romantic for us by setting up the sofa bed and adding freshly washed silk sheets, cushions, rose petals and matching his and hers silk robes. I dread to think where she got the robes. Fairy lights were hung up inside and outside. She called it the glistening cherry sex box, it was a bit over the top but that's Sky and I love her for it.

It's been six years since that night and Josh and I are still together. Everyone was shocked that a young couple could survive a long-distance relationship for such a long time but we have. Even Mum and Dad expected us to part ways when I went off to London. They said it was too much pressure for young love but he came to visit me almost every weekend. The girls say I'm blessed for finding someone so early in my life, someone so committed to me. My life is so different to Sky's wild life. She recently had a threesome with a friend she went to college with and some guy they both knew. Part of me would love to do something wild like that but not as a girl in a relationship; I couldn't share Josh with anyone and I'm pretty sure he wouldn't want to share me either, even if it was with a hot girl.

I'm his world.

'Hey girls,' Molly arrives, dressed as an office worker, except she doesn't work in an office, she mainly works at home. She's carrying a bottle of champagne and three champagne flutes. Mols has become accustomed to all things expensive since she can now afford it, and why not.

'Hey you! I thought you were taking a long time in the toilet.'

Molly swoops towards me and air kisses me on both cheeks. She places the champagne and glasses on the shabby, little table by Sky.

'Yeah, Sky's said she's got some news and it sounds like we should be celebrating so thought I'd treat us. It's my day off tomorrow, you know I'd never drink on a school night.'

'Ahhh thank you, babe. You are too sweet to me. Yes, this is the cause for a huge monumental celebration.' Sky stands up and holds out her arms as if she is about to be crucified.

'Ohh, I'm excited.' Molly pops open the champagne and begins to pour us all a glass.

'Me too, what is it?' I say, taking a glass from Molly. I bet she's won a contract to do makeup for a celebrity or something, I can totally see her doing that. She'll have been whipped up by Dua Lipa's people to do all the flamboyant fun stuff. That will leave my two closest friends with amazing jobs and me stuck at Cool Tours Excellence, the local, outdated tour operators. It doesn't help that my boss, Miriam, appears to not be my biggest fan. In past jobs, I've been told I'm sweet and respectful. What's not to like?

Sky pouts, pleased with herself and begins to open her mouth.

Then, Molly's phone goes off, loudly.

'Oh, shit,' Molly screeches, reaching for her phone. She frantically scrolls, frowns then begins typing at a speed only she could manage.

'What's up? I'm about to do my reveal speech you know!' Sky folds her arms then slumps back down in her chair. The big reveal ruined.

'Urgh nothing, it's just that boy I was seeing, replying to my email.'

'Email?' Why's he been emailing you?' Sky snorts. Luna mimics her snort and Sky smiles down at her dog, her little partner in crime.

'It's nothing, just carry on.' Molly's cheeks pink up and I groan inwardly.

'Not again, Molly. What boy? Let me see,' I say, grabbing the phone out of Molly's hand. The words *you're a sociopath. Please get help* have been typed in response to Molly's email. I scroll down to see an *Excel* spreadsheet attachment.

'Uh oh, it's spreadsheet gate,' I say, looking at Sky as she acts out hanging herself.

'Give it back.' Molly snatches the phone out of my hand. Luna grunts and flops down onto her belly, seemingly sick of our shit, she closes her eyes and begins to snore.

Sky throws her head back and groans, arms reached out backwards. 'Mollyyyyyy! How many times! The boy is right, it does make you look like a complete psycho.'

I widen my eyes at Sky to remind her not to be so harsh. Molly's highly strung and has impeccable attention to detail, sometimes too much, hence the psycho spreadsheet.

'What did he do to warrant the spreadsheet attack, Mols?' I ask, before scrolling down to see the attachment. 'Can I?' I hover my finger over download.

'Yes, go ahead,' she says, with a surrendering wave. 'It's the only way I can get it all out and clear in my head and address every single point exactly how I want to.'

'You literally wrote a post about this last week and how it's toxic to do this sort of thing and now you're doing it again. Such a hypocrite.'

'Stop it,' I tell Sky, who's now lighting up another cigarette from the previous one.

'What did he do?' I rub Molly's arm and she lets out a huge shaky sigh. My poor mate. Sometimes her overactive mind really does get the better of her.

'He listed a few points in a text as to why he thought we were incompatible and I began texting him back but the text got too long and it looked silly. I got myself all muddled up but once I'd typed it all up on my laptop it was just so much easier to reply to him this way. I could then address everything and not miss anything out.'

The spreadsheet downloads and I attempt a kind smile to hide the fact I'm wincing. She's typed out his text and highlighted it in yellow at the top of the spreadsheet. The title reads *In response to your text*, coupled with the date and time he sent it. Underneath, she has listed ten points. His text only listed three.

'This is quite impressive in a way, you should train to be a solicitor or an MP, perhaps,' I contemplate, taking a sip of my champagne.

Sky frowns and continues to blow huge puffs of smoke out of her mouth like the caterpillar straight out of *Alice in Wonderland*.

'I know it's weird, I wish I could stop being so intense about this stuff but it just winds me up so much. I just cannot let him have the last word.'

'Yeah, but there's having the last word and then there's next level stalker, writing him a novel last word.' Sky puffs on her cigarette whilst pouring us all another glass.

'Oh, my God, this stuff gives me anxiety,' I say, whilst beginning to count in my head. The counting is becoming addictive now as much as my superstition for the number thirteen is. Every time I audition for a dance job lately, I appear to be given this number and it has always been bad luck, I never get the job. I was actually number seven in the last audition I went for. I'm still waiting to hear back from them, perhaps my luck is about to change. But other things have happened during my life that have made me fear and avoid this number at all costs. It's just linked to bad stuff happening.

- Started my period at thirteen - worse day out ever with friends and I was wearing white trousers.
- The thirteenth boy I ever kissed severed my lips with his braces – truly awful – I needed stitches.
- I re-sat my maths GCSE to get a decent grade– I did this thirteen times before I eventually gave up – pure torture and all for nothing.

'Everything gives you anxiety, babe,' Sky replies.

'I'm not a stalker. I wish I could just not give a shit like you, but I'm just not wired that way.' Molly offers a little shrug and Sky reaches over to pat her knee.

'I know mate, but we love you for it and it would be boring if we were all the same.'

'She's right, you have an amazing skill for debating, but maybe don't use it for the fuckboy's, they're a lost cause and not worth your time or energy,' I agree.

'Yeah, Dee's right, you should just make money off them instead, exploit them, like I'm doing.' Sky smirks then examines her nails as if she hasn't just dropped a bomb.

'What do you mean?'

'Okay, time for the drum roll,' she says as Molly and I proceed to slap our thighs vigorously, in readiness for Sky's big news.

'I am…' Sky pauses then stands up, she straightens her halo, then Luna's before sticking out her chest and bum to show off her perfect figure. Luna snorts and appears to roll her eyes. Molly and I sit sipping our champagne, waiting with baited breath. Sky inhales deeply, gearing up for her big announcement.

Chapter 5

Amber

'Alright my lovely, happy birthday,' Stella appears and comments, as she looks me up and down. 'Cheer up, it might never happen?'

I purse my lips together and look down.

'Badger, Sofia, why don't you go and play in the park, look the slide's free. Take it in turns remember.' Stella gently pushes the two children towards the park, they hesitate for a second and then run off. 'You alright?' Stella whispers, catching me watching Jayne laughing with the other mums and looking over.

'Yes and no. I've had an email from the headteacher, they want to have a meeting with me next week about Sofia's behaviour, about bullying.'

'Really, that's a bit strange, she's such a sweet girl.'

'Yes, I know, I haven't said anything to Sofia, I can't imagine what they're going to say.'

'I'm sure it's nothing mate, hey you read the latest in the school mums' group chat?'

'No, I haven't, I can't keep up with it all to be honest. It's a full-time job reading all those messages.'

'It is. I don't bother with most of it but latest I saw was that Jayne's arranging a New Year's party at her house.'

'Right, for the kids?'

'No, for the parents, no nippers allowed. She wants all the parents to bond and cut loose.'

'Oh please, no thank you. I'll be expecting a private message on that then if I don't reply on the group. She's done that a few times lately, message me privately.' It feels a bit much.

'Rather you than me. Hey, have you seen she's got new gym attire?' Stella murmurs, nodding in the direction of Jayne who is dressed head to toe in bright yellow *Lycra*. We both snigger and for a moment I feel about as bad as the class bully. But then I remind myself that she can't hear and we aren't saying anything that bad. I'm in the clear – just.

'Clocked it earlier. I wonder if she just goes to bed in those gym leggings, perhaps they do a work out for her whilst she sleeps and that's why she looks so bloody perfect, I might get a pair,' I reply, but I'm genuinely intrigued. I've never seen her out of them, always glued to her like they are an actual part of her body. A mental image of Jayne running in her sleep with her trademark pinched expression enters my mind and I stifle a giggle.

'So, what are your plans tonight? Filipe revealed what you're doing yet?'

'I'm off out tonight with the husband and that's all I know.' I grin.

'Ooooh is Prince Filipe taking you out to be wined and dined?'

'He's said it's a surprise.' I grin, and Stella grins back at me.

'Okay, so inhale a big breath in and hold for, one, two, three, four, five and slowly exhale,' Dylan instructs, whilst I do as he says. We're doing meditating on the living room floor, crossed legs and palms facing up. I've had a wanky day at work. Miriam's been on my case again and I felt so close to a panic attack today that Dylan said I should do this with him to try and relax and find some inner calm. Dad thinks Dylan's gone bonkers. Since he's been back living with us, he's got into all sorts of spiritual stuff, meditating being one of them. He says it helps to quiet the mind so I've started doing it with him. I like it but sometimes I find it quite hard to relax.

'Sky's on FansOnly,' I blurt out, as I exhale. 'Molly and I had to ask her again once she'd said it. We couldn't believe it.' I shake my head and throw my arms up in the air.

'Dee, we're meant to be meditating,' he says, with one eye open, still in his meditating position.

'I know, sorry. But she already has over fifty thousand followers and her account has only been up a week, she's beginning to rake in the money already.' I close my eyes again and begin to breath, half listening to Dylan's meditation speech as my mind begins to wander again. Sky's always had strange side hustles going on. She's always been a bit *extra*. The last one was selling her used tights online and from what I gather it was quite successful but she said she wanted to try something new and was bored of buying and posing in tights. Such a Sky thing to say. When Sky told us, I just had an image of her prostituting herself online and being forced into basically acting out porn naked but she says it isn't like that at all. Far from it in fact. She says she just prances around in her underwear or tight-fitting clothes, doing normal stuff like her makeup and cleaning her bedroom. She chats to them like they're her friends, she kind of acts like she is their girlfriend and they're on a video call. That's the way Sky put it anyway. 'Sounds too good to be true though, doesn't it?'

'Dee!'

'I'm doing the breathing, I'm meditating, look.' I close my eyes again, inhaling and exhaling like a pro.

'You need to try and quiet your mind, relax, not think about the latest gossip from your mates.'

Molly gave Sky a lecture and said she was selling herself short and could easily go viral with her makeup tutorials instead. What would this do for her reputation, selling herself in skimpy underwear to a load of simps and perverts? But Sky simply said the money was too good, so we left it at that. It's usually Sky's way or the highway and no amount of arguing will change that.

Dylan stops meditating and looks at me. 'If you practice this enough you won't have to worry about what your friends are doing, you'll find an inner peace that will set you free.'

'You're such a hippy.'

'I'm not. Okay, maybe I have become one, a bit, but is that such a bad thing? This,' he says. 'May help you find a better path in life instead of fretting about what other people are doing.'

'I'm not fretting, I'm just saying.'

'Okay.'

'Anyway,' I say changing the subject. 'Are you going to tell me why you and Claire aren't together anymore? You need to say it and not fret inwardly, it's been months now.'

'I'm not fretting at all, I'm processing it. There's a

difference.'

Chapter 6

Amber

The rest of the day is spent thoroughly indulging myself. I get my nails done and lastly my hair, in between I even manage to squeeze in a cheeky massage. I do give the house a quick spruce, putting away clothes and emptying and refilling the dishwasher. I don't really like looking at the mess but I don't do any of my usual Friday jobs which consist of hoovering the crumbs from underneath the sofa cushions and cleaning and dusting every single surface. It looks alright, far from a shit hole. I'm sure Filipe won't mind as we're off out anyway so it's not as though we'll be sat looking at it all night.

And it *is* my birthday.

Now, I'm sitting here feeling all fresh and fancy in my bedroom. I spray a few squirts of perfume onto my neck and wrists then spray the air before turning and twirling around in it so as to make sure that I encase my entire body in my husband's favourite scent.

I haven't seen Filipe for a couple of days as he's been away on business so I'm extra excited to see him tonight. I dropped Sofia off at my parents after school to give me a chance to get ready so all I have to do now is wait for Filipe to arrive.

A little glass of wine would go down well right about now, it is my birthday after all. My watch says it's 5.35pm, Filipe should be home around 6pm. I wonder what he's bought me, it's usually something designer and expensive although I'm completely happy with non-designer stuff, it's more Filipe's preference than mine. This watch was from Filipe, it's a Rolex, but I only wear it on special occasions. Jayne and her hareem would have a field day if they saw me wearing it.

I trot downstairs to the kitchen where Olive leaps up and follows me, watching me with her big brown eyes as I grab a bottle of white wine from the fridge. I pick out a nice wine glass from the drinks cabinet before sitting on my bay window-seat, Olive jumps up and lays across my lap and I stroke her soft fur, occasionally scratching her behind the ears as we both gaze out onto the street. Olive and I love to sit here and people watch, she's as nosey as I am. Even though it's pitch black out there the street lamps make it bright enough for me to do my spying. I love people watching but more recently I've become extra curious about the strange characters that pass me by.

I check my watch again and it's coming up for 5.45pm, any minute now she should be walking by, it's been pretty much the same time most nights for the past few months. Just as I'm thinking about her, she appears, a girl of around twenty with long blonde hair and huge startled eyes. As she starts to walk past my house, I wonder if this time she won't do it but she does as she has always done since I noticed her. Her hand flies up to her face to hide it just as she passes the lamppost and she keeps it there until she's well past my house. I wasn't sure at first but I'm pretty sure she's hiding from me. How very odd. Perhaps she knows me. But who would hide from me? I resist the urge to go outside in my finery and demand what the hell is going on but I don't want to get into a fight on my birthday. She also doesn't look at me before she hides, I'm baffled as to what that's about. The door goes and I almost jump out of my skin. Olive instantly starts barking, in protector mode.

'Filipe! You scared me half to death,' I say, as Olive launches herself at Filipe to cover him in licks and slobber. Filipe humours her tonight and half puts up with it before batting her away. He snaps his fingers and points to her place and she obediently complies but with a little groan.

'Why? Why? you know I do live here right?' Filipe smiles his smouldering smile then hands me a bunch of red roses before planting a kiss on my lips.

'Barely,' I joke, but I mean it. He isn't here much at all but it means we can afford the things we have and be comfortable and that's nice. I like that we don't live in each other's pockets. I never understand those couples who end up turning into each other taking on each other's personality and fashion. You see them sometimes, often in the supermarket and they're almost always wearing matching fleeces.

Just no. You have to have your own life.

Most nights, we don't even share the same bedroom.

'For you.' Filipe hands me a medium sized velvet box and I smile at him before opening it. As expected, it's a beautiful gift. A gorgeous diamond and sapphire encrusted necklace with matching earrings. 'I thought they would match the colour of your eyes.'

'Oh, give over, my eyes are green and so are your daughter's.' I laugh and he laughs along with me. Somehow, Sofia has ended up with all my colouring, you wouldn't even guess that Filipe is her father. He jokes that I'm like a fish and I must have impregnated myself. She does have his feet though but that's about it, for everything else she takes after me. Filipe takes the jewellery out of the box as I take off the jewellery I'm already wearing. He gently places the necklace around my neck and I lean up to kiss him as his warm fingers gently touch my neck.

'Time for a birthday quickie?' I ask, grinning.

'No, no, no,' he teases, wagging his finger. 'I have to shower and get ready; our guests will be arriving in exactly one hour. Can you sort the house and lay the table with the best cutlery?' He strokes the side of my face with his finger and I smile a wobbly smile.

'Oh right, I thought we were going out, just you and I?' I say, trying to hide the disappointment in my voice. He has just bought me gorgeous presents so I can't really complain now.

'Whatever made you think that? You're forty today, we must celebrate in style. Lay the table for five guests, I'll be ready soon and maybe just maybe we can have the quickie if the table is ready in time,' he says, leaning down to kiss my neck again.

'Okay, who's coming?'

'Surprise.' And with that he scuttles off to the bathroom to preen himself for tonight. It might not be that bad, in fact he's got to have invited Stella, perhaps Tamsin couldn't come so that will be fun but who are the other two, maybe my sister and her partner? Yeah, that wouldn't be too bad, quite nice actually.

'I'm quite looking forward to it now,' I say to Olive, as I scratch her head then bend down to sniff her fur. 'Not what I had in mind but it will still be lovely.' I smile at Olive and she licks my cheek, taking off half my makeup in the process but I can't be mad at her. She's so damn cuddly and loveable.

My eyes dart round the house to see what minimal cleaning I can get away it. Bollocks, I'll have to hoover under the sofa cushions, he always checks that when we have guests.

After thirty minutes of rapid cleaning and *Febreezing*, I light a few nice smelling candles then pad upstairs to the bedroom to re-do my makeup and claim my birthday quickie from my sexy Spanish husband.

'Ola baby,' I say in my most seductive voice, as I come up behind Filipe and wrap my arms around him. He jumps then quickly composes himself.

'*Ola, churri*,' he replies, slipping his phone into his pocket as he turns to recognise the look on my face. 'We don't have time.'

'We do, we have about thirty minutes,' I whine, sounding a little desperate.

'No, I made a mistake, they just messaged saying that they're on their way.'

'Filipe, you are honestly so rubbish at punctuality. How are you such a successful businessman when you can't arrange a bloody dinner for five guests?' I'm not overreacting, he'll be late for his own funeral and it drives me insane.

'I love it when you get all mad and that fiery red hair flings around your face like Medusa. My queen. My *churri*,' he says, caressing my wild locks. 'And anyway that's easy, I have my PA who sorts all that stuff at work, and a very understanding, caring and competent wife.' He's in a good mood tonight. This is nice, I've missed this, I've missed fun Filipe. I fling my hair at him as I walk away to sort out my makeup, making sure to sway my hips in a way that I know makes him go crazy. He better be prepared for later; we're child free.

I turn back to look at him, certain that he's watching me but he's back on his phone again, probably making the final secret arrangements for my birthday. I wonder if he's organised any entertainment such as a little man on a guitar to serenade us.

That would be special.

Filipe and I met abroad, it was a holiday romance that escalated quickly, well a holiday for me anyway, he lived there. I'd gone with a few girl mates to Ibiza who were less than impressed that I spent the majority of our girls' holiday with hotel head waiter, Filipe. But our relationship was so intense right from the start that we just couldn't be apart. He'd also turn up everywhere we were so it's not as though I had much choice. A persistent Spaniard is hard to ignore and watching the sunset come up with him every day was just magical.

The doorbell dings and Filipe thunders off to answer it.

'Get the wine ready for our guests, birthday girl.'

'Will do,' I shout down the stairs after him. Stella won't be wanting wine, she drinks *Stella*, Stella by name, Stella by nature. I hope we have some in, and Tamsin, I'm pretty sure she doesn't drink. My sister and her hubby do though. Now I think about it, I'm pretty sure we don't have any *Stella*, oh well I can pop out and get some. Stop fussing, stop fussing, Filipe would have sorted it.

I'm sure.

It's my fortieth.

I hear Filipe loudly greet our guests and shout at the dog barking, I wish he wouldn't do that. I shake my head then finish reapplying my lipstick before slowly creeping down the stairs, excited for my fortieth dinner. I pause half way down to listen to the voices.

Voices I didn't expect to hear and one I don't recognise. I force myself to continue down and paste on a smile, preparing myself to greet each one of Filipe's guests as if they were my friends. But they aren't my friends really and it's the absolute worse combination of people thrown together possible.

I wish Stella was here.

I want to scream.

Instead, I paste on my brightest biggest smile.

'Hey, Stephanie,' I say, awkwardly side hugging Filipe's PA who's wearing the red velvet dress. I hope she doesn't bring up the shop incident. If she does, I'll just have to laugh it off. 'And I'm so sorry, I've forgotten your name,' I say apologetically to Stephanie's partner.

'It's okay everyone forgets him, it's Kev,' Stephanie giggles profusely at her own joke as Kevin stands there like an embarrassed, gormless chicken. He doesn't want to be here anymore than I do and it shows.

No-one else laughs.

'Helloooooo.' Out pops Jayne's head behind Stephanie and Kevin.

'Hi Jayne, long time no see,' I say, in a very high voice, attempting a joke because this is what it is. A joke. I can't believe this woman is in my home. Why the fuck did he invite her? What is wrong with him?

'Hi Amber, your house is amazing,' she says, beaming.

'Thank you.'

'When Filipe messaged me, I couldn't believe my luck, I was so thrilled to be invited, so surprised too.'

'Me too,' I say. I'm still in shock. 'But it will be a great opportunity to get to know each other better,' I add, feeling mean. 'Right, I'll go and get the wine, shall I? Filipe, I'll leave you to sort out the coats and get everyone seated.' And make awkward conversation with this strange and ridiculous combination of people. I offer Filipe a smile that stops before it reaches my eyes. I hope it shows how royally pissed off I am at this shit show of dinner guests. Honestly, what was he thinking? Where are *my* actual friends? Stephanie is his PA and Jayne is quite frankly my school mum arch nemesis. It just goes to show how disconnected he is from my life at the moment. He obviously doesn't listen to me.

My dog Olive follows me into the kitchen and I stand there debating which wine to bring in for way too long as I bend down to ruffle her big floppy ears, my one true friend in all of this.

'What are they doing here, Olive? Make them go away please,' I whisper to her, and she cocks her head to one side. If only she could understand how painful this evening is going to be.

'Right, I have red, white and rose,' I announce, as I waltz back into the room and plonk all three bottles onto the table before sashaying off to the drinks cabinet to get the wine glasses. Not one person has brought a bottle with them, that will be Filipe telling them all not to bother, insisting that to bring a bottle would be completely rude of them. He likes to think of himself as the most perfect host.

'Oh Amber, I completely forgot your present,' squeals Stephanie, as her hand shoots up to her mouth. 'I'll give it to Filipe on Monday.' Stephanie looks amazing, her gorgeous brown, glossy hair waves around her shoulders as though she's a contestant from a Miss World contest. Oh, to be twenty-five again. Jayne looks just as good and isn't wearing her gym leggings. Instead, she's wearing a long black dress which hugs her in all the right places. She too has brown, glossy hair, straight out of the salon. She can't be much younger than me but she looks fantastic. I wonder if she's forty yet? She could definitely identify as a twenty-five-year-old; I don't think I could get away with that. It's like these guests were invited to make me feel extra shit on my fortieth, or maybe it's Filipe's hint of "*this is what you could look like if you didn't eat so much and made more effort.*" I'm never dying my hair brown though, it's redhead through and through for me.

'No problem, Stephanie, it's just nice that you guys are here.' Urgh listen to me, so insincere. Why do I have to lie like that, just say no problem.

'Here you go, Amber. I hope you like it.' Jayne hands me a small shiny, expensive looking gift bag. 'Oh, wow, thank you, you didn't have to do that,' I say, feeling terribly awkward and taken aback.

'I wanted to,' she replies, blinking back at me. I reach into the gift bag and pull out my favourite perfume. Filipe must have told her as there's no way she could know. For a brief second, I wonder if she's poisoned it with something before batting the ridiculous thought away.

'Thank you, Jayne, so kind.'

'You're welcome.'

Everyone sits at the table and gets sorted with drinks and then realisation dawns on me. I can't believe the thought hasn't crossed my mind before. I excuse myself from the table and retreat to the kitchen.

'Filipe, can I have a hand with something?' I call loudly.

'What it is my *churri*,' he says, appearing in the doorway. I usher him into the kitchen and close the door.

'What are we actually having for dinner?' I whisper, feeling completely sick at how unprepared we are. I may not want to be at this dinner party but at the very least I want nice food.

'I thought you could make the beef stroganoff, I checked and everyone is a meat eater apart from Jayne but you could just make her mushroom stroganoff. Also, you've only just been shopping so I know you have the ingredients. We can have olives and bread for starter and then maybe I might have bought a birthday cake for dessert.' He smiles warmly, his eyes almost pleading with me not to kick off. He knows he's made a mistake. A big fat one.

'You want me to cook, on my birthday.'

'You love cooking, it relaxes you. Is that okay?' I don't answer for a few seconds, carefully considering my options which are. a. Throw a hissy fit and send all the guests home hungry. b. Politely decline and suggest a takeaway or c. Cook the bloody meal because it will be amazing, I'm starving and I can hide out in the kitchen for most of the night.

I sigh heavily, changing my mind at the last second.

'I'll cook the bloody meal, but you owe me big time,' I say, wagging my finger at him.

'I'll make it up to you later, I promise. Now, get cooking.' He pinches my bum, then marches into the living room to attend to *his* guests. At least I can hide for a bit. Silver linings and all that.

I spend the next hour cooking. It's very fortunate that we have the best of electric pressure cookers that can cook a meal like this so quickly. And at least I have Olive to keep me company, she's so good, occasionally sniffing the air to enjoy the smells but then lying back down again. I throw her a few pieces of beef for a treat and she gobbles them up in nano seconds. She's making me giggle in amongst this extremely shit situation. Every time I so much as lift a bit of beef up, she lifts her head, licks her lips and attempts to stand up, doing a funny little tap dance on the tiled floor. By the time I've almost finished cooking, I only have to say the word beef and she licks her lips, stands up and dances.

It's a case of *Pavlov's* dogs.

I better save some beef for the guests. I command Olive to lay down in her bed and she does for the rest of the time I cook, she's such a good girl and much better company than the dinner guests.

I slowly plate up the starter and turn the cooker off, taking my time to tidy up as I eavesdrop. The conversation sounds the complete opposite of riveting and Filipe has spent most of the time so far talking shop with Stephanie about investment banking whilst the others politely laugh, ask the occasional question and nod along with them. It sounds like I'm eavesdropping on a boring meeting which the director has attended and everyone is on their very best behaviour. I'm actually relieved I ended up cooking, at least I can avoid that for most of the night.

I finally sit down with everyone and we tuck into the starter. I'm slightly embarrassed that it doesn't go with the main course but also past caring. It's my birthday, I shouldn't be doing all the work or worrying about what people think.

'So Amber, what have you been up to lately?' asks Jayne.

Here we go.

'Oh, not much you know, just trying to keep on top of everything here really.' I smile politely.

'Where are you working at the moment?' Jayne asks, leaning forward with a goading look in her eyes.

'I'm not, Filipe is away for work a lot so I'm needed here.'

'Kev, did you hear that? I think it's time you got a

promotion and let me be a kept woman.' Stephanie giggles her little baby laugh and catches eyes with Jayne who chuckles along with her. Great, they've now formed an alliance.

'No chance,' Kev replies, flatly. Good for him.

'Yes, no chance,' Filipe says, glancing at Stephanie. 'What would I do without you?'

'Oh, I'm sure you'd manage,' Stephanie says, nonchalantly.

'I thought you were a trained hairdresser?' Jayne says, not letting this work thing go.

As if on cue, Olive walks into the living room and begins to bark at Stephanie.

'Quiet, Olive,' I say. I don't know what's got into her tonight. 'No, not anymore, I don't have the time at the moment.'

'Of course, you do, I work, I might have to get a second job now that Mia's dad and I are no longer together.' Jayne reaches down and pets Olive, who has now laid down underneath the table by my feet. I should command her to go and lay in her place; Filipe hates dogs by the dinner table, but she isn't begging, she's just keeping my feet warm.

My little guard dog.

'And Sofia is at school now, so you really have no excuse, come and work with me, I'll keep you busy.' She grins. I take another sip of wine and bite my tongue so hard that I taste blood. What the hell is Filipe thinking inviting her?

I've gone from wanting to shag his brains out, to wanting to strangle him.

'No thanks, I'm fine being a kept woman,' I quip. 'So how come you're bringing up Mia not to believe in Santa? Sofia was a bit upset the other day, when Mia told her he wasn't real.' The claws are out.

'Oh, did she? I'm so sorry. I just don't think it's good to lie to children. What's the point? It only sets them up for disappointment when they find out he isn't real.'

'It's not a lie, it's tradition. It's magic.'

'Yeah, but do you believe in God?' Stephanie pipes up.

'No, but…'

'There you go then, I'm with Jayne on this one.'

'You don't have to believe in God to enjoy Christmas, it's about tradition, magic and spending time with family,' I argue.

'And getting a tonne load of presents,' Stephanie says, examining her nails.

Seeing this as my chance to leave the conversation too, I excuse myself and pad over to the kitchen with Olive following behind me, to plate up the beef stroganoff. I serve it with white rice and green beans. With the exception of Jayne's meal, I've wrapped the green beans in bacon. It looks rather delicious, even if I do say so myself. I call Filipe to give me a hand serving the food before he tops up everyone's drinks. I'm really looking forward to eating this, it's much more exciting than the conversation and then after this course we are just one course away from them all going home.

Yay.

Filipe takes Jayne's meal out as I follow after him, carrying Stephanie and Kev's. At first, I feel a cool breeze waft past me as Filipe places down Jayne's plate, followed by a pleading yelp from Olive.

Uh oh. The smell of beef and bacon.

'Beef stroganoff, and mushroom stroganoff for you Jayne,' Filipe announces proudly as if he is the head chef who's been slaving over it. We serve the meals to our dinner guests. Olive pleads again, whimpering by my feet, she hasn't done this in a while.

I shouldn't have fed her the beef.

I place Stephanie's plate down, almost tripping over Olive.

'Leave it,' I command. I know exactly what's on Olive's mind as her eyes begin to bulge out of her head and her nose twitches. I shouldn't have fed her those bits of beef. How stupid of me. Now her appetite is insatiable. Filipe saunters back into the kitchen to grab the water, he's seen this a thousand times and Olive always gives up after a few *leave it's.*'

But I don't normally feed her our dinner scraps.

It's a real treat.

She doesn't normally do funny dances for beef.

Pavlov's dogs.

Olive sits by my feet and groans as the guests tuck into their dinner, admitting defeat. I feel sorry for her.

'Good girl,' I murmur to her and give her a little pat on the head, followed by a piece of my beef. I'm rewarding her good behaviour for not begging.

'Great beef,' Kevin says between mouthfuls.

'Such tender beef,' Stephanie comments.

'Beef does smell delicious, if I wasn't vegetarian I'd devour that in seconds,' Jayne pipes up.

Olive's ear's prick up and her nose starts going.

'Olive, sit.'

I wish everyone would stop saying bloody *beef.*

'Leave it. Down,' I say, a little louder as I gently push Olive down from the table beside me, before smiling back at the guests. She groans a half-defeated moan before retreating back out to the kitchen. Everyone continues to eat and enjoy their meal in peace.

'I make a mean roast dinner, don't I Kev?' Stephanie

boasts as Kevin nods along, chewing his food. 'I don't normally cook beef though, normally gammon or chicken, turkey, I find a bit dry.'

Stop saying beef.

'Beef can be a bit chewy sometimes, can't it? If you don't cook it right.'

As expected, Olive trots back into the living room, summoned of course, by the word beef.

She's salivating. *Pavlov's* dogs.

Olive's nose sniffs the air, now just millimetres from Stephanie's plate and I get up quickly to shoo her away.

'Such a cool dog,' Kev comments, making no attempt to stop her as he pets one of her ears. Stephanie freezes in fear, or is it anger? Her face is locked in a scowl as Olive sniffs and licks her lips right by the side of her plate. I lurch forward to grab Olive's collar.

It's too late.

She's disappeared under the table and I know what's coming, she's going to try a different angle. There's a series of shrieks from Stephanie as Kevin gets spooked by Olive appearing right next to his plate. Kevin knocks his plate onto Stephanie's lap. Olive reappears right by Stephanie's lap.

It's too late.

Olive licks her lips.

'Down, DOWN, LEAVE IT,' I shout, as I hear Filipe mimicking my commands in a much angrier Spanish accent. But it's game over, she's already lurched, paws on Stephanie's red velvet knees and is now enjoying a tasty beef stroganoff right off Stephanie's lap.

After the screams and shouting, there's a split second of deadly silence and all that can be heard is Olive's lips smacking together, enjoying every scrap of Stephanie's dinner.

It's a dog's dinner now.

She's snorting and scoffing like there's no tomorrow.

I barely have time to blink and she's eaten it all, in barely three mouthfuls. There's dinner and sour faces everywhere. Olive gets down from Stephanie's knees and licks her lips with a satisfied smirk on her face. She delights us all with a big, stinky dog fart as she sashays back into the kitchen without a care in the world.

I hear laughter. It's Jayne, and she's snorting into her napkin. If it wasn't my dog and my house, I'd be laughing too. But it is so it's not funny at all. It's horrifying. Excruciating. I guess Stephanie and I are even on the embarrassing incidents now.

I don't know whether to laugh or cry.

Happy bloody birthday to me.

Chapter 7

Delilah

The weekend was spent with Josh, he came over unannounced and it was nice but then he ended up staying the whole weekend, which, if I'm honest got a bit too much by the time the weekend was over. I almost felt like I couldn't breathe, needed my own space. We watched films, and mainly hung out with Dylan, who made us watch this thing called *The Secret*, about manifesting your perfect life and partner. If only. It made me wonder what Dylan is manifesting.

I check my phone. Shitsticks. Five minutes until lunch is over. I better not be late or my boss, Miriam, won't be pleased. I can already tell that she's in a bad mood because she wouldn't let me and Suzie, my colleague, take our lunch break together, so there's no need to provoke her further.

I pack away my lunchbox and walk slowly back to my desk from the staff room. I'm hoping I can just creep in like a mouse and she won't see me. I place my bag back down by my desk, switch my laptop back on and smile at Suzie, she gets me through the days here and if it wasn't for her, I would have walked out ages ago. Anyway, it's not forever, I'll get out of here soon and I'll be dancing again in no time. I just have to work out how, when and where first.

'Delilah, why, why, why Delilah,' Miriam sings in her shrill fake cheery tone and I shudder as she clip clops towards me in her thick, heavy heels. I hate that she takes that song and spoils it, my dad sings it to me but since she's been doing it, I've asked him to stop. He looked crestfallen, the poor man.

'Hi Miriam, everything alright?' I reply, trying to remember Dylan's calm breathing techniques. She sings at me when I've done something wrong so this has become my response to her when she does that now.

'In the nicest possible way,' she continues, not meaning it in the nicest possible way at all. 'This needs to be redone.' She dumps a load of paper down on my desk and I stare at it, blinking back tears. I hate it here.

'Why does it need to be redone?'

'It needs more flowering, puff it up a bit more, use more emotive and descriptive language.'

'Okay.'

'Like Suzie does. Suzie, yours was fantastical as usual, you can go home an hour early today if you wish.'

'Oh, thanks so much but I'm happy to stay,' Suzie says, looking at me and I mouth 'just go' at her.

She doesn't like to leave me alone with Miriam, not since she said she felt like a school teacher having to retrain me again on something I should already know. I explained I'd only been here a few months and was told it can take at least six months to get the hang of it to which she replied it wasn't true. I wish the old manager was still here but she swapped departments and now we're stuck with Miriam who appears to be a wolf in sheep's clothing. All sweet and smiling one minute and then very unhappy the next. I work in the tour department for a bus tour company, Cool Tours Excellence and my job is to put together the tours and basically make them sound interesting. It can be quite challenging at times when the tour is literally a drive around Coolsbay, a trip to the Mermaid's Lair for a pint and a walk along the beach but apparently the Americans love all that shit. Really?

'But you,' Miriam says, pointing a finger at me. One, two, three, four, five, six. 'You'll have to stay on longer and get these finished as the new tours go out tomorrow.' She grins, a smug look on her face.

'I can stay and help, make sure that they are put together properly and get them finished in time?' Suzie smiles sweetly at Miriam as she considers leaving us to it. 'That way you don't have to stay and I can lock up for you?' Suzi is so kind to me and I know all we will do is change a few words and say that Suzie has checked and okayed them.

'Well, if you're sure, Suzie I mean, Delilah should be the one correcting her mistakes, not you.'

'I know but I'm thinking about the company Miriam, we want these ready for tomorrow, don't we?'

Miriam looks at us both and we try our best to look innocent.

'Okay, it would be good to head off early today, I might see if I can get a last-minute hair appointment.'

'You do that,' Suzie replies. 'Spoil yourself, you deserve it.'

'Yes, I do, don't I? Plus, I'm stressed and drained from all the training,' Miriam says, looking at me. 'I could do with a little TLC.'

'Exactly,' Suzie says, and winks at me as Miriam checks herself out in the reflection of the window.

'Thanks Suzie, see you girls tomorrow.' She waltzes

off to her office and moments later we hear the door slam. Both of us heave a sigh of relief and Suzie leans over to turn over the radio station. Miriam insists on us listening to *Radio 2*, even though she isn't in the office with us. Every time she leaves we switch it over.

'Thanks Suzie, you didn't have to do that.'

'I know, I wanted to. I think she might be going through something; she isn't normally that abrupt.'

'Ah it's nothing I can't handle.'

'Yes, but you shouldn't have to.' Suzie grabs the papers then pulls out a pink marker pen.

'I know your work is good, this should take all of five minutes.'

'Thanks Suzie. Hey guess what. My mate has an FansOnly account.'

'Oh my God, who?'

'Sky.'

'Yes, I can totally see her doing that.' Suzie giggles and I laugh along with her. She's only heard about her and seen pictures but I guess she feels like she knows her as I talk about my friends a lot.

'Well, *I* might give it a go, then Miriam can shove this job up her arse.'

'I thought you were a trained dancer,' Suzie says, cocking her head to the side.

'I am but there isn't much out there at the moment, sometimes I wonder why I put myself through all those years of training to end up working here.'

'You've only been here five minutes, have faith and apply for stuff, something will come your way.'

'Four months and counting. I should, I know, I will.'

'Don't let those few auditions be the end of you 'Learn from them and move on and anyway,' she says. 'You're still waiting to hear from the last one, aren't you?

It could be the one.'

'Yes, still not heard. Some of them were so humiliating though. The audition before last, I felt like Julia Styles from *Save the Last Dance,* my knees just turned to jelly and I did a really weird knock-kneed thing.'

'You're just nervous because you're passionate, use the nerves to push through and show how good you are, you never know you may still get the part.'

'Yeah, I know you're right but it's easier said than done.' I stare out of the window and sigh.

'Don't do FansOnly, Dee.'

'I'm not, I wasn't going to.'

'The opposite is written all over your face.'

'Well,' I admit. 'The money would be nice.'

'Yes, but what about your dignity? Don't do it.'

'I won't,' I say checking my phone again for any reply from the dance company. 'Oh my God, they've emailed me.'

'Oh wow, what does it say?'

Dear Delilah,

Thank you for trying out for the Contemporary Elite Dance team. I'm so sorry to inform you that you didn't make the team this year. We had a lot of wonderful, qualified dancers, and the standard was incredibly high.

We appreciated your hard work and dedication, so I'd like to encourage you to keep practicing and try out again next year.

Thank you again for coming out and displaying such tenacity and effort. We look forward to seeing you again.

Sincerely,

Claudia Rivers

Chapter 8

Amber

'You okay Sofia?'

'Yes, mummy, why are we at school?' Sofia's big eyes, stare up at me through her big curly red mane as we stand outside her classroom.

There's a faint smell of damp and the large clock situated at the end of the hall is ticking so loudly, it sounds as if it is inside me. Children's art work is plastered all over the walls and I stand there admiring the children's imagination on the subject of being free. One child has drawn something rather questionable looking and it half resembles a penis. I imagine the teachers laughing amongst themselves and debating on whether to include it on the wall and it makes me smile. I miss the banter that you have with your work colleagues, sometimes staying at home by yourself can be lonely.

'We're just going to have a chat with your teacher sweetheart, she just wants to check everything is alright. These pictures are lovely, do you want to show me yours?'

'No, I don't want to.' Her hands form into little fists and her face clouds over. I say nothing and knock on the teacher's door as I desperately try to remember his name.

Mrs Hiscock, Hercock, Cockburn or was it Cockadge? It was some sort of cock. Please don't be a total brat and prove this teacher right today, Sofia. You're strong, not a bully I think as I stare at my scowling child, trying to insert my thoughts into her head.

'Come in,' a deep voice with a northern accent answers.

'Oh, you're not my cock,' I blurt out as I come face to face with the very face I never thought I'd see ever again.

'No, I'm not,' he answers, smirking before folding his arms and raising his eyebrows behind his designer glasses.

'I'm Mr Thomas.' He speaks with that ridiculous fake accent again. Why is he putting on a voice?

'Yes, I know.' I nod, slightly flustered after being caught off guard by a familiar face. I quietly breathe through the shock of seeing him. After all these years, he still looks good, nowhere near forty. The only give away is the peppering of grey hair that's crept in along his side burns and his eyes look wiser but it suits him and apart from that he's exactly as I remember him apart from the spectacles that look like they might just be for show. He's definitely aged better than me, I look alright, still semi-attractive but I've filled out. All that rich food Filipe likes me to cook has caught up with me.

'I've replaced Mrs Cockbone,' he says carefully, staring into my eyes. Cockbone. That's even worse than what I originally thought. I bet the kids have a field day with that name. Actually, probably not, they are only four and five years old. 'Yes, she's now become a star in the sky hasn't she, Sofia?'

'She's dead? That's awful.' I squawk.

'Well, urrm yes, I believe they announced it on the

school Facebook page? And I was trying to be…' he trails off and looks at Sofia and she smiles sweetly at him.

'We don't all use social media.'

'Sorry, I would have thought they'd send out an email too. I'm so sorry,' he grimaces.

'It's so sad,' I say, shaking my head. 'But Sofia knows about death don't you, poppet? Let's not sugar coat it and pretend it's something that it's not, they really don't become stars sweetheart, you die and then that's it but you might come back as a snail if you're naughty.'

Sofia giggles the tuneful laugh that I love so much and we both smile despite the fact I feel like Jayne, except I'm not spoiling Christmas, I'm potentially scaring a child about death. What am I doing?

'Right, well, yes, of course,' he says, his cheeks pinking. 'Anyway, so it will be me for the foreseeable, I am the replacement teacher.'

'Didn't know you trained as one,' I say, forgetting myself again.

'Umm, sorry I…?' His voice trails away, he looks puzzled.

Oh, shit, he doesn't even remember me. This is so embarrassing. 'Yeah, I didn't know people had to train to be a teacher, not a primary school teacher anyway. Thought it was on the job stuff.' I shrug it off, sounding ridiculously ignorant and arrogant but this wins over having to explain myself. He can't have forgotten me, can he? I take Sofia's hand, holding it in mine and nod curtly at him to continue.

He explains that Sofia, Mia and some of the other girls in class have been *mythering* each other. Yes, he uses that word before he goes on to fill in the detail. He says that one of the mums didn't want to talk to me about it herself as she values our friendship and thought it better if it could be sorted out in class. She's hoping it can be resolved this way.

It can only be Jayne.

'Sofia! How could you call Mia those names and throw sticks at her is just…' I realise I've raised my voice as I make eye contact with Mr Thomas so I take a deep breath then speak in a softer tone. 'You know names can hurt people's feelings, sweetie.'

'No, you always say stick and stones can break my bones but names can never hurt me so I wanted to see if that was true,' she answers, her little face contorted with angst.

'Oh, Sofia.'

'I wanted to see if it was true because Mia and sometimes her friends call me names and that makes me sad so I wanted to see what hurt Mia,' she continues. These girls are being mean to my child. And she's retaliated in kind. My heart drops into my stomach.

'But why didn't you say anything earlier, sweetheart? We could have avoided this. I'll have a word with Mia's mum.'

'I don't know.' Sofia's eye's well up like pools of swishy sea water and I scoop her up into a big hug. Those little shits. Trust Jayne's child to be the ring leader.

'What names do they call you?'

'Is that really relevant?' Mr Thomas asks.

'Yes, it is. Completely relevant,' I say.

'They call me orange head and biscuit face.'

'Biscuit face?'

'Yeah, because they say I have skin like a broken biscuit, like crumbs, they said.' I stare at my daughter's beautiful ginger hair, and tan coloured freckles, dotted perfectly across her clear pale skin.

How dare they.

'You're beautiful, so beautiful, people are sometimes scared of true beauty, it makes them feel ugly inside and want to be bad to people, isn't that right, Mr Thomas?' I say, hoping that she understands my crap explanation as to why people are arseholes. The sad truth is some people just enjoy making others feel crap. Some people are just arseholes but how can you say that to a five-year-old?

'Yes, or they might be feeling a little insecure in themselves and they think that putting others down will make them feel better. It's not that they're ugly, everyone is beautiful in their own way but they might be feeling a little sad themselves and want others to feel the same,' he says, sounding much more diplomatic and grownup than me. 'It doesn't make it right though. I'll be talking to Mia's mum too.' He nods to me, as though he's telling me to back off and not go off on one at Jayne. I feel like I've been slyly and expertly told off.

'Like when Olive snarls at dogs bigger than her?' Sofia asks.

'Who's Olive, Sofia?' Mr Thomas asks.

'She's my dog, she does big stinky farts but gives the bestest snuggles too.'

Her teacher and I laugh, he catches my eye and I swear his eyes twinkle. I decide it must be the obligatory silver tinsel decorated around the classroom reflecting in his multicoloured eyeballs.

There is a lot of it.

He definitely recognises me though, despite implying otherwise earlier.

Being in a classroom and seeing him is making me feel rather nostalgic in spite of the reason why I am here.

I wonder if Mr Thomas is married, has children. Probably. Olive is my first child, my fur baby. Filipe and

I tried for years for a baby but it just didn't happen so in the end Filipe gave in and let me have a dog, under the condition that I take full responsibility, including taking her on all walks, sorting vet visits etc. which I more than happily agreed to. Then I unexpectantly fell pregnant with Sofia and they've pretty much grown up together.

Filipe got the snip a year after Sofia was born, probably due to the severe sleep deprivation, but I mean he still gets sleep, it's me that gets up. Olive's almost six now and she loves people just as much as other dogs, always coming over for a cuddle or carrying a toy in her mouth to get you to play with her. She gets me out of the house and into the fresh air and I enjoy talking to all of the other dog walkers, if it wasn't for her, I wouldn't know half the people that I do. Having a dog is good for the soul, even if they do embarrass you on the odd occasion.

Sofia continues to talk to Mr Thomas about our dog as I muster up everything in me to try and act logical and like a grownup about the situation.

'Now, let's get home to give that big soppy dog a snuggle. She'll be missing you,' I say, standing up. There's nothing more to say now, Mr Thomas is going to talk to Jayne and Mia and organise a class talk on bullying. That should nip it in the bud. And if it doesn't, I'll just have to confront her.

'Yes, Olive makes everything better,' Sofia grins.

'Yes, yes she does.' If only she could fix it for Mr Thomas not to be Sofia's new teacher, I think to myself as I get up to leave. I offer him a small smile and he politely nods at me, the way he used to when we would pass each other along the school corridors.

Chapter 9

Delilah

'Hey squirt, how was work?' Dylan shouts from the kitchen, he somehow knows it's me from the way I slam the door or so he says, either that or the fact I get in later than everyone else every day.

He arranges his face into something resembling pity as he sees my miserable expression. He's wearing dad's apron, the one with the gorilla's body, coupled with pink rubber gloves. I smile as he does a silly dance at an attempt to cheer me up. He's definitely in a better mood today, must be all that mindless meditating he does or whatever he calls it. I lift myself up onto the kitchen counter as Dylan flicks the kettle on.

'Thanks, same old shit, as usual. I hate it,' I answer.

'That is shit. Mum and Dad are out shopping, I'm cooking Spaghetti Bolognese tonight, your favourite.'

'You mean *your* favourite,' I say, smiling at him. 'Don't worry about me, I think I'm going over Josh's anyway.'

'Ah, young love,' he teases but I can see the hurt nostalgia in his eyes. It must be shit living back in your parents' home at his age. Starting from scratch, all over again. He's pushing forty, so even if he meets someone now, it might be too late, depending on the age of the woman of course.

'Ask him to join us, I haven't seen him for ages.'

'Yeah?'

'Yes, it will be nice to see Josh.'

'Hmm maybe, bit cringe though.'

'Why?'

'Because, to be honest, you and Dad interrogate him, and that needs to stop. We've been together for ages now. I don't know what more you and Dad can interrogate him about.' I put a hand on my hip and give my ponytail a defiant swish.

'Yeah, but I'm the much cooler Dad.'

'Only just. I'll invite him, just don't be second dad and interrogate him.'

He nods his promise, quickly turning away to face the kettle.

'Cuppa?' he says with a face much more serious than when I walked in. Did I say something wrong?

'Yeah, go on then.' I stare out of the kitchen window as Dylan clonks about making the cups of tea. A woman with long red hair marches by with her dog, she's walking with such purpose and looks as though she's some kind of high-powered businesswoman. Her dog is walking next to her perfectly in its bright pink harness as it looks up at her every so often for a treat. I wonder if the only time she really gets to see her dog and family is in the evening. She spends those few hours after work rushing around trying to please everyone before she can finally relax with a glass of wine. She looks familiar, I must have seen her at the local Co-op or something, this is Coolsbay so most people look familiar. Dylan comes over to the window and watches her with me. She's mesmerising and we both watch in silence for a few seconds.

'Cute dog, I'd love a dog,' Dylan blurts out, still

staring at the woman. I go to say something about him liking the lady that comes with the dog too but realise it's probably too soon.

'Me too, you know I've always wanted one but dad always says no.'

'I can talk him round,' he says, shrugging, his mood much brighter again.

'Yeah right, and what will happen to it when you move out?'

'Who says I'll move out before you do? We can cross that bridge when we come to it and anyway, it would probably stay with me, go wherever I go. A little companion for life.'

'You're such a *simp* over dogs, you'll move out before me anyway.'

'I might not.'

'You have to, you can't be living at home indefinitely with Mum and Dad at forty. Urgh sad.'

'Urgh, charming.'

'Sorry, I'm just in a bad mood, but a dog would cheer me up.'

'You're not going to let this go now, are you?'

'Nope.' I grin at my brother and he smiles a wry smile back at me, if he can't work the magic on Mum and Dad then no one can.

Chapter 10

Amber

It's only Wednesday and this week is a stinker already, the dishwasher's broken too so that means hand washing the dishes until I can get it repaired. At least it's Christmas soon which means no more school runs for two weeks and some nice quality time with Sofia. Just a few more days of school drop offs, the school play and Jayne's mocking face to endure and then I can relax for a bit.

I march around the block a few times before texting Stella to see if she's free. I've wandered over to her area on the off chance she'll fancy a rant and a dog walk. Filipe came home early for once, so I sweet talked him into letting me go before it gets dark, citing the reason that Olive had a lot of energy and needed to get rid of it before she does something naughty again. He's still cross at her about the meal.

I really enjoy walking the dog for a number of reasons, it keeps my heart healthy but even more so, my mind. There's nothing I enjoy more than going out and meeting and speaking with all the other dog walkers, once you get past the general chitchat and swap niceties about the dogs, they all have a fascinating story to tell and quite often, if you chat to them long enough, a nugget of pure wisdom will escape them. I like to collect these nuggets, keep them close to my heart and think of them from time to time. But today, I just want a bitch with my mate.

I'm still reeling from my birthday dinner.

Relief spreads over me when she says she's free. I know I'll feel better after talking to her.

'I'm so glad you're free, I need to rant. Are you sure I'm not interrupting anything?' I blurt out even before she fully opens the door.

'Hello, my lovely, rant away mate and no no, all fine,' she says, as I step out of the way to let her and Pudding out of the house.

Stella and I walk over to the enclosed fields behind her house and I listen to her finish telling me in more detail about Badger's latest trip to A&E over the weekend after he bumped his head falling off the top of her wardrobe. That boy is always injuring himself. I said he sounds very adventurous and Stella said that he's just a cheeky little shit that takes after his dad and is always up to no good. She does make me laugh.

We arrive at the field and let the dogs off their leads to run about and play. I begin to rant away to Stella about the birthday from hell as the hounds bounce around, playing bitey face, chasing the birds and each other. Stella bends over laughing when I tell her about the catastrophe of Olive eating Stephanie's dinner.

'Ooooooh shit, it sounds like old Olive Oil did you a favour there though.' She wipes tears of laughter away from her eyes and makes an O shape with her mouth to slow her breathing and calm down her hysterics. I didn't think it was that funny at the time but I guess it is now. Sort of.

'Yes, they did leave quite swiftly afterwards. Honestly, what was he thinking? And now *he* is the one doing the sulking? I just don't get it,' I say, as Stella nods at a woman who looks exactly like the little pug she's walking. I look at our dogs, Pudding does resemble Stella somewhat, and not in a mean way but it's the mouth. I guess I resemble Olive a little, a bit podgy around the middle and with long ginger ears.

'Nor do I, I'm baffled as to why he invited Jayne. Maybe you and Filipe need to spend, dare I say it, a bit of quality time together.' She makes inverted comma signs with her fingers on the word quality.

'If you mean shagging then I'd have to convince him first, he wouldn't even shag me on my bloody birthday.'

'What? That's shit,' she says. 'Why didn't you get a birthday shag?'

'Didn't have time, was too busy getting the house ready for the surprise insufferable guests to arrive.'

'Mate, that's shit, Tamsin and I do it every other night.'

'I'm so jealous, if only I had that in my relationship, we used to be saucy, now we've gone a bit salty.'

'You'll get there again; you just need to make the effort with each other.'

'Yeah, maybe. But we've been together twelve years, we've done the quality time. The last time we watched a film together was about three years ago and I definitely fell asleep way before the end.'

'You still have to make time for each other.' She laughs as if I'm ridiculous. 'It's cheesy but you do. It sounds like you've got all out of synch. Why don't you arrange a date night or something and get to know each other again?'

'That might be a good idea but right now I just need

to stay away from him. I left him to put Sofia to bed, he hasn't done that in years. Isn't that sad?' I'll talk to him soon, perhaps tomorrow. After the birthday meal, I went straight to bed and Filipe stayed downstairs until gone midnight, he didn't clear up though, that was left for me in the morning, and we still haven't spoken about it.

'What Prince Filipe? Tend to his daughter and do a mere woman's work?' We both laugh but it's the sad truth. He hardly does anything on his own with Sofia, even if he just took her to the park that would be something. Maybe it isn't just Filipe and I that need to spend some more quality time together. He needs to spend time with Sofia.

Chapter 11

Delilah

Sky: *Hey, what are you doing tonight? Having a few drinks round mine if you're free? Molly's just text, she's coming. P.S. Possible party later too if you fancy it? xx*

I tap reply on my phone and with a heavy sigh I begin typing my message, declining the invitation. Josh, my boyfriend, is here sprawled out on the sofa, he's deep in conversation with my dad and brother about football. They're arguing over some player and whose team he played best in. Mum is in the kitchen making my favourite home cooked meal, lasagne and garlic bread but I'm not in the least bit hungry. I'm so bored, a few drinks with the girls sounds very appealing right now. I don't have to go to the party. I work up the nerve to present the idea to Josh. One, two, three, four. I slowly count to sixty-six in my head, leaving out the number thirteen before allowing myself to speak.

'Mind if I go out tonight?' I say to Josh, once the bantering has stopped.

'No, but I thought we were staying in? Where do you want to go?' Josh replies, running his fingers through his hair. He's so sweet, I almost feel guilty for not wanting to be here. Almost.

'Umm well, Sky has invited me over, think it's a girls' thing.' I shrug my shoulders, insinuating that it's no big deal if I go or stay. But I really want to go.

'She's dumping you for the girls, mate,' Dylan pipes up and Dad laughs softly.

'He can stay here with us, boys' night,' Dad says, ruffling Josh's hair before knocking beers with him.

'Yes, boys' night, we can burp, fart and chat football all night without a worry for the ladies.' Dylan raises his beer to the room as Mum shouts 'Oi' from the kitchen. He's a tad tipsy.

Something came in the post for him today, I'm not sure what it was, but when he began to open the large brown envelope there was a lot of frowning and sighing going on. Since he's moved back, everyone else has moved on, all his friends have families of their own now so no one is free to just hang out. He seems so lonely but I can hardly invite him to hang out with me and my friends, can I? A dog could be his best friend, he really needs to get to work on Mum and Dad, plus I really want one.

'You do that anyway,' I say, as right on cue Dad burps loudly at the TV.

'Uuuurgh, Dad.' I frown and place my hand on my hips, reverting back to embarrassed, grossed out teenager mode.

'Sorry love, boys' night,' Dad says, enjoying himself with the lads. I smile despite my disgust. It's lovely that they get on really, I suppose it could be worse. Yes, it could be a lot worse.

'Right, I think that's my mind made up.' I get up and walk over to Josh, perching myself on the edge of the sofa arm. 'You sure you don't mind hanging out with these weirdos all night?' I say, as I rest my hand on his shoulder.

'No, you deserve it after not getting the part, don't worry about me. These are my family too.' He grins, looking so comfortable on my sofa, in my house, with my family. Sometimes I think they like him more than me. I grin back at him then pull my phone out of my pocket.

Me: *I'm coming girls, be there in ten.*

Amber

It's 8pm, Sofia's tucked up in bed and will be asleep for at least four hours before her ritual of getting up begins. I stretch my legs out then peer over at Filipe who's sat on the opposite sofa concentrating deeply on his phone. I watch his mouth twitch up into little smiles as he reads replies from whoever is messaging him.

Secret smiles.

It's on his work phone so it will be some little in joke to do with work. I used to ask him what the jokes were but now I don't bother, I mean, they are 'in' jokes for a reason. Not really funny if you don't work there.

'Glass of wine,' I say, as I sashay past him.

'Yes, please *churri*. There's a bottle of red on the side,' he says, as he slides his phone back into his pocket.

In the kitchen I slowly pour us a glass each before walking back into the lounge. This was the bottle we didn't drink on my birthday dinner. It leaves a bitter taste in my mouth but I'll drink it anyway.

'Here, you go,' I say, as I hand him his drink.

'Thank you.'

I sit back in my seat opposite him and slowly sip my wine as my eyes drift towards the TV, we're watching a film. Something Filipe picked, set during the war but neither of us are really watching it. We check our phones, sip our wine and occasionally watch the TV. We sit like that, in silence and with the TV blaring for a good ten minutes, I've almost finished my wine when I speak.

'Filipe.'

'Yes.'

'Can I ask you something?'

'Depends what it is,' he jokes.

'What made you chose to invite Jayne, Stephanie and her boyfriend to my birthday meal? I mean, I just thought it quite an odd assortment of people.' I smile, I don't want to sound ungrateful but it was rather strange.

'Jayne was at the top of your list on your WhatsApp. I thought she was a good friend?' He shrugs. He's been checking my phone again. We used to check each other's phones all the time, possessiveness was almost sexy but I thought we'd grown out of it. I don't check his, haven't done for years.

'Hmm she's more of an acquaintance really.' A highly annoying one. 'She's one of the school mums who likes to send me lots of messages about school things. Too many messages if I'm honest.'

'Oh, but she seemed such a nice lady, nice dress she had on,' Filipe says. He smiles and shows his red wine-stained teeth as his phone beeps in his hand again. I run my tongue across my teeth to take off any excess stain. That's the problem with red wine, once you've drunk it, you can't hide it.

'Yeah, Stella and Tamsin are my friends, remember, and I haven't seen my sister and brother-in-law for a while…'

'What are you trying to say? Did I do it all wrong? I thought you liked Stephanie at least.' He sits up straight, his eyes focus on me, looking hurt.

'Nothing, I was just wondering why that's all. I wasn't complaining,' I lie, feeling bad, as the sentiment was there and he did spoil me with the presents. But that doesn't mean the dinner wasn't awful. It was more than awful, it was excruciating. 'Funny when Olive scoffed the dinner off Stephanie's lap though, wasn't it?' I giggle, trying to make light of it. 'Did she say much about it to you? Was she okay?'

'It wasn't the best, was it?' His face clouds over and he throws a look at Olive who is now sitting by my feet. Protectively, I bend down to stroke her, it's not her fault.

'No, I suppose not,' I lie, trying not to laugh but a big guffaw betrays me and escapes anyway. The wine has gone to my head already.

'I'm lucky she still wants to work for me really,' he snaps, annoyed at my outburst.

'Oh, please Filipe, she's got it too good working with you, she gets to do whatever she wants most of the time,' I say, thinking about seeing her at Emmanuel's and toying with the idea of telling him. I decide not to, because she might tell him about me and I don't want my husband to know that I fell through the dressing room curtain like a whale being released back into wild.

'I don't want to lose her, she's a good worker.'

I smile at him, feeling warm and fuzzy from the alcohol. Not wanting to argue over a dinner that's firmly in the past so I change the subject because I can't change the past.

'Mind if we turn this over? It's not really my thing,' I say, eyeing up the Christmas romcoms. Filipe nods, not looking at me then goes back to his work phone.

The secret smiles begin again.

Chapter 12

Delilah

It's taken me thirty minutes to arrive at the shed, it should have only taken ten minutes but of course I got the usual safety lecture from Dad. Dylan also joined in as Josh sat there like a rabbit caught in the headlights. It's been a while since he's heard that speech and Dylan has certainly upped the paranoia in the house since getting into all of those murder documentaries which, I admit, is entirely my fault. Never in a million years did I expect him to behave like this, if I had I never would have got him into them. I told Mum that Dylan needs to stop obsessing over them as it's now massively affecting my life. Mum and Dad think it's a good thing and that my brother is just looking out for me. I wish they would just leave me alone and not try to wrap me up in cotton wool all the time. I feel like such a baby when I'm with them. I swear my parents have become worse since I moved back from dance school. It's like they've regressed.

The door to the shed is closed when I arrive, I stand outside just listening to my friends for a second like a fly on the wall.

'Oh mate, not again, you never learn, do you?' Sky growls at Molly in despair.

'I know, I can't help it, what's wrong with me?' Oh dear, something tells me it's spreadsheet-gate again. Sky has little to no patience for this type of thing. Her personality of don't give a fuck is so far removed from Molly's worrying nature that they often clash and find it difficult to see the other's perspective. That's where I come in, I'm like the mediator in this group.

'I'm going to have to confiscate your phone or something, give it here,' says Sky.

'No.'

'Molly, give me your phone.'

'No.'

One, two, three, four, five, six. I'm going in.

'Hi girls, bottle of wine, Christmas drinks,' I say, entering the shed and shaking it at them in the hope of diverting attention away from spreadsheet-gate.

'Hey, Dee, ahh amazing, but it's a school night so none for me,' Molly says, then presses her lips together, proud of her ability to say no and not give in to peer pressure. I admire that, I'm easily influenced, especially when it comes to partying.

'Stop saying it's a school night, it's not a school night. You haven't been at school in like five years.' Sky looks to the ceiling and puffs on her cigarette as her dog, Luna, watches her then mimics her owner by moving her big googly eyes upwards.

Sky's dressed up again, glitter everywhere, her makeup looks like something out of a West End show, it's stunning. Minus the makeup, Luna is matched with her, wearing a pink, frilly tutu. I don't know if I'll dress up my dog when I get one, Luna does look quite grumpy about it but that might be just her personality. A sassy little bitch.

'How's the new job, Sky?' I wink at her then do my

best twerking impression as the girls laugh. There, I've lightened the mood already, spreadsheet-gate can take a back seat, I won't ask about it for fear of spoiling the atmosphere, not tonight.

'Yeah, it's pretty fucking amazing to be fair.' Sky leans over and reaches into her handbag; Luna starts to snuffle thinking she's getting a treat then lays back down again groaning as Sky pulls out a wad of fifty-pound notes.

'Living the dream,' she says, fanning out her notes and waving them dramatically at her face.

'Wow and that's the money made from your FansOnly page?' I say, with eyes wide.

'Yep, just a week's wage, not even that, five days I think.'

'You've made more than I do in a month,' I say. This is depressing.

Molly folds her arms and shakes her head, seemingly not impressed.

'Yep, and I don't even get my fanny out.'

Molly makes a disgusted face which encourages Sky to get up and show us some of her dance moves. Even though she's not getting her fanny out, she certainly thrusts it about enough, her form is good but some of the moves are a little clunky. I turn the speaker up before getting up to show her some more moves, soon we're dancing in unison, giggling and really enjoying ourselves.

It reminds me of when we were about twelve and we used to make up awkward dance moves to our favourite songs. We'd spend hours choreographing and rehearsing until it was just right. Our poor parents must have been so bored having to watch our performances when we announced that we had yet another one to show them. A memory of Sky begging her parents to let us perform in the pub pops into my mind; they said it wasn't appropriate which of course it definitely wasn't. She knew it wasn't too but craved the attention, even from the pervy old locals propped up at the bar. Molly joins in dancing with us after a while but she does sit down half way through and begin frantically typing away on her phone again whilst intermittently consuming large gulps of wine. She's drinking a lot for someone who didn't want to drink tonight, on a school night. Spreadsheet-gate is even starting to annoy *me* now.

'Give that here, honestly, you're driving me mad.' Sky rips the phone out of her hands and chucks it onto the sofa bed behind her. She pulls Molly up onto her feet and Molly reluctantly joins in again. We dance for another three or four songs until Sky collapses onto the sofa bed with Molly joining her not long after.

'Urgh, that's me done, I need a drink and a cigarette now.'

I'm still dancing though and thoroughly enjoying myself. I've missed dancing. An Ed Sheeran song comes on which propels me into romantically pirouetting around the room, getting lost in the music. I end up performing a whole contemporary piece. The songs ends and I bow to my audience as they clap and whoop me. I open my eyes and sigh; I feel ridiculously emotional.

'Wow, Dee,' Molly says, smiling and still clapping at me.

'Bravo, got any more auditions lined up?' Sky asks.

'Thanks, I miss it so much and no, I'm taking a break for a while, auditions aren't my friend at the moment. I got another rejection.'

'Oh, Dee, I'm so sorry, but don't give up.' Molly rubs my arm and I feel an overwhelming urge to cry.

'I'm just taking a break, earning some pennies until I can give it another shot, I'm not giving up,' I say, not sounding too convincing.

'How about teaching dance?' Molly suggests. 'You'd be good at that.'

'Those who can't – teach.' I hold my hands up, surrendering to my failed dancer fate. We all giggle, but those words have just made me feel sadder.

'Yeah, but is that true? Who says that?' Sky asks, as she scratches her dog under the chin and Luna snorts her gratitude at her owner.

'No, I don't think so, I heard my brother say it once,' I reply. What I'd give to be a pampered pooch, even for just one day. Instead, I'm a molly coddled failed ballerina. Alright, not a ballerina as that's not what I specialise in but it sounds much more dramatic. 'It's not something I would rule out but there's literally two dance schools in Coolsbay and all the teachers have been teaching for years, there's almost never a vacancy. I'd have to wait for someone to leave before I got a job at one of those schools. I could be waiting for years, either that or move to London.'

'No, don't move!' Molly screeches, taking a few more large gulps of her wine. All worries of drinking on a school night, long gone out of the window.

'I won't, I don't want to move but there's not much opportunity here, is there? It's all tour companies, the casino and local pubs, we don't even have a *Butlins* I could dance at.' And I'd happily do that at the moment.

'I could so see you in a red coat,' Molly giggles. 'Or maybe you could be the mascot, is there still a mascot?' She hiccups.

'That's because Coolsbay is snobby,' Sky announces. 'The casino brings in all the money from tourism because all the posh snobs that come to stay in their expensive holiday homes are all hopeless alcoholics and gamblers.'

Sky is still frantically scratching Luna's chin, even though she is now fast asleep, snoring.

'Sad but very true. Urgh this talk is getting too serious for me, I just want to get smashed now,' I blurt out, even taking myself by surprise.

'Let's do it!' 'It's CHRISTTTMAAAAAAAASSSSS.' Molly clumsily raises her glass, slopping wine onto Luna's head in the process. The dog wakes with a start, snorting and barking loudly. She's really not happy. Sky searches frantically for her treats as Luna snorts and barks at her owner, telling her off for disturbing the peace. Sky finally finds them and gives her some fancy looking homemade dog treats with little dog biscuit bones stuck on the top; they look so good *I'd* eat them. Luna barks and demands more treats until the whole packet is completely gone. Sky begins to stroke her and Luna snorts at all of us before staring Sky in the eyes and performing a little low growl. Sky tells us that we need to take this as our cue to leave and that you can't upset her baby like that. Molly and I cry with laughter. I can already tell this is going to be one hell of a messy night.

We arrive at the house party an hour later with a few bottles of the pub's wine in hand. Sky's parents gave them to us as an early Christmas present. It's lethal stuff and my head is already spinning. The party host is one of Sky's friends that I vaguely know from college. We all vaguely know each other in this town, even if you're not friends, you're guaranteed to be friends with someone who is their friend or a friend of their sister, brother, auntie, dad, dog or cousin.

You get the gist.

We spend the first two hours or so catching up with people, dancing, drinking and having a laugh until I feel the need to creep off to find the bathroom and get some much-needed space. I'm having a good night, it's great seeing everyone, but this house is literally swarming with people. I need a breather, a break from the constant chatter and noise and to count myself back to calmness. Even with all the alcohol the anxiety still seeps through. My first thought is to look around for Sky, she might want to go out for a cigarette. It's at times like these that I almost wished I smoked or at least vaped but I can't stand the stuff.

I find her in the kitchen snogging some boy; perhaps not then. I continue through the living room, looking for the bathrooms, I finally find them but the queues, both upstairs and downstairs are huge. I'm not that desperate for the loo so I stroll over to the backdoor, grab my coat and pull on the handle, breathing a sigh of relief when I find it to be unlocked. Stepping out into the back garden, the cold December air hits me, it's also pitch black apart from the security light which thankfully switches on when my feet hit the patio.

It's heavenly quiet and I savour the stillness.

Breathing in a big lung full of cold, crisp air stings my nostrils. I slowly blow the air out of my mouth watching my warm breath fill the darkness. One, two, three, four, five, six. My phone buzzes in my pocket, making me flinch a little. I curse Dylan and his murder documentaries for making me paranoid. I check the time and it's 11:13, a bad omen already.

Josh: *Hey, how's your night? Your dad and brother fell asleep after the game. Got some great photos. So funny. Xx.*

His message makes me smile, perhaps I should go home and get in bed with my boyfriend. I start to reply then panic sets in. I haven't actually seen Molly since we got here and she was pretty drunk when we left Sky's.

Me: *Mols where are you? I'm just outside getting some air, you okay?* I'll just make sure she's alright and then I'll go home, Josh will see me soon anyway so no need to respond to his message. I slide my phone back into my pocket and savour the fresh December air again, taking in another gulp to rejuvenate my soul. One, two, three, four, five, six, I get to number sixty, missing out the number thirteen.

Shitsticks.

This time, I really jump. He appears from the bushes, wearing a long coat and a hood pulled up over his head. He's walking with purpose, fast and determined. I can't move. I count his steps, all thirteen of them. My legs have turned to jelly. It's as if I don't have control over my body anymore. It won't do what I want it to do.

Please move.

Body, you have to move.

I'm sorry Dylan, I should never have rolled my eyes at you.

'Arrrrghhhhhh.' The scream doesn't sound like me but it can't be anyone else. He certainly isn't screaming. 'Arrghhhhh,' I scream again. Please someone, hear me. My limbs suddenly come back to life, the fire in my belly reignited and ready to fight, not flight. I reach into my pocket and clutch the penknife. He stops walking. Now it's him rooted to the spot. Is he going to pull out a weapon?

'Dee, Dee, what are you doing out here?' Molly appears next to me as I turn round with the knife in my hand.

'Arrrrghhh.' We scream in unison and I'm sure the hooded stranger does too.

'Put the knife down,' the stranger says, with a slow steady tone, his voice low and slightly croaky.

'Byron,' Molly squawks at the dark-haired, dark-eyed stranger, who is now standing with his hands up. 'Don't kill him. babe, he isn't that bad,' she slurs, putting her arm around me.

'What were you doing in the bushes?' I ask, aware that I'm not actually in any immediate danger because Molly seems to know him.

'I went for a piss, didn't think I'd get caught, especially by a girl with a knife. By the way, please can you put that thing away.' He points to my knife and I reluctantly slide it back into my pocket but keep my hand on the handle, just in case.

'FUCK.' A guy in his mid -thirties with long wavy hair emerges from the back of the garden, walking with his legs really wide apart. He's shaking his head vigorously but smiling.

'What's going on man? I only went for a piss but ended up crapping myself when you all screamed. Amazing feeling to come up on a pill and take a crap but still, I'm going to have to go home and get changed now.' The guy slopes past and a waft of his insides infiltrates my nostrils as he goes stamping back inside the house.

'Euuw yuk.' Molly pinches her nose then flings her other arm around me. 'Dee is my friend, she cares about me, looks out for me. You,' Molly says, pointing an unsteady finger at the guy in the hoody who we now know is called Byron. 'You.' She points again. 'Don't care.' She leans forward pointing with more force this time. Her body leans further forward, following her finger. She loses balance until she flops on the ground face down.

Clunk.

Shitsticks.

'Mols, Molly, wake up,' I screech, kneeling down on the floor. I slap her face a little to try and wake her. She doesn't move.

'Can I?' Byron crouches down and turns her onto her side, arranging her in the recovery position. He bends down further to check her breathing, pulse and airway. His reaction to an emergency is a lot more helpful and experienced than mine. 'She's breathing, but she's obviously had a lot to drink and has just bumped her head. I hate to be dramatic but we should probably phone an ambulance. I'd drive but I've had a few myself, I think most people here have.' Yep and not just alcohol either.

'Good idea, I'll ring one now,' I say suddenly sober and reaching for my phone. Something tells me, this is going to be a long night.

Byron and I ride in the ambulance with Molly. After a number of checks, they hook her up to all sorts of monitors, measuring her heart rate and breathing. It's so scary seeing my friend like that, my sensible friend too. She never gets drunk like this but I have a feeling I'm sitting next to the reason why she is in such a state.

'I hope she's going to be okay and sorry for… you know.' I point to my pocket, suddenly aware that this could get very serious if I mention I have a knife and one of the paramedics overhears. I don't want the police turning up too.

'I'm sure she'll be fine, it's just a precaution really.'

'Are you training to be a doctor or something?'

'No.' He laughs. 'My dad's a paramedic, he drilled the basics into us as kids.'

'Oh right,' I say, suddenly feeling very inadequate. I should know this stuff. What did they teach me in dance school? 'Molly will be mortified when I tell her what's happened.'

'So, don't tell her.'

'I can't really do that can I?'

'Okay, just looking out for her.'

'Hmmmm, she doesn't seem to think you do.'

'Your friend is high maintenance. I was honest from the start that I didn't want a relationship but she just kept sending me these really long messages trying to argue otherwise. It's odd and a bit scary.'

'Oh, spreadsheet-gate.' I bite my lip, cringing for my friend.

'Yup, it's a whole other level and not one I want to master,' he says.

I suppress a giggle for fear of looking like the shittiest friend in front of the paramedic. Poor Molly, she can be so intense at times, she's her own worst enemy.

'I'm sure she has her reasons,' I say, staring at her.

Byron opens his mouth to say something but changes his mind and closes it again. We sit in silence for the next few minutes.

'Why don't you want a relationship with her?'

'Not just with her, with anyone. I was with someone for seven years; I just want to be on my own for a bit now. Be my own man. Be free.' He shrugs.

'Fair enough.' I study his face, he can't be much older than me which means they must have been childhood sweethearts, just like Josh and me. At least he's been honest with her, a lot of guys I know would ghost a girl that's come on too strong, or worse, string them along. But is he a fuck boy?

'How is it then? Being free?' I ask.

'It's good, I don't have to pretend anymore, if you know what I mean?' he says, searching my face. 'Yeah, that's where I struggle, when it becomes effort, it shouldn't be that hard should it?' He looks at me with intense dark chocolate, brown eyes and I look away. I can see why Molly is attracted to him.

As if she senses my thoughts, Molly begins to stir and writhe around. She leans over and brings up big chunks of pink vomit. The paramedic, who's been sat next to her the whole time holding a shallow cardboard bowl, expertly catches most of it, swapping another bowl halfway through as the other one fills up. He cleans her up and then Molly lays back down, looks up at the ceiling then closes her eyes and begins to snore, blissfully unaware of the situation.

Molly is taken to the hospital; they think she's fine but wanted to keep an eye on her as she wouldn't wake up so she's staying overnight to be observed. I want to stay with her but they won't let me. I send her a text to call me as soon as she's up and follow Byron outside to wait for our taxi. She is going to die when she finds out about Byron being there.

Maybe I won't tell her.

Byron and I wait for a taxi which takes almost two hours to arrive, *high demand, Christmas parties every night*, the operator says when we call up to ask where it is for the fourth time. Byron and I talk about Christmas, living with our parents and our jobs, he's an electrician. I tell him I dance; he tells me he loves surfing and breakdancing, watching it mostly but he can pop and lock. He gives me his jacket. I ask him to show me some moves but he won't, it's too late, we're too sober. We talk more about music, surfing, Coolsbay, friends in common, murder documentaries and older brothers. We laugh about the man who crapped himself in the garden. The taxi arrives and oddly, it feels like it's been two minutes, not two hours. I give him back his jacket.

We say goodbye.

I get home and crawl into bed to find a sleeping Josh. He's out for the count, snoring loudly. It's so late but I'm still not tired, adrenaline still pumping through my veins from tonight's fiasco. I turn over and reach for my phone, scrolling through Instagram until I eventually find Byron and stalk his profile. There are lots of artsy shots of Coolsbay beach and quite a few of him surfing, looking really attractive in his wet suit. I can see why Molly likes him and even why she's been a little psycho over him. I force myself to put my phone down, then watch Josh sleeping for a while. I wonder what Bryon looks like asleep?

Uh oh.

Chapter 13

Amber

We get through the morning school run before I come home and begin to attack my Tuesday list. It's so long as I've let a few things slide recently.

I really can't be arsed.

The motivation to do anything is a real struggle at the moment. I tell myself I'll tackle the jobs in a minute as I make a latte with our new coffee machine. Plonking myself down on the sofa, I begin to scroll through social media for a while, I hardly ever use it but ever since our delightful dinner I've wanted to snoop on Jayne. It appears she doesn't use it much either, there's a photo of her and her ex-husband smiling as the profile picture but her profile's set to private so that's all I can see.

I carry on scrolling, sucked in by people's various posts on weight loss saying it's all down to Juicy Juicy or some other well-known dieting company that makes you join their pyramid scheme and be your own girl boss. Tempting, because the women's transformations do look good but at what cost? No thank you. I end up clicking on a video of a sweet looking dog that can do loads of tricks and make a mental note to try some with Olive, she's so smart. Then, I inadvertently fall down a rabbit hole, staring mindlessly at cute photos and videos of dogs for two hours.

Whoops.

This is why I don't do social media; it sucks valuable time out of my life. I click out of the dog videos and continue to scroll. Google must have been reading my thoughts, there are animal jobs popping up left, right and centre. I've always fancied working with animals but let's face it, I can barely control my own dog, the dinner party proved that. No. don't be so hard on yourself; Olive is a beagle and anyone who owns one of those understand that their brains are all in their noses which can make them incredibly stubborn. As long as I have nice treats, or a bit of beef, she'll do brilliantly. I click on a link about dog courses anyway and there's a whole array of attractive looking courses, including dog grooming.

Dog grooming, why didn't I think of that? It's basically the perfect job for me. As a qualified hairdresser, surely I would already possess some skills, I could at least hold a pair of scissors correctly. I mentally redecorate and install dog grooming furniture into one of the spare rooms that we have never used, then mentally strip it all out.

Filipe would never allow it.

Is this me, wanting to feel like me again? A bit of independence? A bit of joy that doesn't involve keeping house all day? Feeling like a suppressed 1950s housewife, I peel myself off the sofa and begin my jobs, starting with the monumental pile of washing up. When it's time, I pick Sofia up from school, do the normal routine of homework, dinner and bedtime and then go to bed early myself. I hear Filipe come home just before midnight.

Filipe's getting ready for work, he got up at 5am this morning and is now thumping about like a bloody elephant. He stayed in my bed last night which means I must be forgiven for the dinner party, not that it's my fault Olive ate off Stephanie's lap, well, not entirely. I wake up feeling weird after having a strange dream about Sofia's teacher, Mr Thomas. There's a vivid memory of us watching a film in his classroom but the film is of the two of us when we were young. Old us watching young us on an old grey, thick eighties style TV. Then he cracks out the popcorn and fizzy drinks and tells me this is when the good bit happens but not before the earthquake starts and the whole class room collapses around us, that's when I wake up and realise Filipe is the earthquake and I'm not going to get to watch the good bit.

Bollocks.

I shut my eyes again, half trying to get the dream back, half hiding from Filipe. I didn't sleep well last night which is probably why I can remember my dream so well. They say if you've had a good night's sleep then you shouldn't remember your dreams. At the moment, I'm dreaming a lot.

The door slams and I wait a few minutes before creeping downstairs to make myself a strong coffee. I'm looking forward to enjoying it in peace before Sofia's alarm goes off and I have to let Olive out for her ritual 7am shit. I tell Alexa to stick on some Alanis Morrissette. The eighties TV in my dream has got me feeling very nostalgic, even though Alanis is very obviously from the nineties, perhaps my dream like brain couldn't recall a nineties TV, were they that memorable?

Alanis's first album was basically the soundtrack to my youth. I sit there for a good while, hugging my coffee cup whilst reminiscing about my teenage angst and all the wild and fun times we had back then. It was just after this album came out that I met him, properly met him because I'd noticed him years ago. I close my eyes, smiling, then cringe a little. We both had so many dreams, we bared our souls to each other that night, both sharing swigs out of a large bottle of *White Lightening* cider, the smell of cider still makes me heave now. Little did I know that would be the last time that I saw him.

Looking back, it was like an English council estate version of an episode of Dawson's Creek. We thought we knew it all back then and tried so hard to speak differently to the adults around us, to create our own identities. I guess that's how Sofia will be soon, she's already starting to come home using made up words like yeet and she's only five. It's already started, I don't want her to grow up. He and I discussed everything, I always knew I wanted to work with dogs but people laughed and asked me how, I couldn't answer properly then.

I think I always said a vet but I always knew my grades would never be good enough. I just knew I wanted to work with dogs but doggy day care or doggy grooming wasn't really a thing back then, I guess I felt self-conscious and silly. But he didn't laugh, he was genuinely interested or at least I thought he was. He told me that he wanted to be a professional footballer or at the very least to coach football, I guess it wasn't just me who lost track of their dreams. A couple of friends were doing hairdressing so I ended up doing the same and continued until I met Filipe. I'm still not working with dogs, far from it, but at least I own one now; Olive looks up at me and I scratch underneath her chin for her.

'Such a beautiful pooch, aren't you? I'd be much more lonely without you.'

'Mummy, I had a bad dream.' Sofia appears, standing in the doorway, she's rubbing her eyes with one hand whilst holding her snuffle blanket with the other. I must get rid of that old thing soon, try to ween her off it.

It stinks.

'Oh sweetheart, me too,' I lie.

Delilah

'Hello, you're home early,' Dylan says, as I walk into the kitchen and dump my bag on the work top. 'Cuppa?' he asks. He's wearing that jumper again, the navy blue one. It's just so baggy on him, so bland. He's also wearing matching navy-blue trousers and let's not even go there with the shoes.

My phone beeps a message notification in my bag and I choose to ignore it, it will be Josh wanting to come over again. Since coming back to Coolsbay he hasn't given me time to breathe.

'Yes please. We had our Christmas lunch meal and then got told to go home, it's too much to expect us to work on big full stomachs,' I say, patting my usually flat but now slightly rounded stomach.

'Nice one, that Miriam doesn't seem too bad after all then.'

'Doubt that, she still gives me anxiety. It wasn't her who told us to go home anyway, it was the big boss.'

'Ah.'

'What are you up to tonight?' I ask, studying a hole in the back of his jumper as he turns to finish making the teas.

'Not much, but I have to go back to school in a couple of hours. I have a meeting with one of the mums.'

'That's plenty of time then.'

'Plenty of time for…?'

'Plenty of time for me to take you clothes shopping.' I fold my arms as I appraise him.

'Take me clothes shopping? What are you trying to say?' He looks down at himself and I bite my lip, feeling slightly mean at being so blunt but not mean enough not to be honest.

'Bro, I've got to break it to you,' I say, a bit more delicately. 'I love you, but you desperately need a makeover. Those clothes are a huge no no.'

Dylan chucks his head back and roars with laughter, when he's finished, he shakes his head at me. 'No, these clothes are fine thanks, and besides I don't care what I look like, I'm not a teenage girl.'

'Neither am I, but you should care, don't you want to feel good about yourself? Because you have a big hole in that jumper and I can't stop looking at it. Some things have got to go, including that.' I point at the jumper and half expect him to decline again.

Instead, he takes the jumper off and turns it around examining it until he finds the hole. He wriggles his finger into the hole and winces. Realisation setting in that he's been walking around like that all day and possibly even longer; God knows how long it's been there.

'Okay, I do need a new suit for my Christmas works do and I guess it can't hurt to get a few other bits, but I'm drawing the line at those skinny jeans.'

'Dylan no one even wears them anymore.'

'That's alright then.'

Amber

'Is it the school play tonight?' Sofia looks up at me, clearly confused as to why she's the only one at the school. She's already asked me twice why we're here but is having trouble getting her head around it.

'No sweetheart, that's on Friday. That will be your last day and then it's the Christmas holidays, countdown until Santa comes,' I say, trying to sound as excited as I should feel. She's five, this should be the most magical year for Christmas yet. I should be savouring all the fairy-tale moments and creating magic everywhere she looks. Instead, I'm ragingly cross at her father. I feel a pang of guilt about Filipe, perhaps I should arrange that date night soon and try to shift some of this resentment. It's not fair on anyone, he's never been that thoughtless before, in fact it's the very thing that I always thought he was, thoughtful. He must have a lot on at work.

'Yay! Santa!' she says, perking up with a little jump.

'We're just having a little chat with your teacher this evening, make sure everything's alright.' We've been invited in again and to say I'm dreading this meeting in more ways than one is a massive understatement.

'Okay, Mummy.' She blinks back at me, her sweet face simply trusting my every word. I try to remember when that stops and you start questioning everything your parents do and say?

'Come in,' he answers. I push open the heavy door and Sofia runs in to him.

'Hi Mr Thomas, I made you a Christmas card,' she says, handing over her painting of reindeers flying in the sky doing shits all over the town.

She told me that the brown blobs were presents being dropped into the houses but they really do look like shits. My cheeks pinken up, half embarrassed for the shit thought and half embarrassed that I'm embarrassed. Plus, Mr Thomas, looks even hotter than the last time I saw him. He's wearing a grey roll neck jumper which accentuates all the colours in his eyes, and his biceps, they look pretty good too. He takes the card and turns it over in his hands, examining it like it's a lump of treasured gold. My embarrassment of my child handing over a shitting reindeer card slowly turns to pride as I quickly swallow the lump that's forming in my throat.

'Oh wow, thank you, Sofia, that's so kind of you.' She stands with her hands behind her back and beams at him, so proud of herself. 'This will take centre stage right here.' He puts the card up on the shelf behind him, in front of a few of the others. The shitting reindeers taking pride of place.

'So,' he says, knitting his knuckles together as his biceps flex underneath his jumper. 'I've had a word with Mia and her mum and since we spoke we did have a class chat about bullying and I arranged for an old pupil to come in and speak about the effects of bullying. Touch wood,' he says, tapping on his desk 'it's been a lovely atmosphere in the class ever since then. Would you say that's true, Sofia?' he asks my daughter, as I examine his hair. It's much shorter now, doesn't frame his eyes anymore but they are still his best feature, the colour of them is almost non-descript because they appear to be all the colours. Colour changing, almost.

'Yes, me and Mia are friends now and she doesn't say I'm ugly with orange hair or a biscuit face anymore.'

Ugly? Biscuit face? I'm still fuming about the name calling. I'm quite pleased Mr Thomas has taken this so seriously, if it wasn't for him, I would have had serious words with Jayne by now. This is way better and more professional than a mum stand-off at the school gates. I hold Sofia's hand and smile warmly at her as I blink back tears of hurt. Kids are so forgiving. She best not mess with my kid again or I will be going straight to Jayne and this time, she will be held accountable for it.

'That's good, Sofia. I'm glad you're friends now,' I say soothingly, giving her hand a little squeeze.

'Thanks for sorting it out and for arranging the class chat, Mr Thomas.' I smile warmly whilst hoping there isn't anything stuck in my teeth.

He nods and smiles, not breaking eye contact. 'No problem, if there's anything else, please email me directly.' He hesitates for a second then scrabbles around for some paper before scribbling down his email address. 'Here you go,' he says, handing the piece of paper to me, his fingers brush mine and static energy makes us both pull away quickly. Did he feel it too? It all feels very nostalgic yet extremely awkward. A note with his hand writing on, isn't this how it all began?

Twenty-five years ago.

We all line up outside the assembly hall. Somehow I've ended up being sandwiched between the girl who constantly eats tissue and the class mute. My friends are nowhere to be seen; they've been leaving me out a bit lately. The bitches. I feel a light tap on my shoulder, hopeful it might be them but then it's even better, it's him.

He stuffs the note into my hand.

My fingers tingle with charged electric energy. I don't look at it but grip it tightly, holding my breath as he disappears further back down the line to find his mates. Discreetly, for fear of someone seeing it and worse, it being confiscated, I shyly tuck the note inside the top of my skirt belt. I can't stop grinning, without sounding too sure of myself, I already know the gist of what it's going to say. You see, we've been engaged in a clandestine magnetic attraction for weeks. Even when the bullies pick on me, he finds some way to divert their attention.

His eyes are always on me.

Usually, all he needs to do is be there, most of the girls at school flock around him and turn into giggling messes at his very presence. But other times, when he isn't that close, he'll do something funny like kick a football at them or shout at one of them to come over to him. And they do, every time, because it's him. How can a boy be so beautiful? In more ways than one.

We finally get called into the assembly hall to sit down, the note burning a hole in my side. I touch my lips with a finger and smooth around the remains of my Heather Shimmer lipstick as my eyes search for him. They swivel in every direction but I can't see him. I feel so compelled to turn around but I also don't want to draw attention to myself.

Someone coughs, so I use this as my opportunity to turn my head. It doesn't take long for our eyes to find each other across the sea of heads, giving into his energy, forever pulling me back to him. His light brown hair parts neatly down the middle, framing his multicoloured eyes and dark eyelashes perfectly. I want to touch that hair so badly; he has the best hair in school. We gaze at each other for a good two seconds as I use my finger to rub my lipstick around my lips yet again and he smooths down his curtains. A secret smile spreads across our faces, then he simply mouths the word 'alright.' The end of Assembly can't come soon enough, I hope we don't get questioned on it as I have absolutely no idea what's been said.

A while later, I turn my head again, this time, more slowly. He's watching me again, I'm sure his cheeks pinken as I smile at him.

When assembly is over, I rush to the toilets to hide in a cubicle and read the note. His scribbly hand writing makes my heart race.
Hi Amber,
Fancy going to the cinema tomorrow night?
Write back

x
Hell, yes I do. A little shriek escapes me as someone bangs on the door telling me to hurry up. The most popular boy in the school wants to take me out. This, is going to be the start of something

special. I feel it, I know it and I can't wait for it.

Chapter 14

Amber

The last day of school, it's finally here. Mr Thomas is doing a good job of being Sofia's new teacher and an even better job of pretending that he doesn't know who I am. I'm almost beginning to believe that perhaps he actually doesn't. Just because he was a significant part of my life growing up, doesn't mean I was a part of his. It was twenty-five years ago, that's a lifetime and a lot can happen in-between.

I hug my coffee mug and gaze out of the window, there she is again. As soon as she gets to the corner of my house her palm flies up to the side of her face, it's as if she's hiding from me.

'What it is?' I say, banging on the window. 'Why are you hiding from me?' I continue in the hope that she can hear me or sense my lips moving at the very least. All a bit pointless, but there you go.

Padding over to the kitchen, I make myself another strong coffee before cooking up some poached eggs on toast with a sprinkling of paprika. Sofia's donkey outfit hangs sadly on the living room door handle. It's the school play later. I had to sew on the tail again last night, my poor sewing skills not standing up to the rough and tumble of primary school life. I pull on the tail to check it's secure and it comes off in my hand, all lank and woolly. Bollocks. I must have been tired last night. I'll have to do it again.

'*Buenos dias, churri*,' Filipe sings, as he enters the living room. We finally had sex last night after weeks of a drought. I did have to seduce *him* and it would have been nice if it was the other way around but it was still good. I really can't complain, because just before I pounced on him he revealed that he's booked us into a hotel tomorrow night for some 'us' time. This could be the beginning of things looking up. I'm really looking forward to the hotel stay. We never do anything like that anymore, since he got his dream job that's all he breathes, thinks and talks about. I'm hopeful he's starting to realise that he's let other areas in his life slide, either that or it's guilt for the shit dinner party, whichever it is, I don't care.

'Ola, darling, you okay?'

'All the better for seeing you my *churri*.'

'Stop it.' I smile but I don't want him to stop it. 'I have to get ready for school and sew a donkey's tail back on.'

'You're such a pain in the big massive ASS.' He smacks my bum on the word ass as I put my hands on my hips and smirk. His poor dad-jokes always make me laugh but I think he may have just given me a bruise.

'Hey, it's not that big, is it?' I say, straining my neck over my shoulder to check out my bum in the living room mirror. A flashback of me falling through the dressing room curtain lights up in my mind's eye followed by Jayne and Stephanie's perfect physiques at the dinner party.

Oh, get over it, Amber.

'It does look a lot wider than usual but I wouldn't say fat,' I continue, answering my own question. I mean, it's still a nice shape, isn't it?' I say, not exactly fishing for compliments but massively dangling some maggots.

'Big, fat and juicy, but it's fine. You're my Christmas pudding bum.'

'Oh please,' I say, looking in the mirror again. Hmmm perhaps it is a bit lumpy actually. 'I guess it wouldn't hurt to eat a bit healthier.'

'Well yes, the arms are a little bigger, I know you complain about them. Hey, you could take a look at the meal plan and make dinners with less fat in.' He shrugs his shoulders and turns his mouth down. If it was that easy, with an extremely picky daughter and a husband with a penchant for rich food, I would have been doing it all along.

'Yeah, good plan.' No point in arguing.

Sofia appears so I busy myself saying hello to her and finding the sewing stuff. Depressed at the thought of making bland mundane meals for the rest of my life and the fact that my husband called my arse a big fat Christmas donkey, pudding bum. He certainly won't be getting seconds on the stuffing this Christmas after those comments.

'Well done,' he says, patting me on my donkey ass as I fight the urge to throttle him.

'Morning my lovely, it's the last dayyyyy,' Stella sings, and rubs her hands together, grinning and jigging from side to side as her breath meets the air and turns to steam. She's still wearing shorts, albeit a bit thicker material than usual.

'Morning, yeah, thank God.' I touch Sofia's hair and twirl her silky ringlets around in my fingers before stroking her soft cheek. Sometimes I feel bad that she doesn't have a sibling, someone to play with and keep her company but it's too late now. I'm too old and Filipe's had the snip anyway, I don't know why he had to do it, I probably wouldn't have got pregnant even if we'd tried. But having the snip is so final. He's snipped off my right to another child.

I join in on Stella's side step jig to jolly myself up and chuck in a couple of fist pumps for good measure. 'Can you tell I'm excited for the last day?' Soon we're jigging about like lunatics and the kids are joining in too, cheering and singing jingle bells at the top of their lungs. The other mums look on, some judging, some smiling. I'm savouring this moment, in just a few years Sofia will no doubt be dying of embarrassment every time I so much as breathe.

'Good morning, ladies, well aren't you cheerful this morning? Pastry?' Jayne trills, and holds out a plate of what looks like home-made mince pies.

'Oh wow, they look amazing Jayne? Did you make them yourself?' I ask merrily. If our kids are okay with each other then I need to be okay with Jayne. Life is too short to hold a grudge and after seeing her profile picture I feel a bit sorry for her. She's probably just lonely, hence why she accepted the invitation to my birthday. I mean there really could be no other reason, could there?

'Yes, I did, thank you,' she smiles, and flicks her hair as she marches off to offer them to all the other mums.

'Badger! You dirty little shhhhhugar puff.' Stella uses all her will power not to swear at Badger who's farted, cupped it in his hand and wafted it in Sofia's face.

'Oh yuk, Badger, what *did* you have for dinner last night?' Sofia whines, pinching her nose delicately with her fingers. Stella and I make eye contact, trying not to laugh at the comedy duo.

'Baked beans, they're good for your heart,' Badger shouts over his shoulder as he runs off towards the playground, farting again as he does so. Sofia runs after him giggling. 'The more you eat them the more you fffffffffaaaart.'

'Sorry about that, he's a dirty little so and so. Gets it from his dad.'

'Don't worry, it was funny, Sofia's just as bad.'

'I dunno if he's coming down with summat, you know there' s been a sickness bug going around?'

'Oh great, just in time for Christmas, shall we just bin off the school play tonight? Say they're ill and do something else?'

'I know you hate that stuff, don't you? I don't mind it but I can't be arsed at the moment either. Badger's only playing a sheep anyway so it's not like he has a big part on stage and Tamsin won't come with me, she's still very low, can't bring herself to leave the house.' Stella stares off into the distance, frowning. I open my mouth to ask her about Tamsin then notice Jayne making a beeline for us again but there are no smiles this time and Mia trails behind her, crying dramatically but without any tears.

'What's she coming back for?' I say, under my breath as Jayne's pinched face moves closer and closer.

'I dunno, but I feel like I want to do a runner,'

'I dare you.'

'What's funny ladies?' Jayne demands. 'The fact that Badger just pushed my Mia over or the fact that Sofia just watched and let him do it?'

'Urrrm what?'

'Yes, that's right. Your son is a first-class bully and he just physically assaulted my child.'

Cheek. All feelings of feeling sorry for her disappear

as I fight the urge to get into a slanging match at the school gates.

'No, no way that happened. BADGER!!!!'

Badger stands still, a rabbit caught in headlights, it takes a second for his brain to reach his feet before he's pelting over to us with Sofia not far behind. Stella kneels down to talk to him, his little red cheeks flushed by the cold weather.

'Badger mate, did you push over little Mia here?'

'What? No? I didn't even know she was there.'

'Honest?'

'Yes, honest Mummy,' he says, blinking back at her.

'Sofia, is that what happened?'

'Yeah, I think she just got in the way of his elbow.' Sofia shrugs and widens her eyes.

'There we go, Jayne, I think that's cleared that up, an accident. Badger did you say sorry after you accidently caught her with your elbow?'

'Yes.'

'There we go then, case closed.' Stella folds her arms at Jayne and gives her a menacing stare. I bite my tongue.

'I think they're all just as bad as each other aren't they,' I say, trying to smooth things over. 'Let's not spoil the Christmas cheer, last day and everything, the kids should be enjoying it,' I continue a little too brightly. Part of me wants to give Jayne a piece of my mind too but it's not worth it. Mr Thomas has dealt with that and what example am I setting to my kid, shouting and screaming in the playground.

We're saved by the bell. Jayne turns on her heels, stomping off to the school with her mini me in tow, seemingly as manipulative as her mother and just as I was starting to feel sorry for her.

Why oh why does there always have to be one?

Chapter 15

Delilah

Work was an early one today, Miriam demanded that *in the nicest possible way*, I come in two hours before my start time to sort out some mistakes I'd made the previous day. When she spoke to me to tell me of my errors little bits of spit flew out of her mouth while white foam formed in the corners. I counted the spit globules, one, two, three, four, five, six, seven as they danced around and toyed with landing on my face. I mentally blew them back towards her, willing the spray to land in her eyeballs and blur her vision for a second.

I've been on my own for the first hour of the day which was actually quite nice but now I have her company. Thankfully Miriam retreated to her office straight away and hasn't come out since. Suzie is on annual leave already so I don't have my work mum to look after me. This is the last day before the holidays and then I get the whole of Christmas and New Year off. Everything shuts down in Coolsbay at Christmas, we get over two weeks off, which is a luxury I know. A lot of my uni mates from London are working right up until Christmas Eve and those that are lucky enough to be in shows are working all over Christmas. Although, I'd give anything to be working all over Christmas dancing rather than being here with the witch.

My phone beeps in my pocket, making me jump. We aren't allowed our phones on and Miriam would go mad if she saw, *gross misconduct* she'd remind me in the nicest possible way. I steal a look at Miriam to check if she's watching then swiftly turn my phone to silent before taking a sneaky quick look at my messages.

Josh: *Hey you, what do you fancy doing later?*

Byron: *Hi, how are you? Just wondered if Molly was alright and if you'd heard from her? You're a good friend staying with her and it was nice to have some company.*

I drop my phone back into my bag as if it were a hot piece of coal. What is Byron doing messaging me? Surely it would just be easier to message Molly rather than have me as the go between. I quickly check to see if I accidently followed him on Instagram. I didn't but he must have been stalking me too. The image of Josh and Byron sending me messages at the same time sends searing pains of anxiety across my chest as I'm reminded of my encounter with Byron the other night.

I can't stop thinking about him, the way he knew just what to do with Molly when she fainted and the closeness of our bodies in the ambulance. I'm a bad, bad friend for thinking of him like this and an even worse girlfriend. Molly was fine in the end; I got a phone call from her the next day at 6am to go and pick her up from the hospital. She'd woken up in a little box room with a cardboard bowl next to her face and monitors stuck all over her chest but she wasn't hooked up to anything else.

Molly told me that when the nurse came to check on her in the morning, she merely said. *'I think you had a bit too much to drink last night, don't you?'* And that was it. No explanation from the doctor, nothing. She asked if she could leave and she was told, yes. Molly text me last night and said she still has a banging headache; she must have hit her head pretty hard on the patio. I didn't tell her that Byron was in the ambulance with me, I don't know why, it just felt weird and I didn't want her to feel horrible that he had seen her like that. So, the upshot of this is I've lied to my friend and I've also lied to Josh, who came with me to pick her up. Another surge of panic overcomes me as realisation sets in that I better reply to Byron quickly just in case he does decide to text Molly. Oh what a mess. I fish my phone back out of my bag to reply.

Me: *I'm ok. She's doing alright, a bit sore. Let's keep it to ourselves that you were there, she would absolutely hate that. Maybe give her a text to see how she is? She would love that.*

Byron: *No problem, our secret. X*

Our secret? My cheeks burn red just at the thought of us sharing our own secret. I quickly scroll to his Instagram to have another snoop at his photos. After a few minutes of scrolling back a few years, I find his ex-girlfriend. She's pretty with long dark brown hair and also surfs. Within milliseconds I've found out her name and am now stalking her Instagram. Oh, why am I doing this? My life must be super boring right now.

Why, why, why, Delilah, sings the voice in my head. It takes me a beat to realise that the voice in my head is not my own, it's actually Miriam's and a not very happy Miriam at that.

'Delilah, Delilah? Hello? Is there anybody in there?' Too busy staring at my phone all this time to notice that Miriam has managed to ninja across the room and is now standing over me with hands on hips and a face like thunder.

Shitsticks.

'Umm in the nicest possible way using your phone whilst at work is a sackable offence.' Miriam glares at me with a pinched expression, and then her narrowed eyes turn to my phone. I take the hint and slowly lower the phone down, placing it gently face down on the table.

'Sorry.' I chew the inside of my lip and wait for the lecture. Am I cowering? I think I might be. Despite my fear, in my head I begin choreographing a fight dance scene between us. It starts with her fake slapping me, using big dramatic arm motions.

'Good. I take it you'll be staying until 6pm this evening then? We have to get those tours out before the end of play today.'

The dancing me in my head grabs her slapping hands and pushes them down and away from me but she rises again and starts to bring her hands towards my neck.

'The tours for January?' I ask in a squeaky voice.

'And the spring tours too,' she replies.

'Yes, of course, no problem, I'll aim to get them all done by six,' I squeak again.

'You won't aim, you'll do.' The Miriam in my head is squeezing my neck tighter as the physical one smiles.

'Okay,' I gulp. Looks as though I have ten new tours to design and put together by the end of the day, this will be a challenge, if not impossible to achieve. The Miriam in my head squishes my features with her fingers, whilst grinning.

'Fantastical,' she sings, before marching off back to her office. I mentally smack her across the back of the head, willing her to fall over. She doesn't.

Amber

A couple of hours later and I'm back at the enclosed field

behind Stella's house with Olive. I'm looking forward to a good old stomp. Our dog meets have become our therapy as my marriage becomes increasingly more difficult and Stella deals with her partner's poor mental health. I let Olive off to stretch her legs and watch her run fast, trying to catch an unsuspecting pigeon. She's very close but the pigeon teases her, flying off at the last minute. She's fuming, barking at the pigeon and giving it a piece of her mind. I chuckle to myself as a voice cuts across my thoughts.

'She's lovely, how old? Beagle?' A small, smiling woman in her sixties with dark frizzy hair appears with her mini-me black miniature poodle trotting by her side. 'I love Beagles but they're naughty, naughty dogs. Beautiful though,' she continues, as her dog sits at her feet, guarding her. She's not wrong there, in the first few years Filipe nearly had Olive re-homed due to all the destruction that she caused and she got worse when Sofia was born. I kept most of it secret from him, including the following:

- ✓ Ate baby's dummy tips – several times, shat one out that she managed to eat in secret – the other two were trips to the vets and drugs to make her vomit them out
- ✓ Stole baby toys and tried to eat them on numerous occasions
- ✓ Chewed up babies' nappies
- ✓ Stole, then dragged brand new baby shoes through the mud and dog shit – they had to go in the bin
- ✓ Stole Filipe's work shoes and chewed them up – I immediately went out and bought a replica replacement pair
- ✓ Stole, then ate almost a whole loaf of bread

✓ Shredded loo roll multiple times and still does on the odd occasion
✓ Chewed up the TV remote multiple times
✓ Barked and barked at anyone that came to visit the baby ad sat by her like a little guard dog
✓ Stole my maternity bra to sniff and lick every time I tried to get it out of the wash basket to put in the washing machine
✓ Eats and rolls in fox poo – still does this one but I bath her as soon as we get home - shhhh don't tell Filipe

She's mainly good now, a combination of training it out of her and growing up has meant that she's calmed down a lot. Apart from the odd mishap, but like any human, no dog is perfect.

'Yes, she's six now, still mischievous but past the worst,' I say, as Olive's ears prick up and she comes bounding over to see what's going on. As she gets closer, her pace slows down as she susses out the situation, tail high in the air and wagging, eager to please the dog, but more so its owner. The lady puts her hand out for Olive to sniff whilst the poodle's lip begins to curl and her tail slowly starts to wag.

'Yeah, I can see that,' she chuckles. 'Be nice, Shadow,' the owner continues, sensing the aggression in her dog. Olive submits to the older dog and lays down, rolling onto her back for a belly rub. 'Aren't you just gorgeous, yes you are.' She strokes Olive's belly as her poodle sniffs. 'She has beautiful markings, I bet you'd win a few shows,' she says, continuing to stroke Olive who laps up the attention. 'This one's an old codger, almost fifteen. Have to start thinking about getting another one soon.' She pats her dog on the head. 'We got him not long after my husband passed.'

'I'm so sorry.'

'Oh, it was a long time ago now but it was a shock. I was ten years older than him and his dad lived to ninety-three so we always thought he'd be here long after me but that wasn't how it went, sadly.'

'I can't imagine how that must feel,' I say, as I watch the dogs sniff each other, both now wagging their tails. Olive has seemingly won the old grumpy dog around.

'Yes, some days are harder than others but that's why you have to do what you want to do. Buy the new outfit, go for that promotion, kiss the man. Everyone says it I know, but life is so very short.'

I smile at her, there's much to be said for the wisdom that comes from the people you meet on dog walks. I used to see an old guy called Michael, who had a little Yorkshire terrier, out a lot but haven't done for months. I remember him telling me he was almost ninety. I used to love listening to his tales of Coolsbay and what it was like all those years ago. He once told me to always do nice things for people, even if you don't like them, because it makes you feel better and one day they might repay you when you least expect it but usually just when you need it. I wonder what happened to him?

'I think I want to go back to work, it's been a while but I think I'm ready,' I blurt out to this stranger.

'Oh, so you should then, do what makes you happy. As long as you aren't hurting anyone else in the process, do it,' she urges. 'We must go, he's getting cranky, needs his lunch.' She gives her poodle a little tug on the lead and they walk off, leaving me wondering when she'll have to get another dog.

'Alright my lovely, so sorry we're late, Tamsin was a bit upset,' Stella says, looking uncomfortable as she traipses past the lady with the poodle. Her brow is furrowed and her skin looks a little greyer than usual this morning.

'Oh no, what's up?'

'She's alright, I've booked her an appointment at the doctors though, I think she needs a little help, just to chat it through with someone who isn't me and emotionally involved. I get so worked up about it, I don't know if I help sometimes.' Stella lets Pudding off the lead and I do the same with Olive, we watch them start chasing and wrestling with each other.

'Poor Tamsin, I'm sure you do help, could she not appeal the decision, I thought they normally sided with the mother anyway?'

'No, he's gone all in on her, saying she works too much and he can be there for the child more. Also, I don't know if she's got it in her at the moment. We'll get her feeling better and then plan our next step, which will be potentially thumping her ex if I get my own way.'

'Wishful thinking, hey.'

'He's such a cockwomble, Amber, still bitter than she chose me and moved over to the dark side.' A glimmer of humour sparkles in her eyes for a second and then it's gone again. 'I swear this is his way of getting his own back. Gutless knobhead.'

'Really? What a dick. Why's he so bitter? It's been years, hasn't it?'

'Yep, almost four years now and her little girl misses her mum, it's heart breaking for both. Ah shit, don't look now but two o'clock, *Gobbler*. I don't think we can avoid unless we run away.'

I groan, probably a bit too loudly then feel bad. I love talking to people but a *Gobbler* is Stella's code for someone who likes to bend your ear off for way too long.

The sort that makes it very hard for you to get away and you end up having to make up many excuses for having to leave. It sounds horrible but she's right, I can already tell this woman's on one, I can see it in her eyes. There's no way out, we're trapped.

'Hi Stella, who's this then? Well, I say.' She's tall and slim with rosy cheeks and long dishevelled hair. She marches over to us leading her two border collies. They trot beside her, each carrying a green tennis ball in their mouths. She retrieves the balls from their slobbery gobs and launches them both into the air. I'm quite impressed at how far the balls go.

'Yes, yes, this is my friend Amber and her dog is Olive.' Then Stella turns to me. 'Stella, this is Carol.'

'Hi Carol, lovely dogs you have.'

'Yes, I know. Aren't they just delightful, lovely dogs but not interested at all in any other dogs. Just don't want to know, happy with a ball, that's all they want. Give them a ball and they will play all day, not like your beagles they don't like balls do they, much more into sniffing the ground and each other I see… When my dogs were small they didn't mind…' Carol continues to give us her monologue about when her dogs were pups as Stella gives me the side eye. We're there for another forty-five minutes before we can get away. I don't mind the talkers, there must be a reason why they like to bend your ear off so much, perhaps it's their only chance to talk to people all day and I can kind of empathise with that. But sometimes, sometimes…

By the time Stella and I get away from Carol it's time to race home, drop the dogs off, grab a very late lunch then pick the kids up from school again. We just have to get through pick up and the school play and then it's time for a glass of celebratory end of term wine.

It can't come soon enough.

Chapter 16

Delilah

I work my arse off for the rest of the day. Brain storming ideas and clandestinely messaging Dylan for help whenever Miriam goes to the toilet. He's good at all these types of things and knows all the little gems of Coolsbay, places I wouldn't even have thought about using for a tour. I've even come up with quite a few innovative ideas myself. Definitely more than just a beach and pub visit. If it wasn't for the pressure of having to get so many done today, I would have quite enjoyed putting these together.

About five hours into the day, I can't stare at the screen any longer and take myself off for a short walk around the block and to wolf down a quick sandwich. Fifteen minutes later, I get back to my desk and power on through the rest of the tours, I don't make ten but eight is a very impressive number. The most I've seen Suzie complete in a day is six and she's a whiz at it. Quality is better than quantity, right? And I've even been a little adventurous with one tour in particular, it involves dancers and possibly a few of the school children for the cuteness affect, but if the parents and school agree then I think it could be pulled off.

I email the tours off to Miriam and hold my breath, waiting for her response. I was hoping she'd finish early and leave me to it but no such luck. She's literally been here all day waiting to mark my work, pacing up and down like Miss Trunchbull out of *Matilda*. She replies with just a *thanks*, simultaneously the printer comes to life, beginning to make whirring noises as the knots start to tie in my stomach and Miriam gets her red pen out. Moments later, she marches out to collect the printed tours before disappearing back inside her office. I hold my breath again as she emerges from her office half an hour later, making her way over to my desk with a stack of paper in her hands, there's a lot of red pen on them. She reaches my desk and sets the paper down in front of me, standing still and breathing loudly for a few seconds but saying nothing whilst I sweat under her presence and silently try to count back to calmness.

'You have some good ideas here,' she finally says, in a slightly kinder tone than earlier. 'This one in particular is very unique, some are actually *fandabidozi* and I'm impressed that you've completed eight tours,' she continues. 'Ten was a bit steep of me to expect in a day from a newbie.' She smiles, almost apologetically, I think. 'But.' There's always a, *but*. 'In the nicest possible way.' Here we go. 'The grammar isn't great and some of the tours need flowering up a fair bit. In fact, a lot, they need a lot of flowering. They need to really sound special. Coolsbay is the heart of the south west and we really need to encapsulate that.'

'Oh, okay.'

'Yes, oh. I'm going to have to stay late and finish these off now,' she says, tapping the paperwork in her hand with a long fingernail and a frown. The sound of the nail scrapping along the paper makes me cringe.

'I'm sorry, I tried my best.'

'I know you did.' She softens. 'And I appreciate that and don't get me wrong, you have improved, you've done a more than average job.'

'Okay, thank you, so what would you like me to do now?'

'Go home, go on, get yourself home for Christmas and forget about work.' She smiles with a little twinkle in her eye. Is this a trick?

'I will, thanks. Have a nice Christmas.'

'You too.' I wait until she has disappeared into her office to text Josh back. She may not mind as I have officially clocked off but you can never be too sure with Miriam even if she does say it in the nicest possible way with sparkly eyes.

Josh: *On my way over now, take away?*

Me: *Yes!*

I leave the office feeling relieved that she didn't go ape shit at me. Am I actually starting to enjoy my job? I pace home, counting my steps as I do so and also count twenty-five large Christmas trees on the way home, ten medium, and five small. It's dark but the street lights and the lights coming from people's houses coupled with the twinkling Christmas lights indoors and outdoors make it an enjoyable final walk home before Christmas. Except, when I get home, the lights aren't on. It's completely pitch black. What have I walked into? I fumble around in my bag for my keys then use my phone as a torch to find the lock. I'm finally inside and it's eerily quiet.

'Hello?' I shout with a shaky voice, as I enter the house.

Nothing.

'Hello?' I shout in a much higher tone. I tread slowly towards the light switch, feeling along the wall for it. This is my death; this is where I meet my murderer. But not without putting up a fight first. I fish around in my handbag searching for the knife and grip onto it with a tight pulsating fist. The counting begins in my head, I'm almost certain that by the time I get to ten one of us will be dead. Whoever the other one is. One, two, three, four, five, six.

'Arrghhhhhh.' I hear myself shriek a blood curdling scream, as the lights turn on and a small black ball of fluff runs towards me at lightning speed. I lift my arm up ready to swat the flying object just as everyone shouts.

'SURPRISE.'

I freeze. My hand in mid-air.

'SHITSTICKS.'

'STOP,' Mum, Dad and Josh shriek. I push the knife back down into my handbag as Dylan bundles up the ball of fluff into his arms. In nano seconds, my heart goes from beating like a drum to skipping several beats. I sit down on the floor and the most adorable creature I've ever seen with fur as black as night is staring back at me with its tongue hanging out to one side. Its big black eyes stare softly at my face as it pants and snorts. He's just adorable.

'Oh my.' I put my hand over my mouth and study him whilst slowly reaching out with my other hand to let him sniff me. He sniffs then gives my hand two big sloppy licks as if he's approving of me. Is this the feeling people describe when seeing their baby for this first time? Instantly, I love him. I mean, I would completely do anything for him, even if he did look like a Tasmanian devil upon meeting him and scare me half to death.

'This is Loki, he's our new rescue dog.'

'And I bet he wants to be rescued again after that.' I say, sniffing back tears of overwhelming joy. 'Dad, here you go, I can't keep carrying this around, it's going to get me in serious trouble. I could have murdered my own dog.' I pull the knife out again and Dad sheepishly takes it as Mum folds her arms and glares at him with an *I told you so* look in her eye, even though she was as much onboard with the idea as he was.

'Worst idea ever, surprising her, I told you guys,' Josh says, as he puts his arm around me, pulls me in close and kisses me tenderly on the cheek.

'We wanted to cheer you up, as we know you've been having a tough time with auditions and work,' Dylan says, looking smart in his new clothes. I did do a good job, the shop assistant even asked for his phone number after seeing him in the suit he bought for his works do. I'm not sure if he gave it to her as I was trying on a few things myself. He does look different since the makeover although he hates me calling it that. He's definitely standing taller, more confident but it's Dylan that deserves the cheering up more than me, after all he is the one going through a divorce.

'How did you convince them?' I ask my brother, who just taps the side of his nose and grins. 'I wanted to get him before Christmas, didn't want him to be a Christmas dog, it's bit bad taste, isn't it?' He winces.

'Of course. This is the best day ever! Thank you so much.' I reach out to my family and pull them into a group hug, giving them the tightest squeeze. This little guy is going to get so much love, I just can't wait to get to know him and for him to meet everyone.

Chapter 17

Amber

'All ready for the play then Sof?' I ask in an ultra-cheery tone. The end is almost here and I can almost taste the champagne and the chocolates that Filipe and I will be enjoying in our hotel room tomorrow night. It will be nice to relax tonight after the play but tomorrow night is the down time I've really been waiting for.

'Yes, is Daddy going to be there?' she asks, swinging her donkey tail from side to side. She looks so sweet, the cutest donkey ever and she has mastered the donkey bray down to a tee.

'No sweetie, sorry, he has to work,' I say, as a pang of guilt drops in my stomach. I didn't even ask if he wanted to come, I've become so used to him not being able to that now I don't give him a second thought.

What a bad mother. Looks like it isn't just Filipe that's disconnected and thoughtless. We are both to blame here.

'Ohhhhh,' Sofia whines, stomps her foot then folds her arms. 'He hates that I'm a rubbish donkey. I wish I was Mary.'

'Of course, he doesn't, he's very proud of you, we both are. A donkey is just as important as Mary,' I lie.

'Look, you'll see him when you get home and I bet he'll have a special present waiting for you to say well done on the school play.' I stroke her cheek then tap her on the nose, making a beep sound. She giggles, it always makes her giggle.

'Yay!' she brightens and I make a mental note to message him to grab something for her on the way home from work. I should have invited him. It would have been nice to have him there with us, to watch Sofia as a family, then all go home together.

Sofia and I arrive at the school, and she's whisked away to get ready for her performance. I find Stella chatting to a few other mums, we have a laugh and take bets on who will be picking their noses, who will cry and who will shout and wave for their mummy. We find our seats and get comfortable for the show. Ready for school-play bingo.

The play ends up being very cute, sweet and rather funny, Badger picks his nose, a few of the more-timid kids look like they're caught in headlights but surprisingly no one cries and Mia ends up shouting and waving for Mummy, much to Jayne's utter disgust. I bet she's had Mia practicing her lines and rehearsing at home every night like she's preparing for a West End show.

The best part of the night was when a little boy called Harry, who played Joseph, scrunched up his nose and told the whole room that Jesus had just farted when he handed the baby over to Mary. His acting was by far the best although by the look on some of the other kid's face's I'm not sure if the fart wasn't forced out for authenticity.

We end up managing to avoid Jayne and have an all-round really pleasant evening. We're finally home and Filipe greets us with a toy for Sofia, it's a cuddly Santa and she is over the moon. She goes to bed happy and on a high. An hour after I put her to bed, Filipe and I settle down with a bottle of wine. Twenty minutes later as I pour us both another glass I hear the dreaded noise of retching and crying. I run up the stairs to check on her and my thoughts are confirmed.

She's decorated the room nicely, in vomit. Poor Sof has even managed to get some vomit on the ceiling.

I've been up with her all night, holding back her hair as she pukes into a bowl and I wipe away her tears. Stella text me this morning to say that Badger's been the same.

Great.

The nasty sickness bug has well and truly found us just in time for the Christmas holidays.

It's 6am and I've just put her back to bed, but this time in my bed as her bed and bedroom is pretty much covered in vomit and I'm too exhausted to sort it out right now. I don't know how she's been so sick all night because there can't have been anything left in her stomach after the first few times. It's only a matter of time before the nasty bug takes down me and Filipe who is the most dramatic puker of all time.

Last time we had a sickness bug in the house, I woke up at 2am to the dulcet sounds of Filipe vomiting loudly, next to me in bed, small mercies, he did have a bowl. I partly felt sorry for him but the other part of me was fuming at him for not having the decency to go the bathroom to do it. I know if it was me, I wouldn't lie there with a bowl in bed when there's another person next to me. I guess that's the bonus of not sharing a bed much these days. He sounded like one of those really raspy heavy metal singers when he was vomiting, I'm talking like when they really go for it on the mic, except he's twenty decibels louder, slightly sweatier and disgusting fluid is coming out of him. Come to think of it, he actually sounds like Gollum from *Lord of the Rings*, yes, a very loud Gollum.

I lie here in silence, waiting for that dreaded sicky feeling or the sounds of Filipe retching to kick off the next round of vomit wars. I've been up all night going between our bedrooms, mopping up sick and tears from her poor little face. I'll admit some of those tears were mine as my dreams of staying in a fancy hotel tonight disappear into the night. They're replaced by nightmares of copious amounts of washing, scrubbing floors, walls and ceilings clean of last night's dinner.

I leave her sleeping in my bed and pad downstairs to make myself a well-earned extra strong coffee. I have a feeling it's going to be a very long day and whether Filipe is ill or not he is going to be minimal help, he always is in a time of crisis or illness.

'Mummyyyy,' Sofia shouts, ominously. I set my coffee down, just two sips in and sigh deeply. Olive looks up at me as if to ask *what's going on?* I stroke her soft fur, cherishing my last few seconds of peace.

'It's gonna be a long day okay, please don't be a dickhead, yeah?' I croak, as Olive slops back down again in her bed and shuts her eyes as if to say *fine, I was only saying hello, you moody bitch*. I instantly feel bad for calling her a dickhead, but she does seem to have a sixth sense for these things and finds a way to get herself into trouble or much worse, she will probably get the sickness bug too.

Oh God, please no.

'Mummmmyyyyyyy, Mummmyyyy.' Sofia wails again.

'I'm coming Sof.' I pad across the living room and up the stairs to see her and when I get there Filipe is sat, cuddled up to her in my bed. He's stroking her hair and mumbling to her. I rub my eyes, am I dreaming?

'Hey, how you feeling?' I say, sitting the other side of Filipe and putting my hand to her head to check her temperature.

'Fine, Daddy's looking after me now. You took too long.' She scowls at me.

'Oh, I see.' I smile, half hurt, half ecstatic.

'Yep, this will be where I will stay today my *chicca*, by my daughter's side, while you go and enjoy the hotel stay.' He smiles and closes his eyes, seemingly pleased with his own generosity.

'What?' Am I dreaming?

'Yep, there's no use both of us staying at home when that's all booked and paid for, you go. I can take care of her, my little Sofia *mija*. We will have fun, won't we?'

He does a thumbs up to Sofia who sticks her thumbs up back at him, grinning like a Cheshire cat. Even though she's drained of colour, it's clear to see that she's shining with glee at the chance to spend time with her dad. It's just a shame it took a sickness bug for him to want to spend any quality time with her. But I mustn't complain, it's lovely to see, so lovely in fact that my smile begins to quiver as I blink several times too many to hold back emotional tears.

What is wrong with me?

'Back in a minute, just popping to the loo,' I say, overly brightly and flashing them both a big toothy grin.

I have to excuse myself because I need to hide and cry in the bathroom like a baby for a few minutes, okay let's call that a good half an hour as I had to have a shower to try and help with my protruding puffy eyeballs. I'm so emotional at the moment, I wouldn't normally cry over this type of stuff. When I leave the bathroom Sofia and Filipe aren't in my bedroom anymore. I pad downstairs to find them both sprawled out on the sofa. Filipe has retrieved a sick bowl for her which has been placed on the other side and *Bambi* is blaring out of the TV. So far, he's doing a good job.

'You feeling any better Sof?' I say, as I rest my palm on her forehead again.

'Get off. Daddy's looking after me.' She pushes me off with enough force that it causes me to stumble a little. Sofia and Filipe look at each other and burst out laughing. I feel like I've stepped into some kind of alternative universe, since when was he the favourite? It's me who does everything.

'Right okay, no worries. Daddy's the doctor today, that's fine,' I say, extra brightly. Filipe reaches his hand out to me and beckons me over as I begin to retreat back over to the other sofa, a little unsure of what to do with myself. I look at Olive, who's lying out on her dog bed, for some reassurance. She cocks her head to the side and barks once. Is she telling me to go too? No, she would never do that.

'I meant what I said about the hotel, really, you should go. There's no need for us both to be here,' he says, taking my hand. 'And she clearly wants me for a change which let's face it, is extremely rare these days.'

I hesitate for a second, looking at Sofia and then Olive. The overprotective mother part of me doesn't want to leave my child. But, she's his child too and I know this isn't about me, it's about what's best for her. If she wants him to look after her and he is willing then I can't argue with that. It should be encouraged; she is her dad.

'If you're sure? I mean, it would be really nice, thank you.' Inside a little voice is beginning to scream with joy.

A night to myself?

A whole night of sleep.

I'll take that, absofuckinglutley.

This hasn't happened in years, in fact I can't remember the last time it happened. I can't wait to be in a hotel alone getting the most glorious night's sleep ever. Hardly containing myself, but not wanting to show it to him, in case I jinx it somehow, I meander off upstairs to finish getting ready and pack. As I climb the stairs I scream silently, punching the air, I mean I must be making the strangest and ugliest of faces but I don't care. This hotel stay is a little bit of me, even if it's for only one night I'm going to make the absolute best of it. Two hours later my bag is packed and my shoes are on, I'm hoping for an early check-in.

Delilah

'Loki, Loki,' I sing, then stroke underneath my precious pup's chin as he lays between Josh and I in bed. We've been up and had breakfast and now we're back up here chilling with the dog as Dad is watching some crap on TV that neither of us wanted to watch. I can't take my eyes off him, Loki, I mean. His black shaggy fur and dark eyes are so lovable and he has thirteen silvery coloured hairs on his chin. I counted them all but this time that number didn't make me panic because when I touched them, Loki licked my hand then rolled onto his back. It was as if he was telling me it was all right and I didn't have to worry anymore. He has such a calming effect on me, it's unreal.

I have a puppy; I can't quite believe it.

'Wow are you gonna be like this when we have kids too?' Josh asks, as he scrolls through his phone. If I didn't know any better, I'd say he was a bit jealous.

'Probably, but can you blame me, just look at his little face.' I stroke Loki's chin again then ruffle his ears as Josh goes to half-heartedly pat him on the head, Loki doesn't like this and nips Josh's hand.

'Ouch.'

'Don't put your hand all in his face, it scares him, here under the chin.' I move his hand and get him to stroke under Loki's chin. Loki doesn't try to bite him this time. 'See, you're a natural.'

'I bet you can't wait for us to have kids, have our own home, all of that, can you?' he says, before leaning in for a kiss, not letting me answer. 'Twenty-five, that was the age we wanted to aim for, wasn't it? Only a few years away now,' he continues, as he pulls back from me, giving me heart palpations. I try to count them but they're too fast.

'We have years, ages, there's no rush,' I say, as Loki jumps down, hearing Dylan's bedroom door open. Don't leave.

'No but it would be nice to have a plan, now that you're back we can start planning our future, can't we?' He looks up at me expectantly, I try to imagine what our kids would be like. Our home. It's what we've always planned and what we always wanted.

'Maybe we could try living somewhere else for a bit, move away from Coolsbay?' I say casually.

'Oh, no no. I hate London, if that's what you're thinking. Did all that when you were at uni. You know it's not my scene.' Not his scene and yet he was there a lot, most weekends and he didn't like going out so we just used to stay in and watch films which sometimes got a bit boring, especially when all my friends were out having fun. I didn't really have the full uni experience, you don't when you have a boyfriend come up and stay, they just want to see you. They've missed you and they're supporting you so you do as they please and you stay in, watch films and have lots of sex. That's just what you do, isn't it?

'No, I know it's not your thing, don't worry we won't go back to London.' *How is it then, being free?* The memory of me asking Byron, echoes in my head. *It's good, I don't have to pretend anymore.*

'Thank God for that.' Josh smiles, then plants another kiss on me. I didn't think he hated London that much. Out of nowhere tears sting the back of eyes.

I blink them away.

Shitsticks.

'Right, I need to go and find Dylan so we can go shopping for this puppy, he hasn't even got a bed yet, are you coming?' I ask, untangling myself from him, looking forward to spoiling my new pet. I best catch Dylan now, I'm sure he said he was going out later. Maybe he has a date with that woman from the shop.

'Nah, I hate shopping, you know that. I'll go home for a bit but ring me after and I'll come back over, yeah?'

'Yeah.'

Chapter 18

Amber

Exhausted Mum break - One night stay essentials

- ✓ *Face pack*
- ✓ *Luxury bubble bath*
- ✓ *Shampoo and conditioner*
- ✓ *Hair styling stuff*
- ✓ *Foot filer – I neglect my feet*
- ✓ *Makeup*
- ✓ *Tweezers – may as well give my eyebrows and facial hair a good plucking.*
- ✓ *Good book*
- ✓ *Notebook – for journaling. I believe I must have bought it around five years ago with the intention of doing this. Who knows, tonight might be the lucky night it finally gets some action.*
- ✓ *Comfortable, big, baggy PJs*
- ✓ *Hair bonnet*
- ✓ *Nice outfits - Eating a takeaway or room service hidden away in my room is tempting, meaning that I can eat as much as I like and not get judged for my gargantuan portion sizes,*

however, I really want to dress up and feel special and do something for me. Dining out alone suddenly feels very exciting.

✓ ~~Vibrator~~ *– Let's not kid myself. I'll be too busy enjoying my food and sleep.*

'Wow, you going already?' Filipe asks, as I drag my overly packed suitcase into the living room. I'm only going for one night but I could easily be going for a month judging by the contents of my suitcase.

Wishful thinking.

'No, not yet, just wanted to get everything ready.' Until the hotel emails me back to confirm an early check in. 'How's she doing?' I perch on the edge of the sofa, careful not to wake Sofia who is sleeping peacefully in Filipe's arms. She looks so beautiful when she sleeps, like a little angel. If only she would just do more of it.

'Yes, seems a lot better, just tired.'

'She been sick again?'

'No, not since last night. She woke up for a water but that's it.' By last night he means this morning at 6am when I was in there holding her hair back.

'Shit.'

'What?'

'Sofia's room, it needs cleaning, there's sick everywhere.' I stare down at my clothes, I've done my hair, nails and makeup and am dressed, wearing my nice jeans but now I have to clean up a room full of vomit.

For fuck's sake.

I sigh, and stroke my jeans then check out my freshly painted nails in the hope that Filipe will get the hint and offer to clear it all up for me. It could happen, he is sending me off to a hotel on my own tonight for a well-deserved break so anything is possible.

'Okay *chicca*, don't be too long though, you can make me lunch before you go. I'm so hungry I could eat a horse.'

Oh, can I now? I knew it was too good to be true. 'Okay, I best get on then, don't suppose you'll clear up the mess in Sofia's room then?'

'I have my hands full, a child and a dog.'

I don't argue, I can't expect him to do everything.

I suppose, that's my job.

I trudge upstairs and get changed into some old clothes, then dig out some old disposable masks and rubber gloves. I don't want to catch it and spend my well-earned break decorating the hotel room's walls.

Almost an hour later, I'm still here, cleaning. It's as though Sof had an invisible spray gun fitted to her mouth so that she could give the whole room a good even finish. It absolutely stinks too, even through the two masks I'm wearing. A whole bottle of *Febreze* and several bowls of hot soapy water later, it's finally clean and not smelling of gone off guts. It's probably best Filipe didn't attempt to clean it; bits definitely would have been missed.

I bundle up her disgusting bedsheets and pad downstairs to dump them into the washing machine before racing back upstairs again to finish the job. New fresh bed sheets are fitted before I take my time to arrange her teddies nicely on her bed in order of the ones she likes the most. I'm going to miss her tonight; I don't think I've ever spent a night away from her in her entire life and the same goes for Olive. I get changed back into my clothes and put more makeup on to hide my eye bags, they've definitely got worse in the last year, since Filipe has started working more.

'You were ages, what took you so long?' Filipe

complains, as I come back downstairs, feeling like I've had a big session at the gym already.

'I was clearing up our daughter's bedroom, did you even go in and see the state of it?'

'No, it can't have been that bad though, you don't take that long to clean the whole house.'

'Filipe, she covered the whole room and just so you know, it takes a lot longer than an hour to give the whole house a good clean.' He really has no idea.

'Okay, okay, sorry *chicca*, my bad.'

'It's fine, I'm going to go now if that's alright,' I say, smiling at Sof who is still asleep. I go to stroke her cheek but then pull my hand away at the last second for fear of waking her.

'But, what about my lunch?' he whines.

'Are you alright to make yourself a sandwich?' I smile and clasp my hands together, pleadingly.

'Oh *chicca*, I could but Sofia is asleep on me,' he says, as he pathetically tries to free his arm from behind her head. It's almost comical. Almost.

'Okay, what do you want?' I give in.

'An English breakfast would be perfecto.'

'Filipe, you're pushing your luck.'

'You're staying in a swanky hotel for the night, on me.' He looks at me pointedly.

'I don't have to. I could stay here with you guys and help look after Sof. I don't mind,' I say, playing him at his own game and yet genuinely meaning it because the excitement is fast wearing off. I'm knackered and spending some quality time on my own seems like way too much effort now. It's also at the back of my mind that any mess won't be cleared up and I'll be coming back to a whole day's worth of cleaning.

'No, no, no,' he argues. 'You must go, I haven't paid

for the hotel for nothing, one of us must enjoy it.' The corners of his mouth turn down.

'You sure?'

'Yes, I'll just have a bacon roll, save you doing a full English breakfast.'

'Alright, I guess you have a deal.'

The smell of bacon wakes Sofia up and we spend the next hour feeding her dry toast and water then watching her puke most of it back up again. I tell Filipe I'm not going; I can't leave her like that but Sofia insists that I go away as she wants to be with her daddy. She says she doesn't want me to look after her, she wants Daddy. She never wants him but here she is wanting him, over me, her mum, her main caregiver. I can't help but feel that she must be angry with me for something but God knows what. Eventually, after Filipe's insistent guilt tripping and Sofia's resentful scowling, I reluctantly give in.

It had better be worth it.

The hotel isn't very far, just three junctions north up the motorway but when I get there, it feels as though I'm on holiday, I could almost be in a different country. The buildings are different, everything is whiter, brighter. Most of the houses in Coolsbay are painted in a variety of different colours which, even though I'm from there, can look a bit garish. Our house is a dark blue, so not too eye scorching but a bright pink or yellow house wouldn't look out of place in Coolsbay. Although this city is mostly white, the hotel I'm staying in isn't and looks more like an old English country manor house that was once a large farm, perhaps. Either way, it's stunning and made even more stunning by the fact that it's all dressed up for Christmas.

'Hello, how can I help?' The receptionist smiles warmly at me as I walk up to the desk. This is going to be lovely I think to myself as I spy a mini-Christmas tree sitting on her desk and next to it, a plate of chocolate truffles. They look homemade. My mouth waters.

'Help yourself,' she says, probably noticing me salivating.

'Thank you.' I grab a napkin, wrap up a couple and pop them in my handbag, for later. 'Umm check in for Mrs Ramos, please,' I say, as the receptionist taps away on her keyboard.

'Room for two?' she asks, stretching her neck to look either side of me.

'No, just me today.' I smile, clutching my bags a little too tightly. 'It was two, but just me now.' I close my mouth then open it, then close it again. I wanted to explain about Filipe but what would she care. Too much information, Amber. You're on your own and that's that, no one cares, no one is judging. It's perfectly normal.

'Okay.' She smiles again, hiding any sympathy that she might have for me being on my own as she continues to tap away on her keyboard again.

'Yeah, night off. Night off for me, husband's idea,' I say, feeling the need to justify myself as a crowd full of people enter Reception. Suddenly it's very noisy, the atmosphere charged with excitement and festivity. They're all dressed up in beautiful Christmas outfits, many of the women in ballgowns and the men in smart suits or tuxes.

'Wow, what a good idea. Just a moment.' She stops typing then saunters off, leaving me standing there. I begin to eavesdrop on the various conversations going on around me about who will be embarrassing themselves this year and who will be snogging who. One woman has an incredibly loud laugh and I wonder if they've all had a few already.

As casually as I can, I swivel my head around to nose at who's talking. A few of the guests look familiar, but they must just have those kinds of faces. The receptionist comes back and informs me that there's a few Christmas parties going on tonight. She makes an uncomfortable face and warns me that it might be a bit noisy but to compensate the hotel would like to offer me a free meal. The only thing is, the free meal is at the Christmas party and I will have to go down to collect it as the waiters are all busy serving the food for said parties.

'That's okay, so I just go down, show my room key and I can have a free dinner?'

'Yes, exactly that,' she says, offering me another truffle.

Girl after my own heart. I'm sold.

'Here's some free ear plugs, just in case you need them later.'

'Thank you, sounds fair to me.'

'Have a wonderful stay, Mrs Ramos. Enjoy your *me* time.'

'Oh, I will.' I grin.

I catch the lift up to my room with promises from reception that the porter will bring up my bags shortly. My room is gorgeous, it has a balcony with a beautiful view of the lake and gardens and a stunning four poster bed. Filipe certainly didn't scrimp here I think as I eye up the marble bedside tables and crystal chandelier.

A big happy sigh escapes me.

I'm quite excited at the prospect of trotting down to claim my free Christmas dinner in all my finery. The porter arrives with my suitcase and I unpack everything before running myself a nice hot bubble bath. After some scrubbing, feet filing, soaking in the bath then showering to wash my hair. I heave myself out, smother my hair in curling cream then whack on my bright red silk bonnet to stop my hair from frizzing, next, I put on a face mask and feet masks. I slip into my bright red silk PJs, feeling festive and glorious as the silk material dances over my skin. The TV is set to the 90s music channel. *I Need a Miracle* by Fragma booms out of the speakers. I smile. Perfect. My body begins to bop, enjoying the freedom and although it's completely forgotten how to dance, I still give it a good go. My silk bonnet bobs round on my head as my feet swish in their feet mask bags. Moments later there's a knock at the door. Just in time.

I take the wine off the young waiter and tip him.

'Thank you,' he says, taking the tip before his eyes fall to my feet. 'What the?' I step from side to side, my feet rustling like two massive packets of cheesy Doritos dying to be opened.

'Sorry, excuse me,' I say, retreating back inside my hotel room as my feet continue to rustle. 'It's all part of the getting ready process, it's normal,' I reassure, as I start to close the door on his frowning face. Poor lad, I think I may have just scared him for life, not that it's any of his business.

'Thank you.' He scuttles off, eyes wide.

Someone once told me that what a woman does to get ready should be kept discreet, a secret, even. Perhaps this is why. The reality is Rome wasn't built in a day so most women can't get ready in ten minutes, especially if they want to look fancy.

A while later, I'm ready, wearing the navy velvet dress that I bought from that nice shop assistant at

Emmanuel's and wore to my birthday dinner. I've contrasted it with a silver bag, pashmina and shoes. The dress didn't get much wear out of it the night of my birthday party, and I don't want it to be cursed so I'm taking it out to have a better night tonight.

On my own.

I admire my reflection in the mirror. Red hair curls and waves down my back complimenting the smoky eyes I've spent ages perfecting. I practice my smile, turning from side to side as I observe myself, unsure if it's the wine giving me extra confidence or if I'm just feeling good about myself today. I don't really need to lose weight, not much anyway but I should take better care of myself and eat better. I let out a little giggle, I must have shaved a few pounds off when I filed my feet. It's all about how I carry myself. Shoulders back, tits out. There we go. I look bloody good. I send a quick text to Filipe to see how Sofia is and he immediately texts back telling me she's fine and not to bother them again as they're busy watching *Toy Story 4*. I almost send him a photo of myself all done up but at the last minute decide not to. We don't do that anymore.

Fine, you do that and I'll do me.

I swish out of my hotel room and trot down the stairs before following the signs to where the Christmas party is taking place. It takes an age to get there. I go up several staircases then down a few before I see the entrance to the event. The red double doors are propped open and there's a sign on the door as to what companies are attending the party. I don't bother to read it all, what does it matter to me? I'll grab a seat in the corner somewhere and wait for my meal. No-one will even notice me. I show my room key to the man on the door and he tells me to sit wherever I like and that food will be brought out in ten minutes. Perfect.

I help myself to a glass of red from the drinks table then scan the room for somewhere to sit, a small round table with just six seats catches my eye. There's nobody sitting there yet and I realise that rather than feeling a bit nervous as you would expect, I'm excited. Excited at the prospect of meeting new people. I get comfortable in my seat and watch the door, admiring people's outfits as they filter through into the room, smiling and laughing. 'Umm excuse me.' A waitress appears next to me making me jump. I accidently spill a little wine on the bottom of my pashmina. Shit. 'The buffet is coming out now, feel free to help yourself.'

'Oh hello. Buffet?' I say, slightly disappointed that I won't be waited on but it is a free meal, I can't complain. She nods and smiles. 'Yes, lovely of course, thank you.'

I leave my, now dirty, pashmina on the chair and head over to the buffet table. Oh, this wasn't what I expected, everything is beige. Oh well. Beggars can't be choosers. I begin to pile my plate up with sausage rolls and sandwiches, I'm just eyeing up the jar of pickled eggs when a finger taps me on the shoulder. I turn to face the tapper.

'Mr Thomas,' I gasp in horror, as I come face to face with him dressed in a beautiful navy suit, holding an empty plate. He looks, and I hate myself for thinking this, breath-taking.

'You can call me by my first name you know, Amber,' he replies.

So, he does know who I am.

'You know who I am.'

'Yes, of course I know who you are, you're Sofia's mum.' He blinks and with his free hand, undoes the top button of his shirt. Is he flustered? 'Yes of course I do,

I'm teasing, how could I forget you?' He looks at me for a moment with warmness and humour in his eyes.

I should have stayed home, it's actually ridiculous I'm here. Filipe and I could have had some fun together, but on my own I almost feel scared now. Is it that or is it him, Mr Thomas? I'm so out of my comfort zone and yet I'm on my own all the time at home, so busy cleaning, tidying, cooking and running Sofia about. I crave this quality time on my own, so what on earth is wrong with me? The person standing right in front of you is what is wrong with you, my inner voice goads.

'Nice dress, it really suits you,' he says.

'Thank you, I wasn't expecting to see you here, at the buffet.' I glance down at my plate, my desire for a pickled egg diminished.

'Yeah, it's not great, is it?' He laughs softly. 'I guess that's what you get when you work in the public sector.'

'Yeah, public sector.' I tut and roll my eyes, like I know all about it.

'So where do you work?'

'Me?'

'No, her over there, yes you.' He grins, making me feel like a school girl all over again.

'Work?'

'Yes.'

'I don't at the moment. I'm here because, I was supposed to be here with my husband but not at this party in particular. I got offered a free meal by the hotel because of the noise.'

'So, you're here on your own?' Is that pity in his eyes?

'Yeah, thought I'd make the most of it, you know. Us mums don't get much me time so tonight, I've gone all out.'

'Yeah, why not, hey? Good for you and I mean you

look, really great. Really.'

'Thanks.' I clamp my teeth down to stop the words from pouring out. He doesn't want to hear about Sofia's sick spray and the awful time I've been having at home but I somehow feel compelled to confide in him. Like we used to. Except, I don't.

'So, what brings you back to Coolsbay?'

'I broke up with my wife, so back with the parents for a bit now, until I find my feet.' He takes a bite of his sausage roll then makes a face.

'I'm so sorry to hear that.'

'Don't be, my parents are cool and it was lucky I got that job, well not for Mrs Cockburn of course, that was very sad.'

'Yes, do you know how she died?'

'I hear she choked on a pickled egg.'

'Really?' I say, eyeing them up again, 'The deadly pickled egg.'

'No.' His eyes crinkle. 'You're still as easy to wind up.'

'You shit.'

We stand at the buffet table, nibbling on the slightly dull buffet and chat about the old times, who we see, who we don't see, what he thinks of Sofia and how lovely she is. The waiters circle round offering house red and white wine and we both take a glass and then another as we continue to reminisce and catch up. A couple of times, I mention that my pashmina is still at the table and to remind me to get it before I leave. What we don't talk about is why he originally left. Why he never came back. Why he didn't say goodbye.

'After playing semi-pro football for a few years, I got a bit too old for it, you know the knees got a bit creaky, too many injuries so instead, I started coaching kids' football teams. That's when I fell in love with them, especially the three-to-five-year-olds. I love their inquisitive minds, the funny things they say, so decided to pursue a career in teaching, much to my ex-wife's horror.'

'Why the horror?'

'Oh, she didn't think it was right for me for some reason. But I love it. No regrets. They cheer me up, make me forget my problems.'

'Hmmm, same with dogs,' I muse. 'You're very good at it, Sofia likes you, that's an accomplishment in itself.'

We smile at each other, then as if on cue the DJ begins to play *Kissing You* by Desire. For a moment, we both stand, rooted to the spot, just listening. Remembering. He smiles, the same boyish smile he used to use all those years ago. Does he remember?

'Do you remember this song?' he asks.

'Yes, how could I forget?' The song stops halfway through, the DJ apologises for playing the wrong song and then starts to play *Ooooh Ahh Just a Little Bit* by Gina G.

'Oh my God, I haven't heard this song for years.'

'Yes, and I wish I still hadn't, it's truly awful. What is the DJ thinking?'

We giggle to each other as I do my mum bop side step, it's still bad but I don't care, the wine is helping. Something better begins to play, something I recognise that's been playing on the radio recently, he pulls me onto the dance floor and that's where we stay for the rest of the evening until my feet can't take any more and he walks me to my hotel room.

'Wow, you got the swanky side of the hotel,' he says, as we approach the door.

'Yes, it has a balcony. Very nice views. Thanks for a fun night, it was good, it was more than good. Just what

I needed.'

'And did you get your *me* time?'

'I felt like me again, yes.' The old me, in more ways than one.

'Good, sorry if I intruded on it.'

'No, it's fine, it was nice.' He leans in towards me and brushes his lips softly against mine. I arch my back, avoiding him.

'Goodbye, Mr Thomas, be good,' I say, as I push him back. Be good? I slide back and close the door on a frowning Mr Thomas and lean against the back of it for a few minutes, trying to steady my breathing. He doesn't walk away immediately; I hear him mutter to himself, swearing but I can't make out the words before he skulks off, probably back to his Christmas party. How dare he kiss me, I'm a married woman. The absolute cheek and nerve of him, Mr Bloody Dylan Thomas.

Chapter 19

Delilah

The weekend has been spent enjoying Loki and popping out to buy him things that he needs like a cage, bed, puppy pads, food, various squeaky/annoying toys and the rest of the stuff that goes with looking after and spoiling a puppy. Dylan may be a teacher but he weirdly isn't that organised in his personal life. I can't complain though, I'll be eternally grateful to him for persuading Mum and Dad to get our dream dog. We've had a lovely time as a family, enjoying our new bundle of joy even if Josh is a little jealous of all the attention. He didn't come over later on, said he was busy but I'm pretty sure he was sulking. Loki is still only a puppy even though he's a rescue. From the sounds of it, the family that first bought him couldn't cope with his puppy behaviour, I wonder how much Dylan has told Dad as he'll be the one looking after him the most. Luckily, Dad and Loki seem to be getting on like a house on fire, despite his years of protests.

After a lovely weekend the impending Sunday gloom is setting in for the evening as I chill in my bedroom with Sky.

'Urgh, so not looking forward to work tomorrow,' I

say to Sky, who's sitting at my dressing table opposite me, painting my nails with red nail varnish.

'You have work? Thought you'd finished?' she says, frowning, not looking up, concentrating on painting my nails.

Hang on a minute…

'Yes! You're right, I have no work, it's Christmas! I'm officially on holiday baby!' Elation spreads throughout my bones as I jump up and down with my hands, spread out high in the air, careful not to ruin my nails. Sky looks at me as if I'm crazy. Don't you just love that feeling? When you think you're going to have to do something you don't want to do but then it turns out those plans have changed or were never even happening in the first place. Amazing!

I'm feeling pure joy that I don't have to spend the whole day with the not so fantastical Miriam. She truly gives me anxiety when she speaks to me in the (not so) nicest possible way. Although, she is beginning to thaw, just a little. I sit back down, my heart still racing with euphoria at the thought of no work when my phone beeps on my bedside table. I slowly lean over with my free hand to grab my phone and my heart's pace quickens again, it's a text from Byron. I wish he would stop messaging me but I wish even more for me to control myself and not reply.

Byron: *Hey, what are you up to?*

One, two, three, four, five, six.

Me: *Wouldn't you like to know.* I scream a little inside then gently place my phone down on the dressing table whilst glancing at Sky. It's too exciting not to reply.

'Can you just sit still. Who was that? Josh?' Sky asks, inspecting my nails then wiping off a smear that's got onto my skin.

'Nah, just a mate,' I say nonchalantly.

'A mate, you do that face for a mate?' There's no fooling Sky.

'What face?'

'This one.' Sky presses and pouts her lips together, goes cross eyed and wriggles her head.

'If I look like that then please shoot me.' I giggle then grab the bottle of prosecco that Sky bought over before topping up our glasses. It doesn't matter if I have a hangover now.

'Sit still woman. Well, who was it?'

'No one.'

'Dee, tell me who it is or I'll just simply grab your phone and take a look for myself.' She sets the nail varnish aside and hovers her hand over my phone. 'We're friends, you don't hide shit from me. Especially who you're texting when you're making faces like this.' Sky does the face again and I hang my head in my hands, careful not to smudge my nails, the red hood I'm wearing covering my entire head and face.

'It's Byron,' I mumble.

'Brian? Who's Brian? Sounds old as fuck,' she says, grabbing my hands again for their hopefully, final inspection.

'No, Byron,' I say, in almost a whisper, lifting my head up.

'Molly's Byron?'

'Yeah.'

'Why's he texting you?' The *you* is so accusing. I hesitate on whether to tell her the truth.

'He was with me the night she passed out, he put her in the recovery position. I wouldn't have known what to do if it wasn't for him. I didn't tell Molls because I didn't want to embarrass her. She'd hate that he was there and saw her in that state.'

'She'd also hate that he's texting you.' Sky laughs then frowns. 'So, why's he texting you?'

'He just does, asks how I am and stuff.' I shrug, becoming increasingly aware of how it looks but not wanting to admit it.

'Ohhh be careful there, hun.'

'Why? It's totally innocent, I'm allowed to be friends with a boy.'

'Yeah, but this is a boy who your best mate loves, remember. Just, be careful, don't fuck him.'

'I won't.' I grimace 'How's the guy you're seeing?'

'Yeah, good but we aren't putting labels on it, too much pressure. Anyway, where's that ring light? Let's set this shit up. You look stunning.'

After a bit of persuasion from Sky I've decided tonight is the night, I'm going to give this whole *going live* thing a go. It was all a bit of an accident really, more intrigue than anything but now I'm sitting here in saucy underwear whilst my friend does my hair and makeup. It was after 8pm when Sky realised that she'd promised her fans that she'd go live at 9pm tonight. *'There isn't enough time,'* she'd said. *'I'm going to have to do it here and you're going to join me.'* I'm sure little Miss Extra has set this up. I would normally have said no to doing this at my house, but Mum and Dad are out having a meal so it's just Dylan chilling downstairs, nursing his hangover with the pup. His works Christmas party must have been wild for him to be still recovering this late. I caught him all bleary-eyed cuddling into Loki and a silver blanket, he looked dreadful, tearful even. That must be some mammoth hangover. The sooner he starts dating and forgetting about Claire, the better. I must set him up on some dating apps soon.

I turn my phone off and go and grab the ring light box from on top of my bedroom wardrobe. It's just a cheap one from the local supermarket that I bought months ago when Molly was trying to persuade me to film my dancing and become some sort of dance influencer. I couldn't do it, I would film them and then watch the dances back over and over again, critiquing myself until, in the end, I just deleted them all then sat and cried for hours. It's ironic because I am using the ring light for that very thing now, dancing. Except that this time I'll be wearing minimal clothing, it will be quite dark and little kids won't look to me as a role model. Little kids won't even be allowed to watch it because it is strictly for over eighteens. I pour our glasses of prosecco and take a few gulps of mine; I'm going to need this for confidence.

'You do look fucking fit,' Sky says, as she assesses my eye makeup then my outfit, well what there is of it. I'm wearing matching red underwear with a short floaty red skirt over the top which leaves little to the imagination; I'm also wearing a cape. Yes, a big, long red cape with a huge hood. Sky gave it to me, she said I can give off this image of being a slutty Little Red Riding Hood. She said that men love that shit, innocence and sluttiness sells. Personally, I kind of like it as I can hide my face if I want to. Sky's wearing all black, showing off her tattoos, especially the one of a lion on her hip. She has no cape. She looks amazing, but it's her confidence that the viewers will go wild for.

'You don't think it's too much?' I look in the mirror, impressed at the magic she has worked on my face. A sexy minx stares back at me, I don't know her or recognise her, she isn't me, but someone else, perhaps. Yes, that's it, I'm playing the part of someone else.

'Yep, red really suits you, it's so stunning with your hair.' She applies another coat of red lipstick to my lips and then hers.

'Thanks, you look stunning too,' I say, awkwardly touching my wavy blonde locks. I've seen her on the beach in her bikini but there's something a bit embarrassing about seeing your mate in their underwear, sexy underwear at that. I feel like a pervert.

'I'm so excited for you to do this with me and when you've had a bit of practice you can branch out on your own, then you can start earning the big bucks like I do.'

'Okay,' I agree, over stroking my hair, feeling boiling hot all of a sudden. I hope I don't pass out. What if I pass out on camera and wee myself? I might do that. Already the intrusive thoughts and countdown is beginning in my head as Sky fiddles with the lighting. She moves the ring light around the room several times to get the perfect spot, tidying up furiously around her, making sure there are no clothes or mess in the shot. I'm not particularly messy but Sky it seems, is a bit of a pro at this. It has to be perfect.

'There, come have a look.' I'm not sure what I'm supposed to be looking at but I go over to her to see what she means. Sky points into the phone that's now held up by the ring light. Staring back at it are two girls, correction, two very attractive, sexy women that mean business. Something clicks within me, either that or the alcohol kicks in and a new found confidence emerges. I look at Sky and give her a slow grin.

'Let's do this shit.' She taps the screen and we're live.

We spend the next few minutes prancing about in our underwear and sipping our prosecco, it all feels completely normal until Sky leans over to check the messages. She beckons for me to come and see them as they start to fly in one after the other. One, two, three, four, five, six. Stay calm, I'm calm. They can't see me. They can't see my face.

John: *Good evening, ladies*

Stewart: *Looking amazing*

Ian59: *Hey, what have you been up to today?*

User23154891666: *Wow, let the show begin.*

James54: *I'm shy, be gentle with me.*

'Good evening, guys,' Sky says, in a weird Essex accent that I haven't heard her do before. 'Aww thankkkkk youuuu.' She giggles whilst I laugh nervously, half at the situation, half at Sky's ridiculous accent. I think she's going for Molly Mae off *Love Island* but she sounds more like Dick Van Dyke from *Mary Poppins*. What on earth am I getting myself into. Will I have to do that accent? I make an executive decision not to speak, I'll be her mute friend. Yes, that will work.

Ben87: *Who's that with you, tell her to take her hood off?*

'Hi Ben, this is my friend Chardonnay, she's a bit shy so going to keep the hood on for a bit if that's okay?'

Chardonnay? What the actual… I give the camera a little wave then blow a kiss to the camera, playing along for the laughs. Chardonnay? Where the hell does she get these names from? I wish she'd warned me about this, we didn't discuss names. For the next twenty minutes, we carry on drinking and having a laugh, stopping occasionally to see what people are saying then replying to their greetings and requests on camera. Because I can't see them, the people sending messages don't seem all that real after a while. Some of the requests are a bit strange like tell me your most embarrassing story, another one requests that I slap Sky around the face. This isn't so bad, I could get used to this, not slapping Sky around the face, just chatting on camera to bots for money. I know they aren't bots but it makes me feel better thinking that they are.

Ben87: *Give Chardonnay a kiss then*

User23154891666: *I want to see more than just a kiss*

'Ooooooh, you want us to kiss do you?' Sky flirts as I pull my hood further over my face. A flurry of messages appear on the screen as Sky and I flirt with each other and the camera, she ends up giving me a kiss on the cheek and her phone blows up with even more messages. Next, she puts her hand over the camera for a few seconds, whilst simultaneously motioning at me to be quiet. She takes her hand away and starts fanning herself with her hands. I assume she's making out like we've just shared some raunchy kiss. The screen blows up again.

Ben87: *I want to see more.*

Ian59: *Hey girls, looking gorgeous, what have you been up to today?*

Stewart: *Private show.*

'Hi, Ian, not much, just been working, had a wonderful winter wedding today. I'm a makeup artist.'

Ian59: *Nice, cool job.*

User23154891666: *Bet the groom loved that.*

Sam: *Bet the bride was fuming when she saw you.*

'Yeah,' Sky laughs. 'Well it wasn't the groom getting his makeup done, silly.'

Somebody is typing, she leans forward to see User23154891666's reply.

User23154891666: *Haha, I meant if he saw you.*

'Wouldn't that be funny, heeey,' she says, all Essex girl. 'If he recognised me off here. Okay, Stewart, I'll private message you. Private shows start at 10pm okayyyyyy. And no, the bride was an absolutely stunning babe.' Sky takes my hand and nods 'Right, my girl here Chardonnay is a professional dancer. Who wants to see her dance?'

My heart begins to pulsate as little beads of sweat form on my forehead. One, two, three, four, five, six.

User23154891666: *Yes, she's way better looking than you even with the hood on you, fat, ugly bitch.*

Oh my God, a troll, that took an unexpected turn.

'Okay, blocked.' Sky leans forward and taps on her phone for a few seconds. User23154891666 is no more. She doesn't look phased and I wonder if she has to put up with this kind of abuse all the time. It's not nice, even if you have a thick skin like Sky.

Ian59: *Just ignore him darling, you're not fat at all*

James54: *You're beautiful*

Ben87: *I want to see more*

'Calm down, Benny boy, you'll see more, just be patient.' Sky puts her hand over the camera lens again.

'You, okay?'

I nod at her.

'Choose some music, then it's time to dance baby, yeah?' Her eyes glow. I quickly scroll on my phone choosing the song then Bluetooth it to my speaker. Dua Lipa's *Love Again,* begins and I nod back at Sky to let her know I'm ready. She takes her hand off the lens.

'Hi guys, wanna see me dance?' I say, mimicking Sky's Essex accent, and managing to sound very much like Gemma Collins from *The Only Way is Essex.* Who knew I was good at accents?

'Yes, that's my gal.' Sky raises a glass to me as I stand up. The music builds and I begin to move my hips slowly to the beat, using my hood as part of my act. Dua's chocolatey tones belt out through the speaker and something begins to take me over. This is one of my favourites and I just can't stop dancing to it. Sky gently pulls on my arm signalling at me to stop, that's enough, but I bat her arm away.

This is my time to shine. I continue to dance.

Sky leans forward a couple of time, checking the messages. After a few more tugs, each one getting more half arsed, she eventually gives up trying to reign me in. Channelling my inner Mylie Cyrus, I'm really getting into it, showing off all my moves and my flexibility. I flirt with the camera, being cheeky and alternating between flashing my face and showing off my dance moves. I could get used to this. Confident, I could definitely do this for money. They're not real, just bots. I'm dancing for bots. I turn around once more, feeling a little braver this time and lift my skirt up slowly to show off my red French knickers. I sway my hips from side to side, imagining my imaginary bank balance going up and up.

No more money worries.

Dancing for a living.

BANG BANG BANG

There's someone at the door.

It's not okay for them to come in.

The door bursts open and the Tasmanian devil enters the room

'What the fuck?' Before I know it, I'm on my arse and Loki is frantically licking my face. Somehow, he's managed to get upstairs.

Dylan.

'My brother can't see me like this, yuk,' I shriek. 'TURN IT OFF! GET OUT!' I manage between each loving lick from Loki. 'TURN, OUT.'

Sky lunges for her phone but it's already happened.

Already caught on camera.

She stretches across to stop recording but as she moves Loki decides he's had enough of me and pins her down too. She gets the same treatment as I did. Big, long, happy licks as she screams and laughs hysterically but I'm not laughing and my throat won't allow for a scream. Because you see it would be funny, well, at least slightly funny I suppose, if Josh wasn't standing in my bedroom doorway with his eyes wide and mouth hanging open.

Chapter 20

Amber

The chilled, relaxed *'I've got this'* Filipe that I left on Saturday night was replaced with a rather sleep deprived, grumpy shadow of a man when I arrived home early Sunday afternoon. Sofia had made a full recovery and was running around like a loon whilst Filipe lay sleeping on the sofa. Yes, he was having a nap and I woke him, needless to say he was not a happy bunny. Sofia did her usual trick of being up all night, hence the need for a cat nap.

There were toys all over the living room furniture and floor, I almost broke my foot on the Lego that was left out. Beds were unmade and the washing up in the kitchen looked as if it had been left for a week. It hadn't as I do it every day and never leave the kitchen anything but spotless. It was, of course, spotless when I left it on Saturday albeit the plate and frying pan from his bacon sandwich. But I didn't complain or tut and roll my eyes because he was knackered and I was grateful, grateful for my night away and touched that he offered for me to have a break, who knows if I play my cards right, I may get more of these nights. Nights to myself, not nights of bumping into Mr Thomas.

I can't believe he kissed me.

It was so generous and thoughtful of Filipe to let me have my night. I was looking forward to having a joke and a laugh with him about how hard it is to keep the place tidy fighting against the mess and dirt of a child and a dog. I was looking forward to hearing his stories of the mischief Olive and Sofia got up to as they often do. I was waiting for him to say something like, my God you work hard too. He looked rather sweet there sleeping and being a worn-out dad, it suited him. I was excited to spend the day with my family after a refreshing night's sleep.

Or maybe not.

Filipe didn't talk to me for most of the day and night. It was as though I was being punished for going out for the night, even though it was his idea. When I got home and saw him so tired I felt sorry for him. But since the silent treatment, there's resentment bubbling within me too.

Olive almost knocked me over when I got my foot in the door. You can always rely on your dog to be pleased to see you. They don't ever resent you and if they're in a grump it certainly doesn't last long. Sofia was still a bit offish but I think a part of her was pleased to see me, she excitedly shouted Mummy and came running towards me, before reigning herself back in with her trademark scowl and stiff arms when I tried to hug her. Filipe was just a knackered mess, devoid of any energy and emotion other than self-pity.

Oh, I don't feel guilty in the slightest, despite Filipe's mood, I know I fully deserved a break. My hotel stay was just wonderfully beautiful, despite bumping into Mr Thomas, which was wonderful, until he tried to kiss me. It's awkward, he's just an old flame from when I was a teenager, so why do I feel so happy? No. I have a husband who's let me have a night off, kind of.

I crawl into bed having spent the day sorting out all the mess whilst dealing with a naughty dog and a miserable, tired child while Filipe sulks and dozes in the corner. My head hits the pillow then my eyes ping open. Olive hasn't been out for a walk, all day. I usually walk her in the morning at the weekends but our routine is all out of sync now. I grab my phone off the bedside table and send a message to Stella.

Me: *Fancy a walk tomorrow morning? Also, I have goss.* Stella will love that I gate-crashed the teachers' Christmas do.

Stella: *Yes! Let's meet in the field behind mine at 10am? We could give them a big run out at the beach. It's meant to be mild, not too cold.*

Me: *Sounds perfect, see you then.*

I pop my phone back on the side and turn over in bed to face an empty space next to me; I wish we could get back to how we were. I thought he may want to share a bed tonight, I thought he might have missed me. Maybe I'll treat him to his favourite meal tomorrow, beef stroganoff followed by his Spanish dessert, churros. That will cheer him up but maybe not beef stroganoff, that's what I cooked on my birthday night. And maybe not churros, the thought of frying dough suddenly makes me feel rather nauseous. I close my eyes willing the sicky feeling to go away as my mind drifts back to a simpler, seemingly happier time.

The sun beats down on me as I stand outside Coolsbay cinema, peeling off my Adidas jacket which is covering a tight, tiny white boob tube. On the bottom half I'm wearing my hipster jeans, and of course, I can't forget my very impressive Wonderbra that I'm hiding underneath my jacket. The smell of fresh sea air coupled with fish and chips float up from the seaside, enhancing my feeling of nervous excitement.

Tonight, is going to be such a good night.

It's in the air, I can feel it.

I fish around in my bag and pull out a mirror so I can apply a bit more Heather Shimmer lipstick and black eyeliner. My hair is freshly washed and blow dried straight and I feel quite pretty for once. When I left the house, I made sure to have my jacket zipped up to my chin, Dad would go mad if he saw that I was going out like that, not to mention the belly button piercing I had a couple of months ago. A girl's got to do what a girl's got to do, it's my life and I wanted a belly button piercing.

There, that will do, don't overdo it on the Heather Shimmer, Amber, think more Britney Spears not the goths at school. I drop my mirror and makeup into my bag then glance at my watch which is telling me he's now almost ten minutes late. I made sure I was late to meet him at the cinema, not too late but five minutes and now I'm panicking that I was too late and he's already been and gone. I reach into my handbag again and scramble around in my purse for some change for the phone box. Before I left the house, I was smart and looked up his phone number in the yellow pages. I'll call him if he isn't here in five minutes. I hope he's here in five minutes. The thought of his parents or brother answering the phone makes me feel uncomfortable.

Just as I begin to walk across the road to the phone box, I see him getting out of his mum and dad's car. He walks across the car park quickly with his hands in his dark, denim jean pockets. He looks different not wearing his school uniform, he looks older. His hair is gelled a little more than usual and he's wearing a bright yellow jacket. On anyone else it would look horrible but he pulls it off. He actually makes me feel a little boring and underdressed. I knew I should have worn my new Miss Selfridges dress.

'Hey, sorry, um my dad is so slow at driving.' He smiles as he

gets closer, his aftershave drifting ahead of him, it smells amazing. I'm sure it's John Paul Gaultier. My friend at school bought her boyfriend's bottle of it in one day for us to all smell. I swear by the end of the day we were all high. Suddenly, I feel a bit inadequate, why is he here with me? Why did he choose me to write a letter to?

'It's okay.' I smile back. I'd forgive him for anything right now.

'He gave me a lift.'

'Yeah? I was just about to go home.' I look off into the distance and his head swivels to see what I'm looking at. I'm looking at nothing, just awkwardly avoiding his gaze.

'I'm glad you waited,' he says, turning back, then he bites his lip. 'You look nice.'

'Thanks.' So do you, I'm thinking, but I don't say it. Not this time. We begin to walk to the cinema together and his fingers gently touch mine before pulling them into a firm yet gentle hold. My whole hand tingles. Is this love?

'What do you want to watch?' he asks, as we walk in time with each other.

'Umm I was thinking that car film or something.'

'Oh, the new Fast and Furious? Seen it, it's rubbish. I thought you'd want to see Shakespeare in Love?'

'You want to see that?'

'Yeah, love a bit of romance, me.' He grins with a confidence that only a boy like him could have. If this was at school any other boy admitting that would be made fun of and called gay but he doesn't care, he owns his opinions which makes me fancy him even more.

'Well, yeah, okay then. Shakespeare in Love.'

He goes to the loo then comes back with the tickets and then we head over to get popcorn, coke and a pic'n'mix as I try to remember the best ways to get a boy to fancy you. I read it in Bliss magazine that if you blink three times at him then smile instantly, it sends out a signal that he should fall in love with you. I decide to try that in the cinema, in the dark when he can barely see me. It's too *embarrassing.*

We find our seats and settle down. Throughout all of the film trailers and most of the film all I can think about is where his arm is. He put it there, draped behind me straight away and it hasn't moved for almost two whole hours. What if he's trapped a nerve or something and can't move it? I'm sure he should have tried to kiss me by now but he hasn't. Maybe it's the pain of the trapped nerve, maybe I should kiss him.

Just as Gwyneth kisses Joseph Fiennes, I take that as my cue to kiss him. My hand, that's resting on his right leg, slowly glides down his thigh. He turns his head towards me and I blink three times, smiling, he smiles back then leans forward to gently kiss me, slowly at first but then fast and passionate. Intermittently, we snog until the end of the film. The kind of snogs you only see people my age do. Urgent, hungry, exciting snogs and it's pure ecstasy.

Chapter 21

Delilah

Sky: *Oh my God, our live has gone viral. This could be huge for us and for you as a dancer. I woke up to 2,000 new followers this morning. Ching ching.*

Delilah: *What? Oh my God!*

I curl my knees up to my chest on the sofa and glance across at Dylan who's watching an episode of *Gardeners' World*, he sits up straighter when they begin talking about the bees and what we can do more of to help them.

Sky sends me a link to a blogger who has shared the video to her mammoth platform following, all 3.1million of them. I scroll through hundreds of comments, some saying how funny it was and that the dog should get his own show and others saying what slappers we are and how FansOnly is filth and nothing but a porn site. Others comment on how good my dancing is, in fact there's quite a few of them, that makes me smile for a second before I see the troll comments. The personally offensive comments. Someone has even gone to the effort of screen shotting an unflattering video still of me mid hair flick next to Taylor Swift and written, what I ordered from wish.com on Taylor's photo then, what I got from wish.com on my photo. That one hurt, I'm not going to lie.

Delilah: *I'm cringing hard. I literally want to curl up and die. Good for you though, 2,000 extra followers is amazing.*

Sky: *They can't even see your face, no one knows it's actually you. You could become the famous hooded dancer!*

I zoom into the meme to inspect it and see if that is the case, I did have my hood up most of the time but when I flicked my head around the hood did fall down for a split second, revealing my face. It's very blurry though, people might not know it was me. I could get away with it if Sky doesn't tell everyone.

Delilah: *Honestly, I feel horrible, please don't tell everyone it was me. Shit, Josh! What was I thinking?*

Sky: *Ahh yes, how is he? I thought you would have told him that you were thinking about trying out* FansOnly, *I thought he'd be cool.*

Delilah: *Well, he's not cool. I didn't think I needed permission but I probably should have spoken to him first. I feel awful.*

Sky: *Dee, I'm coming over to yours to pull you out of your pit of self-pity puddle. I'll bring Luna and we can take her and Loki out for a bit. See you soon. I might have to wear a balaclava over to yours so no one stops me for an autograph. Haha.*

'What are you looking so glum for baby sis?' Dylan hands me a fresh cup of tea and I take hold of the handle, pulling it in close to hug and make the most of its warmth. Loki stirs in his sleep beside me as his nose twitches a little at the new smell. I close my eyes, desperately trying to keep the tears from falling hard. 'Dee?' He sits down next to me, peeling my hand away from my face. 'Dee, what it is?' He asks more urgently. 'DEE!'

One, two, three, four, five, six.

'My life is such a mess,' my voice cracks and I try to speak through the tears that are now flowing fast down my face. 'Josh is going to dump me; I've been texting my mate's crush because he's hot and now I'm viral. I've gone viral dancing in my bedroom like a whore but at least I was wearing a hood.' I cast a glance at my brother who is looking at me with his head tilted to the side, he looks amused yet also concerned.

But mostly amused.

'Don't laugh, it's not funny!' I wallop him on the arm to show him that I'm really not joking, then wipe my sleeve across my eyes.

'I'm not laughing, I'm not, I just thought you were going to say something really, really awful like you were seriously ill or something, all these things can be sorted,' he says, kindly.

Not the sympathy or understanding I was after. I give him the daggers.

'Or maybe just focus on you, your career?'

I eyeball him, he's low-key patronising and he's just reminded me of another thing that isn't going so well in my life right now. It's certainly not *fandabidozi*.

'Look, it's all relative, it's just all come at once hasn't it, but you can sort stuff.' He's giving me sage advice, he thinks.

'Yeah?'

'Of course, I'm sure Josh will come around, he worships you. Follows you around like a lovesick puppy. Want me to call him?'

'No, no, don't do that. I can't face him. It's over.' A flashback of Josh standing gobsmacked in my bedroom doorway burns in my mind's eye. I shake my head to get rid of his sweet, hurt face. Did I sub-consciously self-sabotage to end our relationship?

'And texting someone else? Why?'

'Because, I'm just a total shitstick and I was bored,' I

mumble.

'Bored?'

'Yeah, am I an awful person? I don't deserve him. How do people stay married for like forty years? That's you, people stay married for as long as you are old. How?'

Dylan rolls his eyes at my old joke.

'Why did you and Claire split up? Was it the same reason?'

'Boredom? No.'

'What was it then?' I ask, half expecting him to dodge the question again or tell me he isn't ready to answer. He takes a big breath then speaks.

'She owned up that she didn't want children, never has, and that's not what I want. I want a family. She sold me a dream, I guess.' He takes a sip of his drink.

'Wow, you left because of that.'

'Yup, well that was the straw that broke the camel's back, we had our issues before that but that just felt like a huge betrayal. We'd talked about it for years. We were ready, or at least that's what she led me to believe. I was more than ready to become a dad, except it turns out that she never wanted it.' He glances at me and sighs, still bewildered by it all. 'So here I am.'

'Sorry if this sounds selfish but I'm glad you're here. *We're* glad you're here.' I point to Loki who's still busy snoring and Dylan strokes his ears.

'I'm glad I'm here too, it's made me slow down and spend some time to work on me, as cheesy at that sounds. How long have you and Josh been together now anyway?'

'Six years now.'

'Six years and you're only twenty-one. People do say that you either grow together or you grow apart.'

'Do they?'

'Yeah, look at Mum and Dad, they've grown together, they were only sixteen when they met and I bet they've had their fair share of tests and troubles. It's normal to be attracted to other people as the years go by, it's just how you choose to deal with those feelings that matters.'

I think of all the romantic movies I've watched, often with Josh, feeling angry that the idea of love that I've been sold isn't reality, not mine anyway. That's really hard to swallow. It's not just Dylan that was sold a dream.

'I don't know, I don't know what I want anymore, with anything. I'm lost.'

'You'll find a way, there's no rush, is there, Dee? But don't treat Josh like a simp, as you and your friends like to call it, he's a good lad. He deserves honesty but maybe sugar-coat it slightly, what I mean by that is don't actually call him boring, that's harsh for anyone to hear.'

'No, he's not boring, it's us as a couple that's boring. But how do you know when it's really done or if you need to work at it? It's so hard.'

'I know. I guess you don't know, you just have to try to listen to your intuition and not the noise around you. Meditate.' He grins, my brother the new age guru. 'And about this going viral thing, I'm sure it will all be forgotten when the next viral gossip comes along, it will blow over.' Dylan winces then has a sip of his tea. 'Maybe you should report it to the police, whoever's leaked this video of you and Josh. You don't think Josh would do that do you?'

'What? No, no, no. I wasn't doing that, just dancing and not naked dancing. Josh wasn't even there.'

'Oh right.' He shrugs his shoulders like it's no big deal but I'm not about to tell him it was on FansOnly.

The doorbell rings and I peel myself off the sofa to

answer it as Loki springs to life barking and jumping. Dylan holds him back so he doesn't escape outside as I open the door for Sky and Luna, looking all Christmassy in their little matching elves outfits. They look both ridiculous and adorable. Luna snorts, slowly looks Loki up and down then snorts again, jutting her head up. Dylan restrains Loki from pouncing on her.

'Hey guys, well this is quite the welcome,' Sky announces, while Dylan relaxes Loki's lead and the dogs jump all over each other and us. I put my shoes and coat on while Dylan grabs the lead for me and attaches it to Loki's harness.

'Right, let's go,' I say, marching towards the door, feeling slightly better after my chat with my brother. I'm so lucky to have him, I don't want him to move out.

'Dylan you should come with us, get some fresh air,' Sky suggests. Dylan hesitates for a second, really contemplating his decision.

'I think I'll give it a miss thanks, Sky. I've a few more *Gardeners' World*s to catch up on,' he says rubbing his hands together.

'Gardeners' World?' Sky giggles as Dylan grins and shrugs as if to say, yeah so what? He's not ashamed to say what he likes, no matter how nerdy others think it is. He misses his garden; he says he's been getting ideas for his next place. I wonder why Claire got the house. It's not like they have any children so it's not for that reason so why should she have it. I suddenly feel quite angry on his behalf then remind myself that he's not angry so I shouldn't be either. 'Did Dee tell you, we're viral?' she says, flicking her hair and looking pleased with herself.

'Yes, heard all about it.'

'Really? You don't have an account do you, Dylan? Naughty Dylan,' she winks.

'What account?' he asks.

Oh no. Oh no.

'FansOnly.'

Dylan shakes his head and frowns, looking slightly confused as I proceed to drag the naughty little elves out of the door. This is a conversation I do not want had.

We meander down to the beach with our dogs, who play fight and yap at each other on the way. It's a clear day in Coolsbay with a cool winter sun shining brightly through the clear blue sky. I love days like this, equally as much as I love sunny, hot days.

There aren't many dog walkers out but then I spot her in the distance, the red-haired lady with her shit together. She's walking with her dog who has a florescent pink harness, and another woman and her dog. She looks so pretty, her long wavy, red hair cascades down her back as she laughs heartily at whatever her friend is saying. I wonder if I'll have it all together by the time I'm her age? So far my twenties have been full of uncertainty.

We meander along, taking the same route as them before we turn off to walk along the promenade. Sky lectures me a little about speaking to Molly as Luna huffs and grunts along with her. I know I have to tell her that he was there that night, I know that I have to stop texting him back. If only I could.

Chapter 22

Amber

'Alright my lovely, bloody stunning day, you wouldn't think it was December, would you?' Stella says, as we approach her in the field. She's right, it is stunning, the sky couldn't be bluer but it's bitterly cold, I can see my breath and there were icicles on my windows.

I let Olive off to greet Pudding, she gallops over and they touch noses then sniff bums before Olive teases Pudding to chase her. She's right, it is stunning, but also stunningly cold, when I came out of the house this morning there was still ice on my window sill. No doubt my nose is matching the colour of my hair right now. I feel like Rudolph the flame-haired old dear.

'You're chirpy this morning,' I say, with an extra bright smile as we fall into step and watch our dogs having fun.

'Yeah, feeling good mate, things are looking up and it's Christmas soon. You look knackered,' she says, doing a double take, seeing through my extra cheeriness.

The beautiful night's sleep I had in the hotel was cancelled out by last night's awful sleep. Sofia was up a couple of times in the night and then I just couldn't sleep. Thinking about everything and nothing. The nothing being Mr bloody annoying Thomas. I wish he would just stop infiltrating my dreams with his boyish good looks and heady nineties nostalgia. I even ordered some Heather Shimmer lipstick this morning before Googling when Alanis Morrissette is touring again. I'm a midlife crisis waiting to happen.

'Yeah, I've had better night's sleep. That's good, what things?'

'Well, Tamsin's ex has backed down, they've agreed to do a fifty-fifty custody now so we don't have to go through the agony of court.'

'Oh, bloody amazing, how did that come about?'

'I met up with him, and had an adult conversation with him, woman to man. We arranged that Tamsin was going to meet him as he wouldn't have agreed to meeting me but then I turned up and explained Tams wasn't up to it. His nose was a bit put out of joint at first but then I won him round of course, we even ended up having a joke and a laugh about the football. Only me, hey.'

'Only you, Stella, could pull that off,' I agree.

'Yeah, I know,' she winks. 'Just got the charm, haven't I? Anyway, we went over what was best for their daughter and I explained what it was like for me growing up, only seeing my dad every other weekend because that's all my mum would allow. It's not good for a child to be denied seeing a parent and when I was a kid, of course I blamed my dad but then when I chatted more to him as an adult and fitted the pieces together, I learnt the truth. It made me resent my mum for not letting me see him more just because she couldn't stand him for trading her in for a younger version. It's tough but you can't use the kids as weapons, it will only backfire, they will find out what you did, kids aren't stupid, are they? And that's what I told Tamsin's ex.'

'That they aren't, I bet Tamsin is relieved,' I say, feeling happy for my friend. I think of Sofia and her little crumpled face. Can she sense something's up with me and her dad? If I'm brutally honest about it, we've been coasting along for quite some time and now the cracks are really starting to appear. Something or someone needs to give.

'Yeah, she is. As you know we have Badger 50/50 so I've arranged it that we have both kids at the same time, that means that the rest of the time is just for me and Tams. Call me a genius or call me a genius.'

'You're a bloody genius, Stella, can you sort my life out now?'

'What's going on with you then?'

We reach the beach and I fill her in on my sleep deprived life, including my one night of luxury sleep verses the guilt and mess I've had to come back to.

'Sounds hard work, mate. Prince Filipe needs to up his game, doesn't he?'

'It was nice of him to let me have a night to myself though, he didn't have to do that.'

'Let you? He shouldn't be letting you do anything, you are your own woman, tell him you're having a night off, demand it. In fact, do it once a week, it's your night off.'

I throw my head back and laugh at the thought of Filipe's face if I told him I was checking into a hotel once a week to catch up on sleep. If only. 'In my dreams.'

'Dreams often become reality,' she says, wagging a telling finger at me.

'And if you don't ask or rather tell, then you don't get,' she continues, spouting the old sayings that I'm sure I've heard my mother say.

I open my mouth to tell her all about Mr Thomas, the free Christmas buffet and the kiss when I realise that

Olive is quite far away. Too far away. Pudding has come back for a fuss and a treat but Olive hasn't come back with her. Odd.

'Olive, Olive,' I call rattling my treat box, I can see her in the distance, in her bright pink harness, down by the sea but she's just stood staring at me. Shit, I know that look, she's going to bloody bolt it.

'OLIVE,' I call in my *this means business, come back you little shit* voice, this is 90% effective and usually does the trick, coupled with a bit of chicken on her return, which I luckily have with me today.

Again, she doesn't move.

Pudding, TRACE,' Stella commands her dog as she holds Olive's ball under her dog's nose. Pudding, unlike my dog, obeys her immediately and trots off excitedly to find her mate. For a moment, I'm relieved that Stella invested in the trace training that I so ashamedly laughed at. Olive stands there for a second until Pudding gets a few metres away. It's no good, she bolts in the opposite direction, again. Pudding circles around and gallops back to us with a face that sadly says she's tried. I pull out my whistle which I only use for emergencies. Despite, this seeming like one, I'm still fairly calm.

She always comes back to this.

I purse my lips and blow on the whistle loudly. The noise of the whistle excites Pudding and then she is off again, this time in the opposite direction. Olive is even further away, now stood still, staring off into the distance.

What the fuck is she playing at?

If I chase her, that might make it worse, she will see it as a game.

'Pudding,' Stella calls. 'Pudding, Pudding, come here,' she calls again then holds her thumb and finger to her lips to perform an ear-piercing wolf whistle, but Pudding is not playing ball either and she's continuing to run, in the opposite direction to where Olive is.

'Shit, she's heading towards the road,' Stella shouts. 'I've got to get to her.' Stella sprints off to find her dog which leaves me alone to get mine. Why oh, why did I trust her off the lead, I knew this was a bad idea and I bet Stella is thinking the same thing.

Never again.

I look around hopelessly then breathe a sigh of relief as I spot her bright pink harness next to a short woman and a tall man in the distance enticing her over. I hold my hand up above my eyes to shade them from the glaring winter sun whilst waving frantically at her with the other one.

Don't chase her.

'THANK YOU! THAT'S MY DOG,' I shout, waving back at them, they don't look at me as I begin to walk fast towards her. Fuck not chasing my dog, I have to get to her.

This is beyond embarrassing.

Don't chase her.

'HEY, THAT'S MY DOG.' The bloke glances at me for a split second then whispers something to the woman, she doesn't look up and continues to focus on my dog. Olive sniffs the air takes two steps towards the woman then decides to bolt it, again, in the opposite direction. The man lurches forward, trying to grab Olive by the collar.

At least they tried.

Olive circles back round then starts to sprint towards the steps up onto the road, she must be following Pudding's scent. As I run after her hopelessly trying to catch up, my mind starts to think the worse. God please no, not the road. Panic sets in as my heart beats so fast it feels as if it might explode from my chest. It's no good, she's way too fast. I clamber up the concrete stairs, calling her name as I see a flash of bright pink harness in the brambles on the side of the main road.

Thank God.

I've got her.

It must be a fox or something, her ears close when she smells one of those. She is in so much trouble, I'm never letting her off again. The man and woman appear from earlier on the other side of the brambles and a sense of relief washes over me.

She's safe.

'Grab her,' I say as the trees rustle and the pink harness disappears from sight again. 'She's going to come out the other side,' I yell. They can grab her before she tries to cross the road. Just as I thought, Olive comes out the other side of the brambles and the woman grabs her, before the man clips a lead on her then does something odd, he picks her up.

It's all over.

Phew.

I smile at them but then my smile quickly fades when it isn't returned and they don't seem to be bringing her to me, instead they are going in the opposite direction. With my dog on their lead. Why did he have a lead when he doesn't have a dog of his own?

Oh shit.

'Let's go. Now,' the man says to the woman, in a strong Eastend accent as he wrestles to keep Olive still. Fuck, something isn't right here.

'Excuse me. That's my dog.' I run down to the end of the brambles, find a gap and run towards them. They don't respond.

Oh. My. God.

Olive is yelping and squirming and crying. She's looking at me with her big brown eyes, just begging me to save her.

'OI, THAT'S MY FUCKING DOG,' my voice booms.

'Fuck sake,' grunts the man, as Olive bites his hand, he drops her and she manages to wriggle herself free from the harness.

'GOOD GIRL OLIVE, GOOD GIRL.'

The woman reaches forward grabbing her tail as Olive yelps in pain. Olive is panting and frantic. She runs towards me, her cow like eyes locking eyes with mine for a split second as she runs past me. Her eyes say, come with me, Mamma.

I follow her down the concrete steps back towards the beach. I take them two at a time, taking big strides, making sure not to let her out of my sight. The man strides past me and sprints towards my dog, much faster than I can manage. The woman follows after him but not before she stops to punch me in the stomach.

'Ouch.' I bend over and lose my footing, stumbling down the next few steps.

'Back off,' she spits, as she runs down the steps past me and punches me on my arm. I watch it all in slow motion as Olive runs towards the promenade with the man and woman chasing her.

'Quick, grab her,' he shouts, as they run towards a girl with long blonde hair, standing on the end of the promenade. It's the girl who walks past my house. The girl that hides her face is standing there at the end of the promenade to greet them.

Except that this time, she isn't hiding her face, she's young, younger than I thought. I feel my feet give way from beneath me as I slip on a piece of ice. I fall backwards then forwards before gravity takes control. My life quickly and vividly flashes before my eyes, marrying Filipe, giving birth to Sofia, giggling with Mum and Dad as a toddler, a memory I don't even remember until now, and finally Mr Thomas then and his face at the hotel. It all makes perfect sense, she's been stalking my house for weeks, just biding her time. Do they know each other? They're all smiling. This was all organised. An organised dog napping.

Crack.

I hold my hand up to my head and feel something warm and sticky.

Then, there's silence.

Delilah

'Thanks gal, she's a nightmare, always running off,' the man says, between puffs as I grab her collar and tell her to sit down. Both him and the woman hold their hands out towards me. They're smiling and I smile a wobbly smile back as I pat the dog on the head.

When I saw them push the woman down the stairs I told Sky to take both dogs and to call an ambulance, all I have to do is keep them here until she's safe. Sky wanted to face them but I said I would, I know the lady whose dog this is, or at least I feel like I do. In my peripheral vision, someone is walking their dog. I consider screaming and shouting for help but then he turns and walks in the opposite direction. My chance missed.

'Hand him over then, gal.'

I look down at the beautiful dog and stroke her ears. One, two, three, four, five, six.

'You'd know that he was a she if she was really yours,'

I say, quietly.

'He/she whatever, isn't that the fashion these days, gender neutral, isn't it? She's mine, gal,' he says. They both laugh as, this time, the woman reaches out for her.

'Come here, gal,' she says, as the dog cowers and proceeds to hide behind my legs, I hold on tight to her collar.

'Are you sure she's yours? Only she doesn't seem too sure of you,' I say, as I reach around inside my coat pocket. My fingers shake as I find the little can of fake tan spray whilst trying not to lose eye contact with the abductors.

'Yeah, why you questioning us? Course she is.' The woman whines as the guy grabs the lead and begins to tug.

'Give him to me. Give him to me or you may get hurt, little girl.'

I'm not a little girl. It's now or never, I can't wait any longer or they may succeed. Or worse, hurt me or the dog.

I whip out the fake tan and go for it, him first and then her before I run as fast as I can head over towards Sky and the dog's owner.

In the background I can hear their coughing, spluttering screams and swearing as the dog runs with me. I have to pull her along at first but then she quickly becomes faster than me, dragging me along at a speed I normally couldn't achieve on my own, but I'm doing it. Adrenaline, coupled with dog power are making me run at a superhero speed as we head towards the flashing blue lights. We're flying, flying at such a rate that I crash straight into my brother.

'Dylan!'

'Dee, Dee,' Dylan bundles me up in a big brother hug

along with Loki as the elves finish explaining what happened to the paramedics. One elf is particularly vocal in her explaining as the other one barks and grunts by her side. The lady is carried onto the ambulance on a stretcher with an oxygen mask fitted around her mouth, her eyes are closed.

'Oh my God, is she going to be, okay?' I say, my voice tremoring.

Dylan inhales, then exhales a big shaky sigh.

'I don't know, Dee.' His shoulders tighten as his eyes dart towards the ambulance. There's a fear in his eyes, that I've never seen before. 'I don't know.'

Chapter 23

Amber

At first everything smells different, it's a sterile odour coupled with the occasional waft of food. The *Bovril* aroma is particularly strong and thick, I don't like it but my stomach rumbles despite myself.

Where am I?

Have I nodded off on a flight on my way to Spain for a two week all inclusive? It would be wonderful if I was but something tells me that isn't the case. The fact that I feel like utter shit is a telling sign that something bad has happened. My head is throbbing and my arm, I can't move it. I finally muster up the energy to open my eyes and look around my surroundings. Instantly, I want to close my eyes again and teleport myself back to my make-believe holiday in Spain.

The first thing I see is a rather shabby looking and very small Christmas tree by the side of a big white door with windows. There are tiny presents underneath it but something tells me they aren't real presents, they're too perfect, too square. These seemingly empty boxes with huge big red bows are all just for show. I stare at the oversized, shiny red and silver baubles hanging sparsely on the tiny tree and try to remember what happened to get me to end up here.

As my eyes wander around the room, noting a stethoscope hanging on the wall, a sink and various monitors and cabinets, a sinking feeling churns in my gut as a huge sense of loss overwhelms me. Something's missing. I've lost something or someone. Sofia. Where is Sofia?

I'm in hospital, in my own room, is she here too?

A big scream erupts from me as a nurse rushes to be by my side.

'Ah, you're awake. It's okay, it's okay.' She holds my good hand and patiently guides me to breath properly. I gulp in huge breaths before exhaling shorter ones until the breaths become steady enough for me to speak again.

'Where's my daughter?'

'Your daughter? She's at home, she's fine,' the nurse says, smiling. 'How are you feeling?'

'Awful, I don't know what happened.'

'You've got concussion, hit your head falling down some concrete stairs by the beach, it was quite a fall.'

'Oh.'

'You've broken your arm, we've had to book you in for surgery as it's quite badly fractured, then you'll be on the mend.' She smiles again, her eyes squinting with kindness as she proceeds to perform observations on me. I close my eyes and try to remember why I was there, at the beach, but nothing comes. The nurse, checks my temperature then speaks again and I begin to panic.

'You were walking your dog, with a friend? She came to visit earlier, along with your husband and little girl.' I hear her say, as my breathing pulsates inside my head. Olive, where is Olive?

'Get some rest, I expect you'll have guests visiting again in a few hours.'

'Olive? My dog, is she okay?' I attempt to sit up but the nurse puts her hand on my shoulder and stops me. 'Lay down,' she says. And I do as I'm told. 'She's fine, now get some rest.'

I nod and watch her leave the room with her clipboard in hand. Filipe, what will he do? My mind begins to float to made up scenarios of Filipe burning the dinner, Filipe letting the washing and dishes pile up to the ceiling, then finally Filipe shouting at Sofia and Olive, taking all his frustrations out on them.

No. Stop.

I'm catastrophising.

I'm sure they will be fine, he coped when I was away that night at the hotel and he'll cope again, it might not be how I do it but he'll manage, I have to let go and let him be a father. Anyway, we have no choice, he has to cope. I'm stuck in here for however long. But it's Christmas, I can't be stuck in here at Christmas.

My mind begins to betray me again floating away to that night at the hotel and Mr Thomas's face and the way he looked at me, the way he kissed me. Over two decades ago was the last time he looked at me like that, where does the time go?

You really do blink and then the years have gone. If you're not careful you spend those years just wishing them away, wishing away the toddler tantrums, the sleepless nights that I'm still having, wishing away the puppy madness, wishing away the husband's long shifts, the crap TV programmes, the piles of washing up, wishing away the school runs until you've wished it all away and then it's replaced with more stuff to wish away until finally you wish you hadn't wished any of it away. You wished you'd embraced the boring and the hard and made it fun instead of making it a misery for everyone, including me.

This won't be forever, it's only temporary, everything is only just temporary. Back when Mr Thomas and I were together, I was so excited to be alive, I was just in it for the moment, not for the future, not the past. Even more so, I lived for every single second of being with him.

'Amberrrrrrrrr there's a young man on the phone for youuuuuu,' Mum sings up the stairs as I groan at her choice of words. Young man, she sounds like a character out of Harry Enfield and chums, why can't she just say boy? Soooooo embarrassing.

I frown and pad down the stairs, trying not to act too grumpy and clunky for fear of being called a Kevin. It doesn't last long; I grab the phone out of her hand whilst giving her the death stare and covering the receiver for fear of her saying something even more horrifyingly embarrassing. She knows she's embarrassed me but she probably doesn't know how. She quickly saunters off to the living room to dissect my behaviour with Dad as they so often do at the moment, I wait for the door to close until I take my hand off the receiver.

Parents are so incredibly annoying.

'Hey,' I say quietly, turning my back on the living room door.

'Hey, what are you up to?' His voice tickles my ears, making my whole body warm. I could listen to that voice all day.

'Not much, you?'

'Same, want to meet up and do something?'

'Yeah, can do.'

'Okay, I'll knock for you in fifteen minutes.'

'Could we make it an hour, I'm a bit busy at the moment.'

'You mean you're not dressed yet, lazy bones?' I can hear the smile in his voice and for some reason this embarrasses me even more. He's seen me get ready; he knows how long it takes.

'No, I am, I'm just busy cleaning out my hamster cage,' I say

in a squeaky voice.

'Yeah, okay, see you in a bit.'

'Bye.'

I put the phone down and race up the stairs, fifteen minutes is not long enough at all. My heart's racing at the pressure of getting ready and looking good but even more so at the thought of seeing him again. I just can't get enough. His multicoloured eyes entrance me, I could stare into them all day and quite often, that's what we do, at our spot on the promenade, sitting on the third bench along. The bench that the birds don't seem to shit on. I often joke that the birds save the bench for the true love birds.

I've finally decided on an outfit when the doorbell rings. My attempts to get to the door before Dad fail and by the time I've plastered on another coat of Heather Shimmer lipstick and trotted down the stairs, he's already sitting with Dad, having a conversation.

I want to die.

'Hi, ready then?' I say, poking my head round into the living room. If I don't go in then he'll get the hint that we need to abort and run now.

'Hey, Amber, just chatting to your dad about Oasis. I noticed he has all their albums. Good taste,' he says, as he points to all the CDs on the alphabetically arranged shelf. Little does Dylan know that Dad has only just stopped using tapes, they're so old school now.

'Oh yeah.' I look at Dad, who looks chuffed to be the cool dad for once, Mum looks up from her copy of Women's Weekly and smirks. 'Ready to go then?'

'Yeah sure, nice to meet you, umm, Amber's Dad.'

'Just call me John, son,' Dad says, as he pats him on the back looking chuffed to bits at my choice of boyfriend.

'Karen.' Mum smiles and nods over the top of her magazine.

'Bye Mum, bye Dad,' I say, ushering Dylan out of the front door.

177

'Your parents are really nice,' he says, as we reach the end of the street.

'Thanks.'

'Yeah, they'd get on with my parents. You should really meet my parents soon.'

'Should I?'

'Yeah, they'd love you, just as much as I love you.' He squeezes my hand and watches my face. His voice quivering ever so slightly on the last word. I grin, I could literally explode.

'I love you too.' I squeeze his hand back.

'Yeah, so do you fancy bowling?'

Little did I know, that it would be the penultimate time I saw him. Mr Thomas's face floats around in my mind on a giant bowling ball surrounded by psychedelic images of all the things we used to love and do back then. There's us snuggled up in our *Adidas* jackets on the promenade in the cold, me in my pedal pushers and him in his jeans which were quite baggy in style back then, not the skinny jeans you see the teenage boys wearing at the moment, although I hear nineties fashion is making a comeback. No, these were baggy jeans which hugged the bum just right.

Girl's jeans were low waisted hipsters, Mariah Carey style, the lower the better. I dread to think what a pair of those jeans would look like on me now, after pregnancy and over indulgence, it would be muffin top on top of muffin top.

An image of a muffin cake castle erupting out over my jeans penetrates my thoughts as the cakes change direction and head straight into my mouth. I chuck my head back, loving the cakes as I let them all fall in, devouring every single one of them at lightning speed. There are blueberry muffins, chocolate muffins, lemon muffins, followed by chocolate fudge cake and Victoria sponge coupled with lashings upon lashings of cream, custard and chocolate sauce to wash everything down into my salivating gob. The flavours swirl around in my mouth like a washing machine on full speed. I can't get enough. It's not enough. I want more MORE MORRRREEEEEEEE.

'Mooorrreeeeee yummy. More cake, give me all the cake.'

'Well, I haven't got cake but we do have flowers,' a male voice says.

'Huh.' That voice wasn't inside my head. With a groggy brain, I open my eyes to a giant bouquet of roses and lilies.

'Can I eat them? Edible flowers?' I hear myself say as my mouth waters. I'm so hungry. They're truly beautiful but the person peering through them is even more so.

What?

What the bloody hell is *he* doing here?

Meanwhile, I'm laid down shouting at the top of my lungs about cake, whilst drooling profusely. I bet I look quite the picture, a very unflattering, ravenous one.

'It's you. What are you doing here?' I say, blinking. I'm so confused.

Perhaps it's the doctor and he just looks like him, well now I feel stupid. I have Dylan bloody Thomas on the brain. But it's just uncanny. Dylan or Dylan's doppelganger smiles then places the flowers on the table as he reveals another visitor. She steps forward smiling, her long glossy blonde hair shimmering in the hospital's glaring lights. I inhale a big breath of air.

'Noooooo, get her out, get her out.' It all comes back to me in a flash, it's her, the hidey face girl. My Olive. She tried to take my dog. 'Get her out, nurse, nurse! Get her out!'

A nurse comes rushing to my side and whispers to Dylan and the girl to leave. I hear her say something about coming to visit some other time and that I need more rest before I can be coherent.

Then, as quickly as they appeared, they're gone.

Chapter 24

Delilah

'You okay, Dee?' Dylan asks, as he looks up from his phone.

He's been sitting on the sofa for the last thirty minutes since we got back from the hospital, just staring at his screen. I'm not even sure if he's reading or watching anything, his eyes transfixed, unmoving. He repositions himself, turning his body slightly away from me so I can't see his screen. I hope he's not researching FansOnly or even worse, he's on it.

His eyes break away from his screen to watch the TV for a few moments, we're watching one of those Hallmark Christmas films, super cheesy but we needed something light. Besides, Dylan's given up watching documentaries on murderers now, he says that you should be mindful of the types of things you choose to watch and expose yourself to as they affect you more than you know. I asked him if they were making him want to go out and do murders on people. He laughed; I didn't think my question was that silly.

'She screamed in my face and told me to get out.' I whip my head to the side to flick my hair out of my eyes as Loki wriggles in his sleep next to my leg.

'Ouch, that got me.' Dylan rubs his cheek and sets his phone down.

'I saved her dog. I mean, I hope she's okay but I don't get it.' I feel bad that she's in hospital and here I am worrying about me, but still, why did she scream?

Dylan puts his hand on my shoulder. 'She's probably just confused. I don't know, just give her time, we can go back and visit again, I'm sure.' He shrugs then picks his phone up again, to stare at whatever he was staring at before.

'What are you looking at?'

He lets out a huge sigh then reluctantly holds his phone up for me to see. It's a very old school photo of Dylan and his class mates in the late nineties.

'Oh my God.' I giggle at Dylan's awkward teenage stance and dodgy nineties haircut. 'Nineteen-ninety-eight,' I say, reading the text underneath the photo. 'I wasn't even born then. This is vintage. Your hair!'

'Be quiet, you. The hair cut was curtains and I had the best pair in school,' he says, slicking back his hair.

'Dad went bald around thirty you know.'

'I guess I'm lucky then. Recognise anyone else?'

I squint my eyes and focus on the photo, scouring each line of spotty teenage faces for a glimmer of familiarity.

'Oh wow, is that her? Is that Amber?' I point to a red-haired girl, with bright eyes and a sweet, shy smile. Other than her hair being a brighter shade of red, she hasn't changed much at all.

'Yeah, stunning even then, wasn't she?'

'Yeah, she really was.'

'So that's how you know her, I did wonder. Did you simp over her at school too?' I tease.

'Yeah, well a bit more than that,' he says, with a far-off look and I wait for him to explain. He doesn't.

'Were you guys together?'

'I guess you can say that.'

Why does this feel like I'm pulling teeth? 'What happened?'

'Life, life happened, sometimes things don't always go to plan do they?'

I decide not to dig any further and let my brother brood in his own little world. It's been a long couple of days.

'They don't,' I agree, then turn the TV up. Unexpectedly feeling sad about Josh again. Sad that I hadn't thought about him all day until now. Sad that this, us, could really be over. Sad that he's cross with me but I don't want to fight for him. Sad that I don't look at photos of him like my brother is looking at photos of Amber.

Amber

The police came to take my statement yesterday but all I could remember was the girl who hides her face. Her long blonde hair and petite frame etched in my mind like a delicate wood carving. The thing I remember about her most is that she doesn't walk, she glides or rather drifts. I explained about her walking/gliding past my house on the lead up to the attempted dognapping and then seeing her on the day it happened. The police looked at me as though I was a mad woman before informing me that it was that very girl who actually rescued Olive.

She apparently warned off the dog nappers by spraying them both with a face full of fake tan. One of the police officers made a joke that instead of catching them red handed they will be catching them orange faced. I forced out a laugh at a very bad joke then despite myself belly laughed as I imagined two very angry *oompa loompas* running off dog free. I hope they didn't attempt to kidnap any more dogs. Honestly, a few years ago dognapping was pretty much unheard of, especially in Coolsbay, now it appears to be as common as supermarket theft.

The surgeon comes in to check my arm with promises of surgery later this evening, apparently it's not as bad as he first thought, hence the delay, but still needs surgery. We're talking pins and plates.

Great.

I reach for my phone to call Mum and Dad to see how Sofia is, they're looking after her whilst Filipe is at work. I can't quite get to it from the bed as it's plugged-in charging on the table, although it's probably still dead, it takes ages to charge nowadays. I'm lucky the nurse could lend me her charger. I had to call Mum and Dad earlier from the hospital payphone, thank God I know their house number off by heart. My head and arm begin to thump and throb with the effort of moving so I give in and lie back down, I'll call them later. I can't wait to see Sofia and Olive again. I can't wait to be out of here. The fact I'm not home and getting everything ready for Christmas Day is killing me. It's Christmas Eve tomorrow!

I just want Sofia to have a happy Christmas but I'm going to be out of action in all areas. God knows what we'll have for dinner, probably a frozen spag bol ready meal. No, I have one arm out of action, it can't stop me from cooking, can it? Luckily, I'd already wrapped all the presents I had bought and I'll order some more off *Amazon* later so I can do this from my hospital bed.

Thank goodness for online shopping and next day delivery.

I doubt Filipe has bought a thing. He doesn't think I know but I'm well aware that he leaves mine down to his PA, Stephanie, to sort. To be fair, she usually does a fabulous job although it would mean more if he chose it himself, of course, but he's much too busy with work to find time to buy presents.

I put my phone down and let my eyes drift around the ward. The guy opposite me hasn't opened his eyes since I got here and the lady next to me seems to be in excruciating pain. I daren't try and talk to her for fear of making it worse, there's also a nurse or doctor attending to her frequently.

Having a broken arm isn't the end of the world, it will mend. The main thing is everyone is alright and Olive is still my dog, even if she is a naughty little shit hound who runs off at the slightest sniff of something tasty, she's still mine and no one has taken her.

I'm lucky, I'm grateful, I'm alive.

'Alright my lovely, oi oi she's awake.' Stella comes marching in and drags over a chair before plonking herself down onto it, just inches away from my face.

'Stella. It's so nice to see you,' I say, reaching out with my good hand, she looks at it, smiles then pats me on the arm, not knowing what to do with my affection.

'How are you feeling?'

I shrug and make a face.

'Here you go, a little something from Badger.' Stella hands me a drawing of a couple of stickmen, one of them has a knife and is stabbing the other one, there's a lot of blood, in fact it fills most of the page. I study it further, noticing a dog in the bottom left corner with a speech bubble saying 'woof kill him woof.'

'Is this Badger's sketch of the crime scene?'

'It sure is,' Stella beams.

'I love it.' I giggle then my eyes tear up because it's made me miss Sofia.

'Thanks, I'll tell him, he'll love that. So, how are you feeling?'

'Alright, can't wait to get out of here though. Fingers crossed, I'm booked in for surgery tonight and then after they've checked me over, I should be good to go home.'

'Just in time for Christmas.'

'Yeah, just in time but I'll be useless with this,' I say pointing to my wrapped-up arm.

'Don't worry about it, just concentrate on getting better, let Filipe look after you.'

'I know, but it's my favourite time of year, I like to make it all special for everyone, Christmas wreath, homemade jam and shortbread, I'd even started a Christmas cake this year. It only needs icing.' I roll my eyes. All that effort wasted.

'People can do without all that shit. You need to concentrate on you for once.'

'I know. But I miss them all so much. When you guys came to visit, I was so out of it. I hardly remember a thing.'

'There wasn't much to remember really, Filipe didn't say much and I just tried to make Sofia laugh and talk to her about Badger boy and Christmas. Oh, and we organised the dog as I've been looking after her of course, since Filipe's at work all day.'

'Oh yes, thanks for doing that. How is Olive?'

'No worries, I wasn't sure if you got my text about Olive though as you didn't reply?

'Oh no I didn't, the battery was flat but one of the nurses is lending me her charger,' I say, pointing at my phone charging and grimacing. 'And I haven't checked it since then. What did it say?'

'Just that I couldn't have her stay at mine as there's not really space but I'd come and do walks and feed her in the day. And that I moved your *Ring* doorbell indoors so you can keep an eye on Olive from your hospital bed. Call me a genius or call me a genius.'

'You're a genius, yes I think I still have the app as well. Thank you, that will put my mind at rest. She's so used to having me there all day, I bet she misses me more than Sofia does.'

'I bet she does, bless her big, dopey heart.'

'I did tell Filipe what I did with the *Ring* door bell and check that it was alright,' Stella says, pointedly.

I can't help but laugh. The sudden chuckle that escapes me makes my head hurt then I try to touch my head with my broken arm. Big fail.

I let out a groan. 'He hasn't a clue what's it's for, it's always me that uses it if I'm out shopping or on the very rare occasion that I might be out for the day.'

'Ah that will explain his confused expression,' says Stella, doing an impression of a confused looking Filipe saying, *Si mi amiga,* before chuckling along with me.

'Urgh, my head hurts so much.'

'You're just having too much fun in here,' Stella mocks, and I snort despite my pain. 'I couldn't help but get in a few digs about not being invited to your birthday meal. Sorry, I couldn't help myself, he said he'd text me, he definitely didn't.' Stella shakes her head.

'God knows what happened there, he admitted looking on my phone and saw Jayne at the top of my WhatsApp pestering me for something so he just assumed we were best mates.'

'Hilarious. You and Jayne, besties.'

'I know, right. What the hell happened to me?' I blurt out. 'I mean an attempted dog napping, in Coolsbay?'

'I know mate, I can't believe it,' Stella draws her eyebrows together then clears her throat. 'If Pudding hadn't run off I could have helped, I feel so bad for leaving you, I'm so sor… '

'No, no, no, don't you dare, you've been nothing but a good friend to me, it couldn't be helped. Pudding was your priority as Olive was mine. Plus, it could have been your dog too. None of us were safe in that moment.'

'Yeah, I know you're right, I'm just glad you're okay.'

I fill Stella in on the rest of the drama, including the girl hiding her face, walking past my house for weeks right up until the hidey face girl and Mr Thomas turning up at my hospital bedside to see me dribble and drool over imaginary cake and edible flowers and the fact I inadvertently went to his works Christmas party. I decide not to tell Stella about the attempted kiss at the Christmas party. I'd feel disloyal not only to my husband and family but also to him, what if the news got out? It could tarnish his reputation and mine. We laugh hysterically at the drooling incident much to the annoyance of the nurses who hush us for causing too much noise on the ward.

Stella finally catches her breath.

'That's very brave of her and how resourceful using the tanning spray as a weapon. The only thing I have floating around in my pockets is dog poo bags, too small to smother a potential dog napper with,' Stella says.

'Yeah, but if you had a full one you could have knocked them out with the smell of one of Pudding's poos.'

'True, they do stink,' Stella says, pulling a face.

'I'll be forever in that strange girl's debt, but first I

have to apologise for screaming in her face. The whole thing is very embarrassing and odd, and what on earth was she doing with Mr Thomas?'

'Maybe his girlfriend?' Stella offers, with a little shrug like it's completely obvious. Of course, he has a girlfriend or maybe even a wife.

'Maybe, but she looked so young but I guess a man like him is bound to have a younger, gorgeous, glamorous girlfriend. It's obvious really.' She's probably a teacher too and works at the school.

But he kissed me.

'Is it? A man like him?' Stella says slowly, raising an eyebrow. Oh no.

'I know him, Stella,' I admit. 'We were together at school, first love. Dylan and I or at least I, was madly in love. But one day, he just disappeared, the day after we went bowling and I never saw him ever again, until he turned up as Sofia's teacher.'

'Oh shit, you and Mr Dylan Thomas, is he Welsh?' She grins.

'No, but he did used to write me a good love poem.'

'His parents were obviously having a laugh when they named him.' She chuckles.

Dylan's smiling face appears in my mind. Go away. It was bloody decades ago. I should be so ashamed. I deserved this to happen to me, I deserve my stupid broken arm and big bash on the head, perhaps it's the universes way of trying to knock some sense into me. Stop living in the past and concentrate on what's right in front of you.

'I better get off,' Stella says, sensing my sudden misery. 'Filipe and Sofia will be here soon, so I'll let you have your time with them.'

'Yes, okay then, well thanks, for everything, I mean

it,' I reply, swallowing the large lump that's forming in my throat.

'No problem at all, get some rest and I'll see you soon, no doubt with another one of Badger's creations in tow. He's probably drawing you on your death bed as we speak,' she says, teasing me.

'I can't wait,' I say, managing a smile.

Stella gives me a little wave then trundles off down the hall way, leaving me wondering if it was Badger that drew the phallic shaped art that hangs outside Mr Thomas's classroom. There we go again, thinking about him.

Just stop.

'Speak of the devil.' I hear Stella say loudly, as I imagine her patting Filipe on the back.

His contorted face appears by my bedside moments later with our beautiful little girl beside him. She's dressed in a most questionable outfit, I'm sure those clothes are at least a size too small and have a multitude of stains on them, but she still looks completely adorable and I don't comment on it. My beautiful Sofia.

'Oh guys, hi,' I say in a squeaky voice, trying to be extra cheerful for Sofia.

'Mummy. Mummy are you okay?' Sofia says, with her eyebrows raised. Her wide eyes barely blink as she stares at my arm in wonder then concern.

'Yes sweetie, I'm okay, I'll be just fine. I just have to get my arm fixed.'

'I want you to come back home now, Daddy doesn't know how to plait my hair like Elsa so that I can have *Moana* hair when you take it out. He does it all wrong,' Sofia says, shifting her gaze down to her feet.

They both look a little stressed.

'Oh dear, poor Daddy, maybe you can teach him

Sofia, you can do plaits, can't you?'

Sofia nods then scrunches her little nose up. I want to bop it and make her giggle but the grogginess is stopping me from moving.

'Yeah, but not as good as you. He can't make my sandwiches right too. He cuts the cheese too big and then puts his big handprint on them, like this.' Sofia holds her hand up then slams it down on the edge of my bed to simulate Filipe's clumsy sandwich making skills.

Filipe stands there, staring off into the distance, looking as though he wishes he were somewhere else. Tears start to silently fall from Sofia's eyes which quickly turn to huge, uncontrollable sobs. I reach for my baby and pull her in for a one-armed hug as Filipe rubs her back and tries to reassure her. Poor guy, they just have to find their way. They aren't used to being alone together.

'It's okay sweetie, I'll be home soon and then we can all be together and have the best Christmas ever,' I say, kissing her forehead. 'Hey, guess what?' I whisper in her ear.

'What?' Sofia stands up.

'It's only two sleeps until Santa comes.'

'Yay! Santa!' Sofia jumps up and down.

'You okay, Filipe?'

He sighs and looks at me with something resembling pity.

'You're very quiet,' I continue. 'How's Olive?'

'She's good, still trying to steal our dinner.'

'Oh, I thought that had stopped.'

'It's because you're not there, she doesn't listen to me.'

'Naughty girl, sorry, I'll be home soon.'

'Don't say sorry. I just can't believe that I almost lost

you. My *churri*, my English rose.' English rose, he hasn't called me that in years.

'You didn't almost lose me. I've only broken my arm. I'm fine,' I snap. It must be the drugs making me cranky.

'I miss you so much, we miss you. I'm so sorry, so sorry.'

'Filipe, don't be silly, come here. It's only been a few days.' I pull him close to me then whisper. 'Come here you silly man, not in front of Sofia, please.'

'Please, please, forgive me, forgive me.'

'Okay, I forgive you for being such a drama queen now stop, you're upsetting our daughter. It's okay Sof, Daddy's just very tired, it's hard keeping everything juggling, isn't it?' I say, inadvertently making a point. 'Group hug?' I pull my family in as best I can with one arm for a warm hug.

Filipe's body stiffens, how do I feel sorrier for Filipe than I do for myself? He's been on a real learning curve recently; I think he may be starting to realise that being a stay-at-home parent isn't as easy as it appears to be. Sofia starts fiddling with my TV, so I put the headphones on her and find her a program to watch. Filipe shuffles on his feet from side to side and I watch him for a few seconds before turning up the volume on the TV for Sofia.

'Filipe, why haven't you taken any time off work?'

'Huh?'

'Time off, surely work would understand? It's an emergency,' I say, in a hushed tone.

'I have a big project on, I can't,' he says, sounding snappish.

'Work always wins, hey.'

'No, but we need it to pay the bills as *you* don't work.' He curls his lip, showing his teeth slightly. I'm not sure I can deal with his rollercoaster of emotions today.

'Don't make this about me not working and not pulling my weight, you made it so that I *couldn't* work.' And that's it, as soon as my arm is healed, I'm getting a job. I'm not doing this anymore. I don't want to be dependent on him, even if he is my husband.

'Not true, but I guess we'll just have to agree to disagree.' He whips Sofia's headphones off her head so fast that it nips her ear causing her to whine loudly. 'Come on Sofia, Mummy needs to rest now.'

We get several disapproving looks from fellow patients and visitors as he picks her up and throws her over his shoulder marching off with her kicking and screaming down the corridor.

I attempt to get up but by the time I've managed it, it's too late, they've already left the room. I didn't even get to kiss her goodbye.

Helpless, I lay back down and close my eyes, hiding away from everyone. Nineties nostalgia eventually infiltrates my dreams again and I happily immerse myself in the past when life was simpler and resentment was just a word and not a feeling that I've recently come to know all too well.

I wake up to the nurse asking if she can do my observations, it only feels like minutes later. The argument with Filipe is still fresh in my mind as I brood over his resentment for me not working when I thought that's what he wanted. What we wanted. What have we become?

Olive's face pops into my mind and I feel a little lift in spirits when I remember that I can now check on my precious pooch. She's the only one who doesn't judge me and only wants the simple things in life, like cuddles, treats and walks. I think we could all take a leaf out of a dog's book every once in a while, they don't sweat the small stuff, or even most of the big stuff like humans do. I reach for my phone and wince in pain as the other arm involuntarily moves. I must order some presents from *Amazon* too.

The app eventually opens and I spend several minutes watching it update before scrolling through the hundreds of videos of the postman that the camera has stored, Filipe coming home from work and people's feet walking past on the street. I finally get to the day Stella moves the *Ring* doorbell and laugh as I watch her narrate to the camera what she's doing before positioning the camera on a shelf in the living room facing Olive's bed, next to the sofa.

She pets Olive, making a huge fuss of her before finding and dishing out her food, all the while giving a running commentary. The whole thing makes me giggle. She would do great on TV. I can imagine her on one of those DIY programmes or something, not actually doing the DIY but talking everyone through what is happening in a jolly, piss taking kind of way. I watch a few more monotonous videos of Olive sleeping before scrolling through to the ones that show something going on.

There's Filipe and Sofia, having dinner, Sofia and Filipe playing Barbies, Filipe throwing Sofia high up into the air and her screaming with glee *more daddy more*. Filipe reading Sofia a story; they both have big smiles on their faces. So, it wasn't all doom and gloom then, they've had fun too and have bonded really nicely by the looks of it. I smile, it will all be okay. We just need time to get back to how we were and Christmas is the perfect time to do it. I continue to scroll through the rest of the videos, watching the occasional one through to the end to see if Olive has been coping on her own alright. There's a video of her sulking in her bed, and then she jumps up and begins to howl, something that she hardly ever does. My heart sinks. *What's wrong my sweet dog?*

The video stops, I quickly click to the next one where the screen is completely brown. The camera starts to focus on the brown thing as it slowly moves away from the camera to reveal that the brown fuzz is actually someone's hair, someone's brown, shiny hair.

Meanwhile, Olive has reverted back to whimpering after a dressing down from Filipe.

I'm sure I know that hair.

It looks so familiar.

The woman talks in a sing songy voice as the back of her head bobs around on her shoulders and her hands gesticulate around her. I turn up the volume, straining to hear their mumblings on the poor video quality as Filipe's smiling face comes into focus, facing the camera. Olive is still whimpering away as Filipe leans forward to murmur something again to this woman.

Seeing them together, makes my heart fall into my stomach and my head ache.

That hair, I've seen it before, it's glossier than usual, bigger but I'm sure I know it.

They're talking, a little louder now, about what kind of a day they've had I think, so matter of fact, so normal. Except that it isn't normal at all. That woman should not be in my house. Next, I'm hearing him say those words, the words he uses for me. He's calling her my *churri* and tells her that she is his favourite English rose. His favourite, because he has another English rose already. Me.

She laughs, but it's not a laugh I've ever heard her use, it's softer, more feminine, she sounds as though she's trying to be cute. They confirm my worst nightmare and begin to kiss. Hungry for each other it seems before Filipe pulls this woman onto the sofa and I have full view of her arse writhing around on top of him. She's wearing those leggings. The ones off TikTok. The ones that make your bum look great and it does look great because of course, it looks like hers.

Like Jayne's.

They begin to frantically undress each other as a little bit of bile fills my mouth.

Despite all this, I watch the whole thing like a slow, painful car crash whilst silently ugly crying into my bad arm. I give myself a few minutes, mop my face up with some tissues then click onto my *Amazon* app to order the rest of the Christmas presents.

Chapter 25

Delilah

'Merry Christmas Eevvvveeee, how's the Coolsbay hero?' Sky sings, grinning from ear to ear and standing on tip toes as I answer the door to her, a pissed off looking Luna, and Molly.

I haven't seen Molly in a while, perhaps I've been subconsciously avoiding her while feeling guilty about speaking to Byron. My body feels heavy, feeling disappointment for Molly and her constant bad luck with men. Then my stomach clenches as a deeper feeling encroaches causing a pang of guilt.

If only he wasn't so gorgeous and seemingly lovely.

'Oh, stop it! I just gave them a bit of a scare, not a hero at all,' I say, stepping back to let them in before we all bundle onto the sofa. My stomach rumbles, the smells from Mum's buffet reminding me that I must eat and not live off my nerves. Sky and Luna are wearing matching Mrs Santa outfits. Sky's in full makeup as always, wearing a dress almost as short as her dog's. Luna, again, doesn't look overly impressed at her outfit choice, proceeding to snort and chase herself around in circles desperate to bite her skirt off. Sky notices and tries to distract her by popping a couple of fancy looking doggy treats into her mouth. Luna barks a high-pitched bark and Sky feeds her a few more, until they're all gone. I don't count them but simply notice the smell instead and they reek. This pampered pooch is living her best life and has got Sky well and truly wrapped round her little paw.

'Hey Mols,' I say, turning my attention to Molly as Sky continues to fuss over Luna. Molly looks great, rested, radiant even. I hope I don't ruin her glow.

'Hey stranger,' she says, embracing me in a big warm hug. 'How are you? How's the new pup? Where is he? What the fuck happened with the dognapping? What's happened with you and Josh?'

I giggle at Molly's tirade of questions as she stares at me wide-eyed, throwing her arms out and pulling me into another huge hug as I try to decide which question to answer first. She finally lets go of me, waiting for my response as I open my mouth then close it several times, just willing for something, anything to come out.

But I can't speak.

I'm a speechless, gormless little goldfish.

'I I I.' I try to spit it all out, every little thing but my voice becomes choked with tears before I can count in my head to calm down and stop myself from breaking down in front of my friends.

'Oh Dee, what's wrong? Just breathe. It's all okay, everything is going to be okay. Just breathe.'

This may be the last time we speak again. Ever.

'Mols, Josh and I have broken up because I was just well… really I'm over it, it's just like we became friends,' I say, feeling like the world's worst person. 'It's just all gone a bit wrong; we were too young. I feel so terrible. I miss him a lot but just as a friend.'

'What she means is, she got the big fat yucky ick,' Sky says, as Molly nods in agreement.

Poor Josh.

'Yup, definitely the ick, I'd say. What put you off him though? You guys have been together since like forever.' Molly raises her eyebrows then leans in towards me, holding her chin.

Sky raises smirks and raises an eyebrow.

'Nothing, I don't know. Perhaps we outgrew each other.' Or perhaps it took me to meet someone I actually fancy, meaning the insanely hot Byron, to realise my true feelings. 'I feel so guilty for not wanting to be with him. Also, I sort of met someone else and we haven't done anything about it because someone else I know likes him but I guess it just made me realise my feelings for Josh more than anything.'

Sky grimaces in my peripheral vision as the words ramble out of me.

'I don't know what to do,' I wail. I'm most certainly not a hero, I was just in the right place at the right time to help Amber. Did I tell you I went to visit her in hospital and she just screamed in my face? I'm infuriating to someone I don't even know. I infuriate myself. It's just all a big mess, I'm so lost.'

'You're fucking brave. I wouldn't have thought to do what you did; you completely took charge of the situation and got those fuckers. I'll say it again, you're a Coolsbay hero.' Sky stands with her hands on her hips as I sniff into my sleeve, repeatedly shaking my head in disagreement.

'I'm no hero, a hero wouldn't betray her boyfriend and friends like I've done,' I admit, turning to Molly, whose eyebrows are now knitted together. She really has no idea.

I take a deep breath and count to six. It's now or never.

'Mols, it's Byron. We met the night you were admitted to hospital for alcohol poisoning. He helped me look after you and I guess, we like, just clicked. He's been texting me, nothing's happened but I like him. I'm sorry. I'll tell him not to text me again, your friendship is worth way more than a boy.'

The longest pregnant pause happens next, even Luna is holding her usually loud, snorty breath.

'Byron?' Molly considers, as if she is asking herself a question. 'Oh, Byron,' she smiles then surprisingly rolls her eyes.

'Yes, Byron,' I squeak, as Luna let's out an almighty snort. Shitsticks. Even the dog's disgusted in me.

'He's old news.' She waves her hand dismissively and a massive breath of air escapes me.

'What?'

'Yeah, I've been hooking up with Brandon for quite a while now. I thought I told you guys. I definitely told you, Sky.'

'Who the fuck is Brandon? I thought that you were still emailing Byron,' Sky says, using the inverted comma sign with her fingers for the word emailing.

'Sky, you don't listen. Byron didn't respond to that email and then I met Brandon online, we've been smitten ever since, which is probably why you haven't heard much from me. Sorry girls. And, Brandon just loves an email. When we're at work we pretty much send each other long emails all day every day. I'm in love-communication heaven,' she says, with a happy sigh.

'Wow,' Sky mouths, her eyes wide before bending down to kiss Luna who is now perched on her lap.

'So, you're welcome to Byron, really, he's a nice guy but not a great communicator and not a patch on my Brandy baby.'

'There you go, you can crack on with Byron now.' Sky laughs.

'Thanks, but I'm not sure I want to crack on with anyone right now,' I say, taking a tissue from Molly, before I catch Sky smiling. Does she know me better than I know myself? Do I want him?

The front door slams, making us jump as I quickly try to sort out my face and in hushed tones ask the girls if I look like I've been crying. Mum, Dad, Dylan and my middle brother, Ian who's come to visit for the evening, all shuffle into the living room, bringing the cold and a very excited Loki with them. Loki, clearly not that worn out from his walk, makes a beeline for Luna. We all watch on in horror as Loki launches himself onto Sky's knees, his little lipstick out and ready for action, he begins to mount Luna or at least tries to but all he can get is skirt.

'NO, NO, SHE'S NOT BEEN DONE YET, SHE'S NOT BEEN DONE,' Sky shouts, standing up, both dogs fall onto the sofa and lay on their sides. Luna seemingly complicit in this passionate love affair, lets Loki rip off her skirt with his teeth.

Smooth.

Loki is locked onto the back of Luna and he isn't going anywhere. This dog is on a mission.

A mission to mate.

'OH GOD, DO SOMETHING QUICK, SHE CAN'T GET PREGNANT WITH *HIM*, SHE'S MY BABY.'

I try not to feel offended at the way Sky refers to my dog as we all look away.

'Don't worry, it's almost impossible unless she's in season, I think. Is she in season?' Dylan asks, as Sky frets over a potential future with puppies that aren't pure bred.

The dogs continue to fornicate.

No shame.

Mum offers everyone a drink and disappears off to the kitchen, with Dad following shortly after her. Moments later we hear laughter. Dylan looks at me with a smirk on his face and I try not to burst into fits.

My brother, Ian, tries to act the big man and separate the dogs before Dylan stops him, warning him it could result in serious injury.

There's nothing we can do but wait.

Everyone looks away for five whole minutes until the whole thing is over.

Mum and Dad come back into the living room, both blowing air out of their cheeks, relieved that the dirty deed is over. Mum offers us a drink again as she and Dad lay the Christmas Eve buffet out.

'Hey, I really recognise you from somewhere,' Ian, pipes up, and points a finger at Sky as he offers her a slice of Mum's homemade quiche.

'Yeah, I'm one of Dee's best mates, of course you recognise me,' Sky says, a little louder than normal as her cheeks turn slightly pink.

Oh no.

'No, it's not that.' Ian shakes his head, determined to get to the bottom of it. 'I'm way older than you girls, God when I last saw you, you were probably only about five years old, running around naked in the back garden. It's not often I come back to Coolsbay but I thought I'd surprise Mum and Dad and the siblings for the evening, since the old boy is back home.' Ian punches Dylan on the arm, a bit harder than he should have before Dylan gives him the daggers. 'I swear I know you little lady, or are you on TV?' Ian continues, as Dylan can't resist flicking Ian behind the ear. 'Ouch, yeah, that must be it,' he says, unfazed by the ear flick. 'TV, what do you do?'

'I'm a makeup artist,' Sky says, even louder. 'To some very important people, some are *celebrities*.'

'Ahh right, no not that then, makeup artists don't go on TV, do they? More behind the scenes if anything.'

Sky gives him a slow grin.

Oh my God. No. It can't be that.

Stop. Please stop.

If I've worked out how he knows her then he must clock on soon, surely? I don't know what's more cringe, knowing that my brother has a *FansOnly* account or seeing Sky simping at seeing one of her fans in real life. I just want the ground to open up and swallow my obnoxious brother. The thing is, he's probably oblivious as to where he remembers her from, he's really not playing dumb this time.

'Buffet anyone?' Mum chirps, sensing a bit of awkwardness, as Dylan gives me a knowing nod, even he's clocked that something's not quite right.

'Buffet sounds great,' Dylan answers. 'I'm starving.'

'Come this way then kids,' Mum sings, still calling my middle-aged brothers kids. It makes me smile. I do love it when we're all together, even if it is hugely cringy at this very moment.

We all pad, some a bit more reluctantly than others, over to the table where the perfect Christmas Eve spread has been laid out. I take a paper plate and begin to pile my plate high with cheese and pineapple sticks, sausage rolls and anything else that resembles the colour of cardboard. Sky drops a sausage roll on the floor and Ian bends down to pick it up, getting an eyeful of her barely there skirt on the way back up. They lock eyes as he places the sausage roll on the table then I watch his arm drop to his side before his hand forms a fist, he quickly turns away, mouthing the word 'fuck' to himself.

Looks like the penny has finally dropped.

Ian's cheeks and neck flush, turning the same colour as Sky's skirt and I'm so thankful I didn't decide to go down that road. Even if the money is stupidly tempting, I'd rather die than have my older brother accidently stumble across my *FansOnly* profile. Rather Sky than me.

Puke.

Amber

I'm finally coming home, gammy arm, broken heart and all. I close my eyes, wincing at the pain in my arm as Filipe drives too fast over the speed bumps, eager to get me home before Sofia falls asleep in the car and has the inevitable danger nap. He's been unusually chatty on the drive back home, like he's excited. Or perhaps he's nervous.

Yes, that's it.

Guilt.

Nervous guilt.

Why didn't I see it before?

I watch my husband's face, looking comfortably smug and happy as he continues to drivel on about what he's been watching on TV and the even more boring breakdown of what he's got on at work. As he drones on and on, I wonder where it all began. That time he picked Sofia up from the school when I was unwell or maybe that time he invited her for my birthday dinner thinking we were friends or was it neither of those times and she tracked him down online somehow.

'Shall we sing another Christmas song, Sofia?' I interrupt Filipe's droning.

Sofia grins then quickly nods her head. She starts

singing Rhubarb the Red-nosed Reindeer. This always makes me giggle but this time I can't muster up the energy to laugh, instead I smile as wide as I can. It hurts my face to force it into something it doesn't naturally want to do right now but it's worth it just for her. Her sweet little singing voice breaks my heart, she's so excited to have us all back together, so excited to have me home.

However, it started, I'm having a hard time getting my head around it. I'm still processing it, all on my own.

We pull up onto the driveway and a thick sadness engulfs me. He hasn't put the outdoor lights up.

'Where are the Christmas lights?' I ask a still overly cheery Filipe.

'Oh, I don't know, I've been too busy to worry about them. I think they're probably dead now anyway, my *churri*.' He stops the car and pulls up the handbrake.

'Probably.' Every year, we put out the light up Santa and reindeer and decorate the house with white sparkly lights. It always looks so tasteful, so beautiful and magical, but not this year. This year we have no lights, because there is no sparkle, it's gone, for good.

We bumble into the house in the pitch black. I'm both glad and sad to be home, will this be my home for much longer? It will be until I say the words out loud. For now, I can pretend, just for a couple of days, I can pretend and savour that we are that happy little family that we once were. I walk into the living room and gasp at the state of it.

It's an absolute mess.

Before I have a chance to speak. Olive comes bounding out of the kitchen and flings herself at me, I nuzzle my nose into her fur as she licks the side of my face in excitement.

'Oh no, did you do this?' I say to Olive, who is still

frantically wagging her tail in happiness.

I scan the room, she could have done it but she's never been a fan of wrapping paper, always backs away from it so the thought that she would cause all of this mess just doesn't make sense.

'Do you think we've been burgled?' I shriek at Filipe, as I check Olive for signs of injury. I hope they didn't hurt her. 'I'm calling the police.' I shake as I attempt to reach into my handbag and fumble around for my phone with my good hand. This just bloody tops it. They say things come in threes, attempted dog napping, husband's affair and now this, a Christmas bloody burglary.

Please can this be it. I don't know how much more I can take.

'No, no we haven't, we haven't been burgled.'

'What's all this then? We have, there's been a burglar here, see.' I point to the mess all over my living room floor. There's wrapping paper and ripped boxes everywhere. When I look closer I can see the toys in amongst the mess. Realisation sets in and my hand flies up to my mouth to catch my gasp.

'You've opened the presents? Sofia's had her presents?' I move my hand up to my throbbing forehead, the stress of it now, becoming all too much.

'Santa came early didn't he, Sofia? Because he knew you were feeling blue and missing your mama.'

As if the shock and upset of seeing Jayne frolicking with my husband on my sofa wasn't enough, I get home to find that most of the Christmas presents have already been opened without me.

He's given her the ones I'd ordered off Amazon and told her we could give her the rest on Christmas day, it's not all of them thank God, but a good amount.

'Mummy, Mummy look what Santa got me.'

I smile through my tears, trying to act happy as Sofia shows me all her gifts. There's no Christmas tree in sight, nor a card or a candle. In fact, you wouldn't even know it was Christmas if it wasn't for the shredded wrapping paper all over the floor. Felipe has always insisted that I don't put the tree up until Christmas Eve, but he hasn't bothered in my absence.

My eyes fall on the sofa, also covered in wrapping paper.

They did it on my sofa.

'Mummy, this is shit, isn't it?' Sofia says, watching my face. 'Santa was supposed to come down the chimney on Christmas Day, not yesterday. Daddy said he even came through the front door?' She holds her hands up in despair.

'Sofia! You cannot say that word, it is a bad word, an adult word,' Filipe admonishes, but I say nothing, because she's right. It is shit. He's spoilt the magic, just like Jayne did, telling her child to tell all the other children that Santa isn't real.

I bet this was even her idea.

My blood boils.

They're a match made in heaven.

'Never mind, that's so kind of Santa to do this for you, isn't it? He must think you're a such a good, special girl. Shall we go and put out some goodies for Santa and his reindeers? It's getting late and they'll be getting hungry for their mince pies and carrots,' I say, sounding overly cheerful. But something in my expression gives me away and Filipe catches me looking at him, in disgust.

'Yay!' Sofia cheers and runs off to the kitchen.

I begin to follow her but Filipe grabs my good arm, almost twisting it as he tries to get me to face him.

'Not now. Just, not now.' I rip my arm away and

wince as the sudden movement makes my other arm ache.

'I wanted to make her happy, you miserable woman.'

I snort at his insult then lean into him and move my mouth towards his ear.

'Well, you've ruined Christmas. You've ruined everything. Well done,' I hiss, as he stands there heavy breathing, looking at the floor.

'Mummmyyyyyy.'

I march off to the kitchen to help Sofia find the mince pies and to get Santa a very strong drink.

Chapter 26

Delilah

The buffet only lasts a couple of hours before everyone begins yawning and making their excuses to leave. Sky was the first to go with Ian following shortly after. The whole time they were here I couldn't stop thinking about Byron and the fact that Molls has given me her blessing. I kept checking my phone, just willing him to text me but he hasn't so here I go, there's nothing or no one to stop me now.

Me: *Hey, Happy Christmas. I hope Santa brings you everything you want and more.*

Did I really just send that? Oh shit. Yes. It looks like I did. I don't expect him to reply to that, it's probably about the lamest thing I've ever sent to anyone (ever) but within seconds I have a response.

Byron: *Hi! Happy Christmas to you too, hey, I've been thinking…*

Me: *What have you been thinking?*

Byron: *Mainly, if I'm honest, about you.*

I read his text over and over, imagining his sexy voice saying it to me. About me? He's been thinking about me, just like I've been thinking about him. I start scrolling on social media, going through all of his photos as I try to come up with a witty response to that message. I mean what can you respond to that? *What about me, maybe?* No. Or perhaps, *oh that's nice, me too.* Again, just no. So I don't reply, just yet.

No longer than half an hour later Mum shouts up the stairs.

'Deeeeeeee, there's someone here to see you.'

Oh. My. God.

Butterflies dance about in my belly but they're not just dancing they're having a fucking rave in there.

That can't be him, he doesn't even know where I live.

I rush over to my mirror and check my face before giving my hair a quick brush, it falls around my shoulders and cheeks, framing my face like a silk curtain. I study my appearance and decide that I look quite nice, despite the earlier crying episode, my eyes have returned to their normal size and colour and my skin looks fresh and clear.

One, two three, four, five, six.

Footsteps tread slowly on the stairs. He'll be here any second. I close my eyes, inhale through my nose then breathe slowly out of my mouth.

Knock, knock, knock. Three knocks.

My phone pings and I read another message from Byron. *Can I come and see you?*

'Can I come in?' But it's not Byron's voice as hoped for. It's Josh's. 'Dee? Can I come in?'

'Hey,' I say, answering the door, looking and sounding as disappointed as I feel. 'Yeah, sure, come in, I was just, um, nothing, I was doing nothing. Yeah.'

'Not doing your sex show then?' he says, as he sits on the edge of my bed, looking up at me with sad, puppy dog eyes. 'I thought I'd better knock just in case you were up to that again,' he says, sounding as depressed as Eeyore from *Winnie the Pooh*.

'Sex show? It wasn't a sex show, I was dancing, just having a laugh with Sky.'

'A laugh at my expense?'

'No, not at all,' I say, as I sit beside him and entwine my fingers together on my lap before taking a deep breath. I look at his face and I want to cry, he's so sweet. Why can't I be happy with him? 'I'm sorry, Josh. I'm sorry for doing that and for not speaking to you about it first, I realise how it looks now and I'm sorry for humiliating you as well as myself.'

'Thanks, but you didn't humiliate yourself as much as you did me. Sky told me you got offered dance jobs off the back of it so it wasn't all bad, was it? You got your lucky break. You got what you wanted.'

'I did get offered a couple of things, but I turned them down.'

'Why?'

'Because it just didn't feel right,' I say, turning as red as the hooded cape I was wearing, feeling an absolute whore.

'Oh right.'

'You've always been good to me; I don't deserve you.' I look down at my hands.

'No, you don't.'

'I'm sorry.'

'Yes, you've said that. I got all your missed calls and messages. I know I said it was over but I believe that you are sorry which is why I'm willing to give you another chance.'

'You are?' I say, feeling a sudden coldness in my bones. This was not the response I was expecting.

'Yeah.' He flashes me a small smile as he rests his hand on my thigh whilst I fight the urge to slap it away. He searches my eyes for appreciation. 'I think you're

worth another chance, it's not like you cheated, did you?'
I shake my head. 'Plus, your face was hidden so it's only
a few people that know it was you, you little tart.' He
laughs lightly but I can hear the pain scratching through
the laughter. I've treated him so badly and he knows it.
He's been at my beck and call for years, all because I
didn't want to do things on my own. I needed my hand
held and he was happy to do it, he'd be happy to do it
forever. He doesn't deserve this.

'Yeah, that's true, I didn't cheat but I don't think we
should get back together.'

'It's fine, I forgive you. I know you just got carried
away with Sky, she's a bad influence on you, she knows
you're easily led. I've already had a word with her about
it,' he says, inching closer towards me.

'And said what?'

'That she isn't to let you do that again, sometimes you
don't know your own mind.'

'What?'

'Come on, Dee, you've said it yourself, you don't
know your own mind sometimes. You're easily led
astray.'

'Maybe sometimes, but I know what I want now.'

'I'm glad.' He leans in to kiss me and I hold my hand
against his chest to stop him getting any further.

'I know my own mind now and I don't want this,' I
say, with a cracked voice.

'Yes, you do, it's fine, just come here.' He moves my
hand off his chest and pulls it down towards his crotch.

'NO. Get off. Get out. I don't want this,' I say,
motioning between me and him. 'I don't want us.'

'Yes, you do.' He laughs but I don't get what's funny.

'No. I don't want you. I'm sorry but I just don't want
you.'

I bite my lip and blink back tears as the realisation at what I've just said hits me and the fact that it can never be taken back. Ever. After someone's been backed into a corner and is forced to say that, that's it. You can't go back from that, can you? He moves his hands away from me and then there's silence as he processes the words that hang in the air like a bad smell.

He opens his mouth to say something then changes his mind, gets up and leaves. My words ring in my ears then stab me once more when he slams my bedroom door. Six years of us and I tell him that. It must have stung. I don't blame him for being angry, I would be too. Now he's gone but I know I've done the right thing. I trust my own instincts. Next, I pick up my phone, perfectly clear on what I need to do next. I know my own mind better than ever now.

Me: *Hey, I'm so sorry but no you can't. I just wanted to wish you happy Christmas. I think you're lovely but right now wouldn't be right to meet, I've not long split from my long-term boyfriend. xx*

I set my phone down then pick it up again as it beeps and vibrates in my hand.

Byron: *Oh, that's a real shame but happy Christmas to you too. I didn't know you had a boyfriend. Message me again in six months if you still want to, I'll be waiting to hear from you. x*

I look up to see when six months is in my calendar, six months will be summer, it seems so far away when Christmas is tomorrow. But now I'm free, as free as a bird in fact and if I remember rightly, Byron was rather enjoying being free too.

Me: *I don't know where I'll be in six months, take care. X*
Byron: *Neither do I, take care. X*

Amber

Sofia goes to bed at eight, but actually doesn't fall asleep until at least an hour later, not because she's messing about but because I'm there just milking my time with her. Little does she know I'm already overcompensating for her parents' failed marriage. I let her draw Christmas pictures on my arm cast before reading her six Christmas stories and then we sing Rhubarb the Red-nosed Reindeer and other Christmas songs until she tells me to leave as she wants to go to sleep because Christmas day will come quicker if she falls asleep now.

I reluctantly leave her room then go and hide in the toilet while Filipe is sitting at the dining room table on his laptop. He's usually barking demands on Christmas Eve, wanting the house to look perfect and telling me well done but he's obviously reeling from earlier, a tell-tale sign being that he doesn't even look up when I walk past him.

I close the downstairs toilet door and silently let the raw, sore emotion that's been gathering in my throat and lungs, escape. The tears fall thick and fast as I taste the saltiness of them and struggle to quietly catch my breath. At one point my body betrays me and lets out a noise of pure wretchedness. Hearing my own raw sadness, as if it's even possible, just makes me sadder. I clasp my hand over my mouth to stop the noise but I can only turn the volume down slightly, it won't be silenced anymore.

In recent years, I've been so stressed about getting everything perfect, so finickity about the detail because I wanted it all just right and of course, I wanted my praise from Filipe. I've thrown Sofia into bed on Christmas Eve with threats of not getting any presents in the morning if she gets out of bed but tonight, I really took my time with her. It makes me sad to realise how much I enjoy spending quality time with my child. I need to do this more, instead of fretting over everything else. Is this what it takes to realise this? My life falling apart in front of me to shake me into noticing what's really important. I examine my face in the mirror then splash cold water over it. I straighten my shoulders; I will learn how to stand on my own two feet again.

The show must go on.

If I have to move back in with my parents for a while then so be it.

I retrieve the last of Sofia's presents and arrange them in a pile downstairs in the living room. It doesn't look much now, and it looks even more pathetic that they can't be placed under a tree but I have to work with what I've got.

Filipe eventually gets up to help when he sees me struggling one handed but he lets me struggle for a good while until he does help. The bastard. I find some bows and some tinsel and make the pile of presents into a pretty display as Filipe returns to his laptop. I'm sure I catch him shaking his head at me but I don't call him out on it. I'm saving that for Boxing Day; Sofia will be at my parents so there will be no holding back.

Christmas Day goes by in a weird mix of emotions. Sofia, true to form got up at 4am, we both relented and let her open her presents. It was still night time really but I didn't care, she can have whatever she wants before we turn her life upside down. Christmas dinner was even more depressing that I thought it would be, a frozen Christmas dinner. It was from Marks and Spencer so it was of good quality but I had to refrain from crying into the packet as I opened it and put it in the microwave. The funny thing is you would never have known once it was on the plate, all the preparation and hard work that goes into making a roast dinner can be stressful but that's half the fun of it, you've made it all yourself and it's beautiful. When it's made by someone else, some unknown, someone without love for you and your family, it doesn't quite give you the same joy. I know the exact amount of honey that Filipe likes on his parsnips and the way he likes he stuffing – just slightly crispy on top. Marks and Spencer don't know that, does Jayne know that yet? Probably not. There's a fridge full of Christmas food I'll have to cook at some point but…

The good thing about getting up early is that Sofia is more than ready for bed at 6pm. I spend an hour up there again, talking about the day and her toys and reading her copious bedtime stories before I realise that she's fallen asleep in my arms, she was probably asleep ages ago. I decide to go to bed myself and Olive follows in for a cuddle. I try to read for a bit but can't concentrate. I even try to go on social media for a bit and end up messaging Dylan's wife a grovelling apology for screaming at her and a big thank you for saving Olive. I continue to scroll but people's seemingly perfect lives and wonderful festivities depress me endlessly so in the end I just lie there, staring at the ceiling as Olive lays next to me with one paw on my hand, watching me with her big cow like eyes.

She saw what I saw.

'Why, Olive?'

She cocks her head and barks once then begins to shuffle around on the bed, unable to settle, before she starts sniffing the mattress and pillows. Then, the sniffing becomes so loud that she sounds like a snorting pig, determined to find whatever it is that she can smell. She sniffs the whole of the bed in a fast loop, hoovering up the scent in a circle like fashion several times then leaps down onto the floor to do more of the same. She's snorting so loudly, it's not unusual but it's the loudest I've ever heard her do it. Knowing her, she can probably smell a treat that was once there three years ago, that's usually the case when she acts like this. Either that or Filipe has taken to eating in my bed but why would he do that when he has his own bed to slob in. His room's probably a mess and he can't be bothered to tidy it, he's waiting for me to do that. I bet he's been sleeping in here too. She sticks her bum up in the air as her nose continues to stick to the ground sucking up the smell that appears to be underneath the bed. In one big swooping motion she launches half of her body under the bed then returns milliseconds later.

With the grand prize.

Looking very pleased with herself.

'What are you doing in bed so early?' Filipe asks as he walks into the bedroom.

Olive jumps up at him with the prize in her mouth.

Black, silky French knickers.

Dirty knickers.

And they don't belong to me.

'I'm exhausted, must be the pain killers,' I say, watching his face.

'Oh, okay, well I'm going to put a film on...' Filipe stops in his tracks as he finally notices what Olive has in her mouth.

He knows. He's fucked up. Big time.

I don't move a muscle, concentrating on keeping my facial expression neutral just to see what he'll do. Olive is relentless and she just wants to give them to him.

She won't rest until she has.

She's like a dog with a bone or rather a dog with a vile human's dirty knickers.

Her persistence is quite impressive.

'No. Off,' he says, holding his arm up to prevent the knickers being forced onto his face.

She keeps diving at him with the knickers in her mouth like a big kick in the bollocks as if to say, *look what you've done, look what you've done to my mamma.* I'm sure I would be enjoying it if I wasn't so disgusted and mortified; they've done it here in my/our marital bed and I bet he hasn't even changed the sheets. With that thought, I get up and watch the sorry performance standing up.

'No.' He pushes her away again and she comes back with vengeance. 'OLIVE, NO! NO! NO! STUPID FUCKING DOG. GET OFF.' This time, he pushes Olive off him with such force that she finally lets go of the knickers causing him to fall backwards and lose his footing. The knickers eventually float down to land on his face. Olive goes over to sniff them once more, obviously not having had enough of Jayne's odour.

Yuck.

I walk over to him as he lays there breathing in their dirty old stale sex. The knickers still on his face, he's like a child, he won't move because he can't see me and I think part of him wishes that I couldn't see him either. He's glued to the spot as much as his face is glued to Jayne's underwear.

'Oh, don't you want her dirty knickers as a keepsake then?' I manage a small smile as Olive obediently stops sniffing to come and sit by my feet. Filipe sits up and stares at me, bewildered. He still doesn't have a clue how I know. I bend down to stroke my only loyal companion in all of this. It seems Marilyn Monroe was right when she said, *dogs never bite me, just humans.*

'Well done, Olive, good girl.'

Chapter 27

Christmas Day

Delilah

'Moorrrning, Merry Christmasss,' I sing, bouncing down the stairs, feeling my ponytail swish behind me. I pad into the living room to find Mum, Dad and Dylan drinking cups of tea in their dressing gowns. Loki is snuggled up in Dylan's dressing gown, it's become his favourite nap place. I'm already ready for the day, excited and slightly nervous for my new chapter. It's going to be lovely spending time with my family over Christmas, a little strange that Josh won't be here, but nice. Despite over indulging yesterday evening on left over buffet food and copious glasses of prosecco with Dylan, I already feel lighter, much lighter.

And I'm free but not completely, I still have to tell Mum and Dad what's happened. I couldn't bring myself to do it last night, not right after it happened. Josh was like a son to them and I'm not sure how they're going to react. They need to know. Dylan knows, I ran to his room as soon as it happened and made him promise to keep it to himself and that I'd break the news to Mum and Dad in my own time. He told me to do it sooner rather than later, give them time to adjust, like ripping a plaster off, he said. But he also said that it's my life and I can do as I please with it and he was sure that they would support me no matter what. He's become a little less protective of me too, I'm wondering if that was all just his own insecurities getting the better of him and besides, I have just fought a couple of dognappers. I can handle myself. Either way, I'm glad I'm not being babied anymore.

So, here goes nothing.

'You're sprightly this morning, no hangover?' Dylan asks as he hugs his gargantuan mug of tea, squinting at me from over the top of his glasses.

'Well, it's Christmas and nope, all the food must have soaked up the alcohol.'

Despite his obvious hangover, he's cheered up a little recently, he seems to have got himself some teacher mates, which I'm pleased about. I hated seeing him on his own all the time, moping about like a depressed superman, plus he looks better now I've given him a much-needed makeover. He sits a little straighter now, he may not admit it but I can tell he feels more confident. I've made a difference to him and made him feel good, just like he has with me and learning to control my nerves. The counting helps to keep me calm and I'm starting to think thirteen might not be such a scary number after all. It was all in my head.

'Enjoy it, when you get to my age it tends to float on top,' Dylan says patting his stomach and laughing.

'I guess I have that to look forward to then, gross.' I laugh with him.

'Josh coming over today, love?' Mum asks.

'Umm no.'

'Oh, why not? I've got his present here, do you want to pop it round to him later on or is he coming over for

Boxing Day?'

'Ah, shitsticks.'

'Or not? You don't have to,' Mum says, wide-eyed, and shakes her head whilst Dad snores next to her with his mouth wide open, he's still holding his cup of tea, albeit cackhandedly. Thankfully it's empty otherwise it would be all over his lap at this point. 'I just thought you might visit his parents before he comes here this year,' she continues, a hint of a frown appearing.

'Mum, wake Dad up a minute, I've got something to tell you.'

Mum jabs Dad in the ribs; he snorts and coughs then opens his eyes and smiles like he was never asleep.

'What it is, sweetheart?' Dad asks.

I hesitate for a moment and look at Dylan who taps on his giant mug of tea and gives me an encouraging nod.

'Josh and I aren't together anymore.'

'Oh,' Mum says.

'What's he done?' Dad asks, sitting up straighter on the sofa. Mum pats his knee, her subtle way of telling him not to get too carried away.

'Nothing, he hasn't done anything. I just think we've outgrown each other, you either grow together or apart, don't you,' I say, glancing at Dylan. 'And well, that's what's happened to us.'

Mum and Dad give each other knowing looks.

'Well, that's understandable, sweetheart, you're only young, you have your whole life ahead of you.'

'Thanks Dad.'

'Yes, it's up to you, darling. He was a nice boy but a bit wet at times, wasn't he?' Mum says, as Dad nods along agreeing with her.

'Mum! You can't say that,' Dylan says.

'It's okay,' I giggle.

'And there's something else…'

I was nervous about telling my family about my break up with Josh but they understood and they didn't seem that surprised either. I was even more nervous to tell them that I want to put dancing on hold for a while and do other things. It all became too much and I lost my love for it but again, they understood, I'm so lucky they did. Dance school wasn't exactly free but that's not to say I won't ever go back to dancing. Mum said I don't have to put all my eggs in one basket so I'm holding onto that.

'So, what are you going to do now?' Dad asks. Already worrying about my future for me.

'I have a few things in the pipeline, but I think I'm going to move back to London and stay with some friends for a bit. I have some savings from my job so that will help until I find what I want to do. I'm thinking I might try and join the police.' I bite my lip, anticipating their response.

'Oh wow,' Mum says.

'Yeah, I guess we'll see,' I say, not wanting to commit.

'You have to go and figure it out on your own, doesn't she Dad?' Dylan says, as Dad frowns into the distance considering his answer.

'Yes, you do, you're a grownup now, there's only so much we can advise you on.' Mum digs Dad in the ribs again and he nods.

'Have you handed your notice in?' Dad asks.

'I will, when I go back in the new year, then that will give me a few weeks to get sorted in London.'

Susie messaged me over Christmas to say that Miriam has contacted her about a huge event that Cool Tours Excellence has just put a bid in for. She had her working on tours all over the Christmas holidays, I'm glad she didn't contact me although I am intrigued as to what this event is. Nothing ever happens in Coolsbay, apart from attempted dognappings of course.

We spend the rest of the morning opening presents and enjoying each other's company as a family. Ian video calls us and we have a laugh with him which is nice as he never usually makes the effort. Loki even has his own little stocking; he went nuts when he saw the goodies that we had got for him. If we'd let him, he would have eaten it all in one go. Dad said he didn't want to spend Christmas at the vets so we had to restrain him and ended up hiding the rest of his Christmas treats.

I'm going to miss this.

'So, whilst we are on the subject of news, I may as well share mine.' Dylan puts down his comedy cooking apron of a merman that I got him for Christmas and claps his hands together.

'Who's the lucky lady?' Dad asks, and Dylan shakes his head.

'No not that.' He pauses. 'I'm also moving out, not sure when exactly but it's moving along nicely so…'

'Oh my God, where? Who?' I squeal. He kept that quiet.

'Well, not far from here, a stone's throw from the beach. It's a two-bedroom house with a garden for this little guy,' he says, scratching Loki's head 'That is unless, you wanted to take him to London?'

'No way! You can't take a dog to London, it will die of smoke inhalation,' Dad pipes up and Mum digs him in the ribs again.

'It's up to them, remember,' Mum says, then moves her eyes towards me and Dylan.

'No, I mean, of course you take him,' I say, choking back tears. As much as I love him, I hadn't even factored little Loki into my plans. Dylan has been the one mainly looking after him. 'He's your dog really and it makes sense, I couldn't promise him a garden or smoke free air,' I say, throwing a glance at Dad who smiles before closing his eyes again.

'Oh, my babies, flying the nest yet again.' Mum sighs and looks as if she might cry. 'Looks like it will be just me and you again, love.'

'Back where we started.' Dad smiles 'And I can't wait, no offence, you two.'

'None taken,' Dylan and I chirp in unison.

'Oh Dylan, Amber messaged me this morning,' I say in a teasing tone. I bet he wishes she was messaging him.

'She did?' he raises an eyebrow then sips his tea. Is he hiding a smile?

'Yeah, sent me a really nice message apologising for the scream and thanking me for saving her dog's life.'

'That's nice,' he says.

'It is. Where are you going?' I ask, as my brother suddenly leaps into action, taking off his dressing gown and untangling Loki from his arms who jumps onto the floor and instantly begins biting Dad's slippers.

'Taking Loki for a walk, we need some fresh air after all this news, the beach is calling and besides, Loki probably needs a shit.'

'Yes, take him out before that little bugger shits on my floor again,' Dad grumbles, whilst indulging in an unwanted game of tug of war with Loki and his now, very slobbery slipper. As much as Dad is fond of Loki, I think he's very much looking forward to some peace and quiet when we all move out.

'Can we come with you? You can show us your new house?' Mum asks, with a twinkle in her eye.

'Yes, let's all go!' I add.

'Later, I want to do this walk on my own.'

Amber

We arrive at my parent's house the next day, I'm glad of their support and understanding having text them a brief message of what's happening. I'll explain when I see them properly, alone, but it can't be done now. Sofia is super excited for a second Christmas and I'm relieved I don't have to pretend at happy families anymore.

Last night Filipe pleaded and begged with me to hear him out as I repeatedly told him to be quiet. There's no way I was going to do that with Sofia in the house. I would have liked to have done this drive on my own, to carefully plan and think things through but of course, I can't with my arm so Filipe has had to be the driver. After our goodbyes to Sofia, I get in the car and pull out my phone.

Me: *Hi Stella, please can we meet? My marriage is over. I'll be at the beach in an hour with Olive.*

Gulping back tears, I drop my phone back into my handbag. Filipe begins to drive, rage spilling out of him as he takes his upset out on other drivers. This is so not becoming of my husband. The husband that shags other women. We don't go straight back home, first I get him to stop at the local corner shop, the only one known to be open on Boxing Day so that I get some well needed supplies.

'Take me there,' I say, as I get back in the car, armed with calorific goodies, hoping he'll just know where *there* is and I don't have to say her name out loud.

'What? No, no way,' he moans, immediately knowing what I mean. 'Amber, we have to discuss this. You're being irrational,' he says, seemingly more poised after having had a few minutes to calm down whilst I was in the shop.

'Irrational? I'm not the one who had the affair.' I won't admit it but I know he's right. We can't go there; she has a child the same age as ours and God knows who else over. 'Let's just go home, I can't bear to see her face anyway or yours for that matter.'

But he doesn't move, his hands just squeeze the steering wheel tighter before his head jerks then I watch that angry little vein pulsate in his forehead.

Uh oh.

'You're such a miserable bitch. Do you know that? Always whining and moaning about this, that and the other. You don't know how good you've got it,' he spits, as he changes gear.

'Oh, it speaks.'

'Yes, I speak. I speak a lot which is why I'm very successful in business. If you listened, then you would know.'

'Not in relationships though, hey.' I say, fully aware that we are now *that joyful* couple, having an argument in their car on Boxing Day. 'What happened to us? We used to be so happy?'

He just shakes his head, turns the ignition on and begins to drive. We used to laugh so much all the time, until, over time, it just whittled away into this. Two people just living together, living completely separate lives, in separate bedrooms.

'Yes, we did, what did happen?' he says, turning it back on me.

'Her, her of all people,' I say, not able to say her name. 'You know I saw you on the *Ring* doorbell? I already knew, the whole time on Christmas Day and Christmas

Eve, I already knew.'

He frowns then grips the steering wheel, not looking at me.

'Are you surprised? She's there for me, she isn't always miserable. All you do is just bite my head off every time I tried to spend time with you, I try to help but you say it's not good enough. I can't win.'

'Because you do the fucking bare minimum, you do it shit on purpose so that you don't have to do it. And Filipe, I'm fucking exhausted, exhausted from trying to please you, always trying to do *all* the things, all of the time, just waiting for you to give me a well done. I get that you work hard, but I do too and I shouldn't have to do everything at home all by myself, always.'

'You're such hard work, you're a job in yourself, which is why I am always at work. It's much easier there. I used to like it when you were feisty but you're just, you're just TOO MUCH FOR ME, WOMAN.' His hot, venomous breath hits me hard.

I'm too much.

'Yeah? And you're not enough for me,' I say quietly, feeling anything but too much.

We drive the rest of the way home in silence and when we arrive back, I grab Olive and head straight for the beach.

Filipe doesn't try to stop me.

It may end up being a very long walk. Stella rings me when I arrive at the sand steps to say that she's on her way. It isn't until I put the phone down that I feel a sudden panic rise within me. I'm on my own at the very place the dognapping took place. Suddenly, I feel very vulnerable and, very cold. In the hurry to leave the house I didn't put a coat on and am wearing my slightly stained and worn house jogging bottoms and jumper. My arm is hurting a lot; I forgot to take my last lot of pain killers. The burst of adrenaline in the car is subsiding and I feel quite weak. I find a bench to sit on and try to huddle up as I feebly search for a stick on the ground to throw for Olive.

Hurry up, Stella.

Please get here soon.

'Don't you ever do that to me again. You're staying on the lead forever,' I say to Olive, as she looks up at me with big, brown, sad eyes. I stroke her silky soft ears and those pleading eyes beg back at me; she definitely knows what I'm saying.

'Well, not until my arm's healed anyway, okay.' I soften, knowing full well that I will let her off at some point as I'll feel guilty for not letting her run about. She enjoys it too much. I close my eyes and try to steady my breath, to stop the heaviness that's beginning to build in my chest.

Flashbacks of the incident start to come back to me, the dognappers' faces, their accents and the screaming sounds of my own voice calling for Olive. The girl hiding her face. Dylan's girlfriend.

A deep sense of impending doom overcomes me as a voice penetrates my thoughts, rebounding in my ears.

'Amber, are you alright?'

I shudder then jump. The unexpected visitor catching me unawares is Mr Dylan bloody Thomas and he's being dragged over by his dog. He really has the perfect timing. Not.

'I'm fine, I'm just, just…' His hand gently touches my back as I feel the lead slip out of my fingers and I watch him take control of Olive as she starts to sniff his dog.

'Breathe, slowly, inhale, exhale, that's right, just keep doing what you're doing. You're doing great.'

I follow his instructions because I feel I may stop breathing if I don't. The emotion is all too much, everything, just all too much. How ironic that the first person I loved would be here with me now watching my life with the second person I loved fall apart, twenty-five years later. Even more ironic that we're sitting at our old bench, the third one along, that no birds appear to shit on and still haven't.

'Breathe, just breathe, that's it,' he encourages, as I do just that. Breathe. It's all I can do. We sit there for a little while. His hand on my back, his eyes watching me intently. Me, concentrating on my breathing. The dogs, entangled in each other's leads, playing.

'I didn't know you had a dog,' I finally croak, sounding as if I have a huge frog stuck in my throat.

'Yeah, just got him.' He smiles and ruffles the dog's head before offering me his drink again. 'Here.' He hands me his flask of coffee and I shake my head.

'No thanks,'

'You need to drink, go on, it has sugar in it, it's good for after a panic attack.'

'I didn't have a panic attack.'

'It's okay, my sister used to have them all the time. Here.' I reluctantly accept the drink and take a few sips before handing it back to him.

'My husband's having an affair, I've just found out. It's with Jayne. Mia's mum,' I blurt out, feeling hugely embarrassed and angry as the words leave my mouth.

'I'm sorry, that's shit.'

'It's alright, well it's not, but it will be.' It was when you left and it will be when he leaves too.

Life goes on.

'Well, if it makes you feel any better, my wife lied to me our entire marriage saying she wanted children, only to tell me years later that she now doesn't. Sorry, now this is terribly awkward.'

'Wow, no it's fine, I mean it's not fine, for you. Shit, I'm sorry.'

'Yup, it's okay. I've been processing it, it's fine.'

'I'm so sorry she left, she looks so young too, I couldn't even think about children at her age,' I muse. 'Is there a chance she may change her mind?'

'Who looks young? You've met my ex-wife?'

'Yes, the girl, I mean, sorry your wife with the beautiful long blond hair, the one you came to hospital with. She saved Olive, didn't she? I have apologised now. Somehow, I had managed to convince myself that she was part of the dognapping gang. Mainly because she'd walked past my house acting suspiciously in the months and weeks leading up to it, she'd hide her face, like this.' I hold my hand up to the side of my face, mimicking what she used to do and, shockingly, he bloody laughs.

'What's funny?'

'That's my sister, not my wife, sorry ex-wife. She's highly superstitious, does your house happen to have the number thirteen in it?'

'Yes, it is the number thirteen.'

'She doesn't like looking at that number, she's been that way for a while, says it brings her bad luck with her dancing and stuff. Madness, I know.'

'Alright, my lovelies.' Stella arrives with Pudding and perches on the bench the other side of me. I smile then blow air out of my cheeks to try and control my emotions. 'Hello, Mr Thomas, fancy seeing you here. Merry Christmas.' She pats me on the back and leans across me to shake his hand.

'Merry Christmas,' Dylan says, as Stella vigorously shakes his hand for far too long. Is she eyeballing him?

We all sit in an awkward silence, watching the dogs.

'You okay, mate? What's happened?' Stells asks, looking at Dylan like he might be responsible.

'No, I'm not, I'm really not.' And so, I spill my heart out there and then sat in my dirty, old jogger suit only meant for the house to my best friend and my first ever love who has just confided in me as have I to him.

I surprise myself and we laugh at the *Ring* doorbell catching Filipe red handed, we laugh harder at the knicker incident; hell, we even laugh at me having no job, becoming a single mum. We laugh a lot until I can't laugh anymore and the laughter turns to choked up scared, sad, angry tears. I've lost all dignity but I'm past caring.

Shit's just got real, it's hit the fan, sprayed the walls, the ceiling, the floor and covered the entirety of my face in the process. I'm probably at my lowest ebb, so I have to tell myself that it can really only get better from here.

Because, that's right, isn't it?

Chapter 28

New Year's Eve

Delilah

'You all sorted? Self-defence kit at the ready?' Dylan grins then flicks through the channels on the TV, before true to form, he settles on another gardening programme.

He's dressed smart, for him, not teacher smart but going out smart and there's not a navy-blue jumper insight. He's done his hair and has treated himself to a splash of aftershave. He's cheered up loads from the time he arrived here in the summer and is quite clearly getting back to himself again, he's got friends. I'm happy for him, like really happy for him. There's no one that deserves happiness more than my lovely brother.

'I'm sorted. New bottle of fake tan in my bag,' I say, joking, tapping my bag. 'But you're welcome to borrow some before you go out if you like, to complete your look, you are looking a little pasty.' I circle my finger at him and giggle at my own joke, the funny thing is I've been approached by a security company to work with them on developing young people's attack packs. The dognapping story made not only the local newspapers but also the nationals. People were intrigued (some horrified) by my method of self-defence and it triggered an interest in brushing up on safety for young people when out on your own. It's surprisingly fun so far and Molly is working with me to help get a good deal with the security company. After all I am helping to design the tools which include a safe dye spray to mark the attacker as well as market it for them on my social media sites, which have thousands of followers now and are growing fast. The detailed spreadsheets that Molly's so good at and her knowledge of social media are definitely coming in handy now.

I'm already feeling slightly giddy at the thought of new year celebrations with my best mates in the shed and also the idea of starting afresh. I don't know what this year will bring but I know I'll be in a completely different place this time next year and I can't wait for it. There's so much opportunity now, you don't have to assign yourself to one thing for the rest of your life and I think that was part of my problem. I put too much pressure on myself to be a dancer and only a dancer, forever.

It doesn't have to be that way.

For the first time since I was a little kid I feel wildly excited. Instead of dreading being on my own, I know that I've got this, by myself. For God's sake, I took on two bloody criminals and won, I saved a dog from being dognapped.

I can do anything. I can be anything. I trust myself.

A huge weight has been lifted off my shoulders.

Dylan throws an empty tube of *Pringles* at me and I dodge it with precision, my dancing skills coming in handy, even in day-to-day life.

'Don't chuck your starter at me, you're going to need that to soak up the alcohol later,' I say, in jest.

'I wouldn't want to spoil my dinner with some sour cream *Pringles*.'

'Wow, you kept that quiet, a little *romantic* dinner date?' I tease, grinning. I wonder if he has a date, a teacher from work, the shop assistant from *Emmanuel's*?

'No, I'm going out with my work mates for drinks. She's only just split with her husband remember,' he says, shaking his head. Of course, he means Amber. I can't help but think that he looks a little disappointed.

'I'm sure you can work your magic.' I wink.

'I very much doubt that, but anyway, I'm not going to, there's a thing called respect.'

'That's why I love you, bro. Respect.' I walk over and fist pump him and fight the urge to ruffle his perfectly coiffed hair.

'I'm going to miss you when you move out Dylan, but I'm going to miss you more my little ball of fluff.' I bend down and kiss Loki on the head as he sleeps on the sofa, curled up in a perfect cosy little ball. Our little mischievous bull in a china shop, the unstoppable mutt. The one that made me a Coolsbay hero, because if it wasn't for him there's no way I would have been out walking in the freezing cold in December. On my way out I notice a beautiful silver pashmina hanging up, it must be Mum's she won't mind if I borrow it, I think, as I sling it around my shoulders. It will go perfectly with my outfit.

Amber

'Mummy, how long are we going to stay at Grandma and Grandad's house?' Sofia asks, as I finish applying my makeup.

We're in my old bedroom, I haven't slept in this room since I was eighteen and even though they've kept it exactly the same, I bet they never really envisioned their daughter moving back home at forty. I've told Filipe not to speak of what happened as there isn't an ounce of me that wants to hear it. He's respected my wish, in fact he's been very quiet except for the nightly phone call to Sofia, which makes me think that he's probably with her, Jayne. The focus is now on making everything smooth for our daughter and then I'll be filing for divorce on the grounds of his adultery. I should name her too.

Sofia's also done her makeup, copying me as I got ready. Her pink lipstick covers half her face and she resembles a happy, cheeky little clown. I smile and bop her on the nose, smiling at her tuneful giggle as I zip up my makeup bag up and put it into the top drawer of my old dressing table. Olive gently snores on the bed, legs moving like she's on a treadmill, I imagine she's chasing squirrels in her dreams. We'll be alright, I have my two, special girls and they have me.

'Just until we get our own place, I'm not sure. Do you like it here?'

'Yes, because you're not cross anymore and I still get to go back to my old house and see Daddy.'

'That's good then, as long as you're happy, sweetheart. Are you sure you're okay?'

'Yes.' She beams, like this is all an adventure. I've underestimated how strong she is, I've underestimated her. 'Are you happy, Mummy?' I consider this for a moment. Everything has changed in the last month of my life. It's been a whirlwind of events and people but am I happier for it?

Not yet exactly, but I will be.

'Absolutely.' And I'll be a little more satisfied once I've confronted Jayne, the marriage destroyer, but let's face it, my marriage was already breaking, it was over a long time ago. Perhaps I should take a different tack and thank her.

'I'm happy I get to sleep in your bed.' She treats me to her toothy grin.

'Me too, cheeky.' I wonder how long we will have to share a bed?

The funny thing is she has slept like a log since we've been sharing my old double bed, no getting up in the night, no crying for me. I'm here, with her and I'm not about to give up on a good night's sleep, yet, for either of us. She hasn't slept back at our old house yet, having only seen Filipe during the day a few times but that time will come soon and I wonder what it will be like for her. It makes me a little sad to think she'll be unsettled again, I can't see Filipe wanting to share a bed with her, not if he's already sharing it with somebody else. I glance at my phone to see the messages between me and Jayne from earlier on today.

Me: *Hi Jayne, hope you had a good Christmas. I think we need to talk, you probably know what this is about. The sooner we can meet up and get a few things clear, the better.*

Jayne: *Hello Amber, I'm so glad you've text. I've been feeling the same way. Agree, we need to talk asap.*

Me: *Great. Free to meet me this evening? 6pm at the Mermaid's Lair?*

Jayne: *That's fine but I can't stay long, I have the New Year's Eve party that I'm hosting tonight, are you coming?*

Me: *No, I'm afraid not. Don't worry this shouldn't take too long.*

Jayne: *Fab, look forward to it.*

The absolute cheek of the woman, only Jayne could

be so blasé about stealing another woman's husband. Still, I'm not going to lose my cool. I'm not about to enter the room all screamy and shouty. No, I shall hold on to some decorum, especially as it's in a public place which means that she must do the same when I present the evidence.

I'd be lying if I said I wasn't looking forward to that part. Plus, she needs to realise who is boss and that in no uncertain terms is she to ruin any more magic for my daughter. She can spoil it as much as she likes for her own child but not mine. Sofia won't be pleased when she realises that she has a new step-sister in the form of Mia but we will cross that bridge when we come to it. One thing at a time.

'How do I look Sof?' Like a princess?' I ask, as I give a little twirl in the new dress that Mum and Dad treated me to.

'No, Mummy, not a princess.' She giggles and twirls her little fingers around my wavy hair. I'm a little over dressed for the Mermaid's Lair in my glitzy black floor length dress but I don't care. I feel and look good so why shouldn't I show it off? I'm not hiding away anymore, even my arms are out on show tonight. And I've wrapped a black silk scarf around the ugly cast. It almost looks like a part of the dress, almost.

'No?'

'Like a queen,' she says. I high five her, then give her a big squeeze. Yes, my darling, tonight your mother will act like the queen that she is.

The queen she should always have been.

The Mermaid's Lair is busy, buzzing with the excitement

of New Year's Eve. Rather than feeling out of place in my extravagant dress, like I thought I would, I feel very at home at the Bond themed New Year's Eve Party. Even the staff are dressed up in Tux's and gorgeous dresses. When Jayne has gone, I'm looking forward to dinner, plenty of wine and spending time with my friends. I saunter up to the bar and order myself a glass of white wine before managing to find a two-seater table tucked away in the corner. I've arrived a little early, just so I can watch her walk in and see the sorry, sad guilt on her face.

Five minutes later, she waltzes into the pub in a long expensive looking dress. As I scan her face for remorse, I wonder if she's going to tell me where it's from and how much it cost but there is seemingly no guilt, not an ounce, just smugness. I watch her smug face order a drink, then wearing a winning smile and looking beautifully glamorous, she glides over to our table. A man that she's been chatting to at the bar whilst waiting for her drink follows after her. Jayne has a fan.

Great.

'Amberrrr, hi.' Jayne puts her wine glass down on the table then holds her arms out in the air, mouth open, silently shrieking. She seems genuinely pleased to see me. The feeling is not mutual. The man, attractive and in his early thirties, hovers beside her.

'Hi Jayne,' I say flatly, not getting up, as the man continues to drool over her.

'Sorry ladies, can I just say something and then I will leave you to your evening?' He has an eastern European accent which is rather attractive. He turns to Jayne, all doe eyed. 'You're stunning,' he gushes 'You're like, you're just the perfect combination of every single race.'

Wow.

'Oh, thanks.' Jayne giggles and plays with her earrings before smoothing down her dress. 'That's a new one. Is that a chat upline? This dress does look a little exotic I suppose, it was rather pricey.' She touches his arm briefly and he bites his lip. Is she for real?

'Maybe, can I, I mean would it be okay to get your phone number?'

'Ummmm, yeah why not.' She grins and I watch open mouthed as Jayne taps her digits into his phone. 'Text me,' she mouths, as he grins and walks back to the bar, turning back repeatedly to ogle Jayne. I watch her, fluttering her eyelashes back at him and rage boils within me.

'Are you joking?'

'I know!' She shrieks then pulls out the chair to sit down 'How about that hey. He's rather gorgeous too, well you never know, new year, new man,' she says, with a twinkle in her eye and a wriggle of the shoulders.

I'm fuming.

Are Jayne and Filipe already no more? All that for nothing. She arranges her hair, smiling broadly. But the smile quickly fades when she notices my unsmiling face and flared nostrils. My fists clench by my side. I was going to say something later, after we'd discussed the girls but it can't wait now.

My blood is boiling.

'Amber? Have I said something?'

Not trusting myself to speak for fear of losing my shit in public, I reach into my handbag and pull out a zipped-up plastic sandwich bag.

'What's this?' she asks, frowning.

'Must be part of a matching set, thought you'd be missing them by now,' I say, using a carefully controlled tone as I thrust the bag over to her side of the table.

She examines the knickers through the sandwich bag, turning it this way and that. Her nose wrinkling up as she stares at them. Bewildered.

'I I I, what's going on?'

'Oh, forgotten already? Let me jog your memory.' I pull out my phone and tap on the *Ring* doorbell app, scrolling through to the dreaded night I saw them on camera. The night I was in hospital and in pain. I press play on the video and watch her face as she watches the thirty-second long video of her and Filipe.

'Oh my God.' Jayne's hand flies up to her mouth and her eyes begin to well up.

'Yes. Oh my God.' Busted.

'Amber, do you think that this is me?' she asks, with hurt in her eyes as a single tear slowly falls down her cheek. She frantically taps on the screen until it pauses on them frolicking on the sofa.

'It is you.' I tilt my head to the side so I can see better. 'Isn't it?' It can't be a mistake. It must be her.

It is her.

'Amber, I'm so sorry this has happened. Filipe. What a shit, but that isn't *me*,' she says, pointing at the screen. 'I mean, I can see why you would think that, we do have similar hair I suppose, but that isn't me. I would never do that to you. You're my friend.'

'Oh God.' I take the phone off her and watch it again. The slim figure, the brown, bouncy, glossy locks. Of course, why didn't I see it before. It's bloody obvious. *She* too, could be described as the perfect combination of every single race. 'Oh God.'

'Amber, if it makes you feel any better my husband cheated too, almost a year ago now. It was hard but I told him to get lost. Best thing I ever did, and it will get easier.'

'Thanks, yes, it's over.' I nod as I watch the video

again, this must be the gazillionth time but now I see it. The shape of her nose, the subtle golden highlights that Jayne doesn't have, that childish, giggling baby voice. It couldn't be anyone else really. 'It's Stephanie, Filipe's PA.'

Of course it is.

'Oh God, the lady with her boyfriend at your birthday meal?'

'Yes.' Going on under my nose the whole time, for however long.

Months, possibly years. 'I thought it was you and I hated you for it, I really did.' I let out a huge sigh, deflated. Did I want it to be Jayne so badly that that's all I could see?

'Oh, that's awful, I can see why,' she says, quietly.

'I'm so sorry, Jayne,' I apologise, relieved that we're in public so I couldn't release the full extent of my rage.

'Honestly, no hard feelings. So do you want these back? You might want to give them back to the owner.' Jayne dangles the sandwich bag in front of me and we both laugh. 'Oh God, I bet you hated me?'

'Thanks. I did a bit but I also wanted to thank you. You or rather, Stephanie, has done me a favour.'

'Are you alright?'

'I will be.' I take a sip of my wine and notice the man at the bar eyeing up Jayne again. He truly is taken with her.

'I knew you didn't want me there on your birthday,' she blurts out. 'I thought it was strange Filipe inviting me but I wanted to make the effort, I wanted to know more about you because you seemed great, like you don't give a shit about what people think. I admire that you can just dance about and have fun with the kids at the school gates. I could never do that.'

'Really?'

'I worry too much about what people think. I also thought that if we became friends then we could arrange a few play dates and our daughters would stop being awful to each other. In all honesty, I thought you invited me here today to speak about our girls, not accuse me of having an affair with your husband.' Jayne purses her lips and a pang of guilt hits me again. How could I not see it?

'I did, as well. Mia has said some really nasty things to Sofia, about her appearance.'

'Oh, really? I don't know what to say.'

'I should have confronted you after the first meeting with Mr Thomas, but I guess I was a little intimidated by you. You seemed to know all the mums, you're all friends and I wasn't sure if talking to you would actually make things worse.'

'All the little ones went to pre-school together; we know each other from that but how would it be made worse?'

'I don't know, I guess I was angry after Mia told Sofia that Santa wasn't real and spoilt the magic. I didn't think we'd see eye to eye on anything if we didn't agree on that.' A bit immature of me.

'Amber. Sorry, that was shitty of me. I guess I was jealous of you and the fact that you didn't have to work or send Sofia to pre-school. I was jealous of the time you got to spend with your child, your life seemed so much more together and happier than mine.'

'It's okay and if it's any consolation I highly doubt that I was happier than you. And…' I hesitate. 'I was jealous of you too; you always look amazing.'

'Really?'

'Really, thank you.'

Jayne blushes and smooths down her dress. 'Let's

arrange that play date soon for the girls, we can lead by example,' Jayne says, brightly. It feels awkward and I'm not sure I want to meet up as friends but she's right. I think of Michael – the old dog walker, wherever he is. He would encourage me to do this nice thing. Plus, I'm feeling festive so in the name of good Christmas cheer and wise old dog walkers, I agree.

'Sure, sounds great.' I smile. 'Hey, you might want to invite him to your party, a guaranteed kiss at midnight.' I grin and nod at the man at the bar who is still gawping at Jayne. He grins widely when she turns around and gives her a little wave.

'I might just do that,' she says, waving back at him. 'Sure you don't want to come? I have canapes and cocktails.'

'I can't, I'm meeting friends here but thank you and have a great night.'

'Okay, well I best be off. Happy New Year.'

'Happy New Year and new man.' I nod as Jayne trots off to the bar to get acquainted with her new number one fan.

I now have a lot of thinking to do, but it can wait.

Delilah

The bitter air stings my nostrils as I pad to the pub, I knew I should have worn a coat, Mum's pashmina, as beautiful as it looks, isn't warm at all. The pub is crowded which instead of making me anxious, like it normally would, makes me smile and tingle. I swiftly make my way to the back entrance to get to the shed, I'm looking forward to seeing the new year in with my mates. New year, new confident me.

'Dee, over here.' Sky waves and I do a double take as

I see her and Molly sitting at a table in the pub. We never venture inside the pub but perhaps the time has come to join the grownups. Molly has her boyfriend with her and next to Sky, sits my brother, no not Dylan, that wouldn't be so bad, but it's Ian.

'What the hell are you doing here?' I say, marching over to them.

'Oh, nice to see you too, sis.'

'Do Mum and Dad know you're back?'

'Umm no, should they?'

'Actually, he's here with me. He's come to see me, we hit it off after that night at yours.' Sky rests her hand on his knee and I fight against the urge to retch.

'But you barely spoke?'

'We had spoken before, we just didn't realise.' Sky bites her lip and looks up at Ian, simpering. He returns the look and holds her hand. I think I might vomit into my hands at any moment.

'*FansOnly*,' Molly says giggling. 'They met on *FansOnly*.' she squeals into her prosecco.

I stand there open mouthed as two women catch my attention, walking into the pub in shorts. 'Alright my lovely,' one of them says loudly.

'Mental,' I say, tearing my eyes away from the shorts crew.

'Yep, it's pure madness but we like each other,' Sky replies.

'This will take some getting used to, aren't you a bit old for her?' I say, trying to hide my disgust.

Ian shrugs.

'Hey, I like an older man, those young boys can't handle me, you know that,' Sky says, as I watch Ian watching her with intent, stroking her hand. I've never seen him look at someone like that before.

'Anywayyy… this is Brandon everyone, *my* boyfriend,' Molly says, looking pleased with herself.

Brandon does an awkward little grin. 'Hi everyone.'

Great, I'm the gooseberry for the night. I wish they'd told me they were bringing boyfriends, especially since one of them is my brother, yuk. Not that I have anyone to bring, those bridges have been well and truly burned. I glance over at the women with the shorts to see where they've gone and that's when I notice who they're with, Amber. Then, I recognise one of the women, it's her friend.

'I'll be back in a minute; I just need to go and speak to someone.'

'Okay, I'll get more prosecco in, then we can get the party started. Whoop.' Ian punches the air then high fives Sky. If I needed another reason to leave Coolsbay, this would, most definitely be it. It's done, decided, I'm going. My notice will be going in the new year. London is calling and Miriam will have to manage this secret fancy event without me. Wow, I suddenly feel quite liberated.

'Hey.' I tap Amber on the shoulder and wait for her to turn around.

'Delilah, oh my God, come here.' She pulls me into a big embrace, her arm cast digging into my side.

'How's your arm?' I smile widely, still inwardly pleased with my decisiveness to leave my job.

'Not bad,' she says releasing me, whilst making a squinty face. 'Nice pashmina, I had one just like it.'

'Thanks, it's my Mum's,' I say. 'I got your message and I wanted to say thank you and not to worry about you know, the screaming. I did message you back on Facebook but I don't think you saw it yet.'

'No, I don't really use social media, but I wanted to

245

contact you and thank you for saving my Olive, she means the world to me. She's like my other child.'

'It's not a problem, I guess you found me via my brother,' I grin, fishing for more info on their history, but she doesn't bite. Instead, she's staring at Mum's pashmina again.

'Sorry, this may sound a bit strange but are you sure that's your mum's? Only, it looks exactly like mine, it even has the same red wine stain.' She points to the corner of the pashmina where sure enough, there is a tiny red wine stain.

'Umm, I don't know. I think so. But why would it be at my house?' She doesn't answer. 'Oh, you've been to our house?' I grin, so happy for Dylan. He kept that one quiet, the dark horse.

'No, I haven't, I lost it at a hotel.' She blushes. 'It wasn't like that, we bumped into each other. I phoned the hotel the next day and they said it wasn't there.'

'Ah, he took it home, looking after it for you.' My mind flashes to him on the sofa a few weeks ago, smelling and cuddling up to what I thought was a little silver blanket he'd bought for Loki. It wasn't though, I see it now, it was Amber's pashmina. I stifle a laugh but don't tell Amber that bit. Don't want to freak her out just yet.

Dylan would die.

Amber

'Here, I've been standing here wearing it for long enough, this is so awkward.' Delilah giggles then hands me back my pashmina and I throw it round my shoulders as the smells engulf me. It still smells of that night, of him. The kiss plays over in my head and I blush.

'No don't be sorry, I'm just glad he found it. I thought I'd lost him forever, I mean, I thought I'd lost *it* forever,' I reply, wincing at my slip of the tongue, feeling my face blush.

'Alright, my lovelies? Well if it isn't the local dog rescuer, been tangoing any more criminals lately?' Stella chuckles to Delilah, as she appears beside me, putting a hand on my shoulder. 'I know that Amber will be forever grateful for what you did that day as will I. We don't know what we'd do without our dogs, they hold a special place right here.' Stella looks across to me then thumps her fist on her chest. 'Shit the bed, you look rosier than Rudolph's nose, matey.'

'Just the drink going to my head, makes me flushed. I think I need some food,' I say, in an attempt to get away from the conversation, because now I've seen him.

Dylan. And I can't take my eyes off him.

The pull is magnetic, just like when we first met. He's sitting with what looks like a few teachers from school and he's looking over. Our eyes lock and it takes me back to all those times we would steal secret glances at each other.

'It is hot in here mind,' Stella continues. 'Knew it would be, that's why I'm wearing these bad boys,' she says, pointing to her shorts. 'I'm hot blooded, don't feel the cold at all, you see.'

Stella continues to talk to Delilah about winter attire and then the dognapping. Time stands still between Dylan and I as his friends chatter and joke around him, he smiles a little secret smile, just for me and I wonder how different life would be if we had stayed together, as childhood sweethearts. If he hadn't just disappeared that day but then I wouldn't have my girls.

'I'm just going to the bar, top up anyone? In fact,

Delilah, I'm definitely buying you a drink, that's well over due.'

'Ahh thanks, Amber. Prosecco please and please just call me, Dee.' She smiles and flicks her long blonde hair.

'Two pints for me and Tams, please mate.'

'No problem, be back soon.' I really need to get a job. I feel like coming down the pub might become a little bit more of a regular occurrence now that I'm not with Filipe. I head over to the bar and wait patiently in the long queue. The Christmas lights hung up around the bar twinkle joyfully and I catch a glimpse of myself in the mirror behind the bar smiling. I'm going to be okay; we're going to be okay.

'What can I get you love?' the barman asks.

'Two pints of beer and a bottle of prosecco please.'

'Coming right up.'

'I'll get those, mate,' Dylan's voice calls. 'Add two more pints on as well please.'

'You don't have to do that,' I say to Dylan, who is standing next to me, looking divine in a suit. The aftershave he's wearing also smells beautifully heady and rich. His aftershave coupled with the few glasses of wine I've already consumed suddenly make me feel quite tipsy.

'I want to,' he smiles. 'How's your arm?'

'Not bad, getting there, your sister is very sweet, you've actually just bought her a drink.' I grin. 'She gave me my pashmina back too. She thought it was your mum's?' I slur a little, raising an eyebrow.

'Oh yes,' he says, slightly colouring. 'I've been meaning to give it back to you but the timing never seemed right.'

'Why?'

'Though you'd think I was strange taking it home, I should have just handed it in to the hotel.'

'Hindsight is a wonderful thing, we've all done things we wish we had done differently.'

'Yep, I suppose that's true.'

'Like when you left and I never heard from you again.' Oh no, I really am tipsy and the alcohol is making me bold. The barman begins to place our drinks in front of us and Dylan looks at me with his intense multicoloured eyes before turning back to stare at the drinks. I shrug my shoulders. It doesn't matter anymore, does it? It was years ago. A whole lifetime ago.

'Here you go mate, that's forty-five pounds fifty please,' the barman says, as Dylan hands him his card. We stand there in silence as the barman places the beers on a tray and plonks the prosecco into a small bucket of ice.

'Let me help you.' Dylan picks up the tray of beers in one hand and the handle of the bucket in the other. I pick up the two wine glasses and we head back over to my table with me leading the way.

'Well, well, well. Hello Mr Thomas,' Stella booms, as we approach. Everyone takes their drinks and we stand there awkwardly with everyone seemingly looking at Dylan and I. 'Happy New Year.'

'Happy New Year, everyone. Umm, can I just steal Amber for a second, we were midway through a private conversation at the bar.'

'YES!' Dee screeches, jumping up and down, slopping her prosecco a little as Stella and Tamsin chuckle.

'You better ask *her* that,' Stella says.

Dylan looks at me. 'May I steal you please, Amber.'

'You may steal me but not for long,' I reply, in what I think is a prim sounding tone. I hope we're going outside; I could do with some fresh air. All this fizz is going to my head way too quickly.

Dylan leads us out through to the back of the pub, through the empty beer garden, save for a few smokers, and we walk the few feet in silence until we reach the beach and then the third bench along.

Our old spot, again.

'Ooops, we still have our drink.' I giggle as we sit down and I take a sip of my wine. 'I hope we don't get into trouble.'

'I'm sorry, about you know, kissing you that night, I didn't know you were married.'

'Oh, I thought you were going to tell me why you disappeared all those years ago.' I hiccup.

'My dad got posted up north with his work, an opportunity too good to miss. We had to move, there was no other option and they didn't give us very much time either. It was easier just to cut you off. In my teenage boy head I didn't see the point if I was all those miles away. I wasn't up for long distance. And then I met my ex-wife and stayed there, well until she became my ex.'

'Ah, that explains it.'

'Explains what?'

'Why you used the word mythering and of course the change of accent.' I pull my pashmina a little tighter around my shoulders, the cold air causing me to shiver.

'I don't have an accent, do I?'

'A bit, I thought you were putting it on for the kids, you know, to sound more friendly.'

Dylan laughs and shakes his head.

'It's true, it does sound friendlier, like you're trying to be a kids' TV presenter or something.'

'That's funny, you're funny. Look, I'm sorry I was a dick but I was immature, silly. We were so young. I tore up your phone number and sulked for a month when Dad told me we were going.'

'Didn't you know it off by heart? I knew yours.'

'Did you?' I nod and press my lips together. 'I was distraught, confused, heart-broken. But it was a long time ago. I thought I'd done something wrong, I guess it's nice to know it wasn't me.'

'Of course not, I loved you.' Dylan puts his hand on my knee and we teleport back in time; he leans forward and his soft lips brush mine for a second. It feels so good, so warm and tender. I kiss him back. I could kiss him forever but could my heart take it right now after everything that's happened? I touch the side of his face and move my lips away from his.

'I'm a freshly, raw, not even divorced yet, single mother. I may come with a lot of baggage.'

'Same here, the baggage part, not the single mum bit.'

'Let's just slow down a bit then.' I stand up and offer him my hand to make our way back to the pub. He takes it and gently pulls me back down onto his knee. We stay there for hours but it feels like minutes, kissing like teenagers and in between those kisses catching up on all the lost years until the fireworks begin to bang and sizzle around us. It feels the same, but different. We've both grown up, experienced life.

'Happy new me,' I whisper to myself, as a giant multicoloured fire work explodes in the distance over the sea.

This is truly the greatest start to a new year.

'Happy new you,' he murmurs before kissing me again.

Chapter 29

6 months later

Delilah

'In the nicest possible way, Delilah, those dresses are a little garish in real life, in the photos you sent, they didn't look so bright.' Miriam frowns as she stands on the port in her black sunglasses and hi-vis vest, clutching a black clipboard. She shifts her gaze from the team of dancers and stares up at the huge cruise ship, squinting, even through her sunglasses. The sun appears to be shining the brightest it's ever shone.

Suzie, Miriam and I gasp again at the vastness of the cruise ship.

I glance down at the ever-growing crowd forming on the promenade and give a little wave to my brothers, Mum, Dad, Molly and Sky who are up front and centre behind security. It's the first time a cruise ship has ever graced Coolsbay with its presence and it has created quite the hysteria, especially concerning Cool Tours Excellence.

'Miriam, trust me, I'm the creative here and it will work. It's a shame they didn't arrive sooner so you could have seen them before but best laid plans and all that.'

'Yes, well you would know about that, chop and change your mind like the wind,' Miriam remarks, making reference to my ever-changing choice in career.

Right now, I'm living in London, working towards getting a job in the police whilst teaching at a local dance school. I also have a couple of other projects on the go, this event being one of them. I'm loving the variety, the choice and not having all my eggs in one basket.

'Are you completely sure?' she asks, as the girls begin to warm up on the pier and the sudden rush of excitement begins to bubble within me.

'Completely, it's going to be *fandabidozi*,' I reply lightly.

Miriam purses her lips and if I didn't know her better, I'd say she was trying not to laugh. She's definitely excited too.

'Here you go chick, copy of the contact details for the band etc, should you need them,' Suzie, says. 'I won't be here when the ship departs so you want to make sure they all turn back up again,' she continues handing me a sheet of paper.

'Pressure but thanks, Suzie. You've done an amazing job. Thanks for all your help. The port looks absolutely stunning,' I say, looking around at the bunting and beautiful art work displayed on stands. The pretty portable fish and chip shop along with a local arts and crafts store, the freshly brewed coffee stand and pop-up bars sits on the edge of the beach alongside a traditional Punch and Judy theatre. Suzie has worked so hard on this, and Miriam has noticed giving her a well-deserved and long overdue pay rise.

'Couldn't have done it without you, I mean, how would we have welcomed them in? We would have had to have got my dad and his mates to perform their sea shanties,' Suzie says, visibly wincing.

I choke on my coffee. 'That might not be a bad idea for next time. Hey, we could even do both! Dancing and sea shanties. The guests would love it, very traditional.'

'No, their sea shanties are super rude, Dee. You wouldn't want them singing about hairy balls and busty fair maidens to a load of fancy, well-to-do cruise guests. Imagine the horror.' Suzie makes a face and we explode into fits of laughter.

'Ladies, please. Stop talking about balls in front of the guests.'

Suzie and I exchange glances and explode again, even Miriam manages a little giggle. The guests are still on the cruise ship.

'Miriam,' I say in an even tone. 'It's time.' I tap my watch and point to the dancers. Miriam nods and Suzie beams at me before making her way over to the band and dancers, a few moments later the band begins to play.

The dancers get into position.

Five, four, three, two, one.

It's show time.

'Let's do this,' Suzie and I chorus.

The music, combined with the smell of the sea air and the excitement of the event, gives me the most intense goosebumps. I watch the dancers perform their beautiful, striking dance as the guests begin to filter out onto their balconies. Some guests still yawning in their dressing gowns, their faces a mixture of joy, surprise and curiosity.

I'm sure a lot of places include a special welcome but some are bound to make more of an effort than others and we have certainly pulled out all the stops. One hundred dancers including break dancers, children and adults wearing seven brightly coloured outfits give us the performance of their lives to a live band. I'm so proud, because I choreographed it.

I was asked to help during a panicked, grovelling phone call from Miriam on an early Sunday morning. I was so hungover so I probably didn't sound exactly enthusiastic. Miriam apologised for her grumpiness towards me, explaining that she's suffering badly with menopause symptoms which cause her horrible mood swings. I sympathised with her, then counted to thirteen in my head before telling her that I would be happy to help as long as she spoke to me respectfully because I didn't appreciate the way she spoke to me when I worked for her. She agreed and apologised again. Win win.

The tour I'd written all those months ago that Miriam liked, was merely a tamed down version of this. Except it was to be performed for tourists down at the beach, once they'd had their obligatory free drink at the Mermaid's Lair, of course. We involved the local dance schools but Miriam wanted more dancers, *more professional ones* she'd said, so I roped in a few of my old friends from dance school as well a few of their friends. I've heard that Claudia Rivers from the contemporary Elite dance school was going to come down and watch as a few of her dancers are involved, but I haven't seen her yet. The last time we communicated was her telling me via email that it was a big fat no.

'Right, the surfers, are they ready?' Miriam asks Suzie.

'They should be starting any minute now.'

'The weather's perfect, just the right amount of wind.' I hold my hand up to my eyes and squint towards the beach. A sea of black, white and red wet suits sprint towards the ocean, each with a colourful surfboard in hand. My breath is almost taken away as they each catch a wave at precisely the same time then take it in turns to perform a series of flips and acrobatics, dancing with the surfboard, the wind and sea. It's beautiful. 'Wow, that takes some skill,' I say to Suzie, as Miriam goes over to bend the security guard's ears about the crowds getting too close.

'Yeah, they're phenomenal. Not bad looking a few of them either.' She winks.

'I'll have to get a closer look later.'

'Still single?'

'Yeah, been talking to a few boys but nothing special, everyone's so busy and career driven.'

'You must be living the dream in London though.'

'Yeah, I am,' I admit. 'It's definitely not boring. I enjoy the lifestyle but I'm not sure if I'll be there forever.'

'Oooh, are you coming back to Coolsbay?'

'I'll never say never. Coffee?'

'Definitely.'

Suzie and I head to the fresh coffee stand near the beach to watch the rest of the performance, joining in with the crowd's whoops and cheers. An hour later the guests begin to exit the cruise ship, swarming the town and the beach with their smiles and thick wallets. We spend the next couple of hours chatting to the dancers before the crowds disperse.

'Hey, if we keep getting ships in like this, it will do wonders for Coolsbay's economy,' I say quietly to Suzie.

'Delilah Thomas?' A petite, well-groomed lady with a posh London accent holds her perfectly manicured hand out to me.

'Yes?'

'Hello, Claudia Rivers, from Contemporary Elite Dance Company. Your manager told me that you choreographed the dance.' Shitsticks. I refrain from explaining that Miriam is no longer my manager and hasn't been for a while.

'Hello, nice to meet you,' I say, shaking her tiny, elegant hand. 'Did you enjoy the performance?'

'Yes, very much so. Choreographed many other events?' she asks, with a swish of the hand.

'No, but I am a trained dancer. I actually auditioned to dance at your school not too long ago.'

'Oh, did you?' I watch her face study me, trying to remember.

'It's okay, I don't expect you to remember me.' Because it was a truly awful audition. 'I didn't get in but you sent a very kind email and told me to try again.' I smile. 'I think I actually might pursue chorography. Now that I have this event under my belt, I have something to show for it.'

'Well, jolly good for you, you should do just that and if you ever need any advice or contacts, because I have many,' she says, handing me a pristine business card, 'then please feel free to drop me a line or two.'

'Thank you, so much, I will.'

'See you soon.' Claudia glides off into the crowds and I bite my lip at the excitement of it all. When she says she has contacts, she means she pretty much knows everyone in the West End.

'Who was that?' Suzie asks, as she comes back with another coffee and a slice of cake for us.

'She owns a dance school, her dancers dance for all the West End shows.'

'Wow that's cool, did she like our show?'

'Yes, she did.' I grin.

My phone vibrates inside my pocket, it's probably my flatmates arranging another night out. They are party animals, which although I enjoy, it isn't quite my scene so much these days. I've got into all that hippy yoga stuff that my brother introduced me to, I've even bought a few crystals. I know, I'm one of those now but I enjoy it, it helps to make me feel calm. I am amused that I introduced Dylan to murder documentaries and he introduced me to yoga but there we go.

Unknown Number: *Hey, how are you? So I've been wondering… if you're free to catch up? X*

My stomach drops, should I play it cool and wait a few hours? I check the calendar on my phone just to make sure. No. I've already waited, six months to be exact. That's long enough. I don't remember giving him my phone number. Molly. I bet she gave it to him. I told her about our exchange of messages and she said that I must give him my phone number in case I get locked out of my social media for whatever reason. My dear friend, always worrying about the minor details. Luckily there's been no spreadsheet gate with her new boyfriend, that gate has stayed locked so far.

Me: *Hi Byron, nice to hear from you. I am actually in town. Would be nice to meet up. X*

'Good, because that would have been a bit awkward if you'd said no.' A slightly croaky, warm voice comes out of nowhere, it gives me instant chills. Standing the other side of the fresh coffee stand is a very tanned, very toned, gorgeous looking Byron in a red, white and black wet suit.

He takes his sun glasses off and gives me the slowest, sexiest grin.

'Oh my…'

1 month later

Amber

My heart explodes as he walks through the door, just as it does every time that I see him. I can't imagine that sensation ever wearing off because, let's be honest, it never really went away. I watch him fuss over Loki and Olive, both beside themselves with excitement to see their master. He laughs a joyful laugh as their waggy tails go mad for him before making his way over to plant a tingling kiss on my lips as the dogs still fuss and jump around him, encapsulating how I'm feeling.

This time it's different. The feelings, if at all possible, run much deeper than when we were young, so much for taking it slow, although we have tried to.

And failed, desperately.

Sofia has not long been told about us. I waited until the school summer holidays to tell her because we didn't want Dylan to still be teaching her, that's not to say some of the mums hadn't worked it out though. That includes Jayne, who I now see regularly as Sofia is best friends with her daughter, Mia. I was bracing myself for the worst with Sofia but as always, she completely surprised me, she was so happy to have Dylan in her life still. It helps that she knows him and they get on so well, she even made him another card as a kind of welcome to the family but this time without the shitting reindeers, her drawing skills have come on a little since then.

Dylan and I have both grown as people, but predominately I've grown to love myself and not spend so much time and energy worrying about what others think. What they think of me, after all, is not my business and if they want to edit their image of me in their minds and make me have thinner arms, then that's up to them but I won't be hiding them, they are fully out, waving and flapping. Those bloody photographers gave me a complex for so long.

Not anymore.

'Hey, how was it?'

'It was great, she did a tremendous job with the dancers again. The whole event was quite breath taking to watch, there were some amazing break dancers this time,' Dylan says, as he sits down next to me on the brown leather sofa. Loki and Olive jump up onto the sofa and rest a nose on either side of his legs, both sets of eyes staring up at him.

'Aww that's really great, such a shame I had to work again, but maybe next time, hey.' It's Coolsbay's second cruise ship this summer, apparently there was a last-minute change of port and Delilah was drafted in to make it extra special for the guests again.

I don't actually live here at Dylan's house but when I don't have Sofia, I basically do. I've got a job now, too. I'm a receptionist at the local vets, working school hours, so it's just perfect for me. I've also completed a little course in dog walking, which I now do on the side. It wasn't hard to find customers as I know plenty of people who have dogs in Coolsbay.

The next step is to complete my dog grooming course and then finally get premises to work from. It may take a little while, possibly even longer than planned now but I know I'll get there eventually and when I do, it will be fantastic. I have a plan, a vision, I have a new purpose. Life is about to get ridiculously busy, but in a good way.

This time, I won't be rattling around a big house cleaning, polishing and fixing all day long just waiting for a *well done*. This time I'll be doing some stuff for me and looking after my baby. It's just like that lady with the little black poodle once said to me on a dog walk: *Life's too short, you have to do the thing, kiss the man, go for that job and wear that dress because you never know what's around the corner.* I can proudly say that I'm doing all of those things now and much more.

Since Tamsin has cut down her hours for a better work/life balance Stella has expressed that she is keen to join me on my business venture too so when I start my dog grooming course, she is going to do the same.

Dylan rests his hand on my thigh and an electrical jolt races up my leg, I can't wait to get him into bed later. My libido is through the roof these days.

'Well, now that the cruise lines know we're here, I think we'll see more of them. Coolsbay is a bit of an enigma, isn't it?'

'Yes, I suppose it is, just like you.' I tease, a little running joke we still have about him disappearing all those years ago. I said it would be much harder to do that now and I'd definitely track him down. But in the nineties most people just had a house phone and that was it, the internet was only just becoming a thing and there were only three people in my year at school with a mobile phone.

'Have you called him yet?' Dylan asks, studying my face.

'No, not yet, I wanted to wait for you, not to hold my hand but yes to basically hold my hand.' We both laugh, albeit a little nervously. He's nervous too, he doesn't want to get on the wrong side of him, I can tell.

'He'll be alright, he has to be.'

'I know, it just feels weird, I mean I could just not tell him, it's not actually any of his business. I'm sure Sofia would deliver the news just fine but I want to keep some kind of amicable relationship with him and keep some integrity and respect for myself. At the end of the day, he is the father of my child and for the most part, an okay human being.' When he wasn't cheating on his wife and being a quietly controlling slave driver.

'He never deserved you.'

'Neither did you,' I tease.

'No, you're right, I didn't,' he says, dropping another kiss on my lips.

'Right, let's get this over with.' I grab my phone off the coffee table and hover my finger over his name, Sofia is at my mum and dad's so no chance of her hearing him shout. I can imagine his face and the vein bulging on his forehead already. The phone starts ringing and I get up and pace around the living room.

'Hi, Filipe.'

'Ola Amber, how can I help you? Is Sofia okay?' This is how he deals with me now, like I'm one of his clients and not a very important one either. It has its pros and cons and if I think about it, isn't all that different to our marriage, except this time, I'm not letting him be the boss of me.

'Yes, yes, she's fine but I wasn't calling about Sof,' I say, pacing into the kitchen.

'Oh, then why are you calling?' There's a long pause. 'Babe, who is it?' Stephanie squeaks in the background.

Well, I guess she'll be finding out now too then, she won't be happy about it, especially considering the amount I'm getting from the divorce. I'm sure she knows; she's been extra cold recently on the drop offs and pick-ups. Filipe said he won't be telling her but she could easily rummage around and find out for herself.

'Well, I wanted to tell you some news before you hear it from anyone else.'

'What news?'

'I'm pregnant. It's early days and a bit of a surprise but we're very happy. Sofia knows and she is very excited at the prospect of having a little brother or sister to play with.' I take a deep breath in and hold it.

'You're pregnant?'

Uh oh, there's no doubt that the vein is now bulging.

'I am, yes,' I say, fighting the urge to ask him if that is okay. It's more than okay and I don't have to ask him permission for anything anymore.

'Good for you, I know you always wanted another one. Well done.' Well, that wasn't the response I was expecting but then I remember, I'm his client now and he's acting professionally.

'Oh my God,' Stephanie screeches, before Filipe shushes her. I hope she doesn't end up being too much for him.

'Thank you, Filipe,' I say, with an even tone.

'You're welcome, now I must go, Stephanie has cooked my favourite, you know, beef stroganoff.'

'Ahh yes, how could I forget,' I say, holding back a snigger. 'Okay, well enjoy your dinner,' I manage, without giggling. I hang up and slide my phone back into my pocket.

'Well, that seemed to go okay? No raised voices,' Dylan comments, raising an eyebrow as I pad back into the living room. He gives me a lop-sided grin, because I'm laughing.

'Yeah, surprisingly. It couldn't have gone better.'

'I'm proud of you.'

'Thanks, also I think I know what I want to call my dog salon now.'

'Yeah?'

'Yeah. How do you think *The Dog's Dinner* sounds?'

Dylan throws his head back, laughing that wonderful laugh as I grin and bend down to stroke Olive, her big brown eyes gaze back up at me and I nuzzle my face into her fur. I love this bloody hound. I hope she knows that.

'I think it sounds perfect.' Dylan pulls me up onto my feet and moves his hands onto my slightly swollen bump, his face lights up, still getting used to the idea, still really exciting and new. Our whirlwind, second time around romance that has spiralled so quickly has morphed into our very own baby.

A sister or brother for Sofia.

It was meant to be.

'*Dog's Dinner.* Yeah. I mean, how could I not call it that? I owe almost everything to Olive and her impeccable detective skills, she was trying to lead me to Stephanie from the first moment she ate that dinner off her lap, sniffing out Stephanie's knickers, crying and howling on the ring doorbell, seeing you at our spot on the dog walk on Boxing Day. All of those things inadvertently led me away from him and right back to you. Time and time again.' I laugh and stroke his face. And I still thought it was poor old Jayne, what a complete idiot I was, she's actually become quite a good friend.

'And the fact I was Sofia's teacher?' He grins.

'Yes, that had something to do with it, but if it wasn't for this pooch, you would have just stayed as Sofia's teacher because sadly, I may have stayed with Filipe for a lot longer.'

'And what an awful shame that would have been.'

'Truly bloody awful.' My stomach begins to whirl and pop as Dylan starts to kiss my neck. Our beautiful little baby forming and growing, just like our everlasting love for each other.

The End.

From the author

Thank you so much for reading my book, I really do appreciate it. I'm an Indie Author, part of a small family run imprint (Tamarillas Press) so not backed by a big publishing company. Every time a reader buys one of my books, I am genuinely thrilled.

If you've enjoyed my book then please feel free to post your review on goodreads, Amazon or both. I cherish every rating and review, they really do make my day and encourage other potential readers to try my books.

We've worked hard to eliminate typos and errors but if you spot any please let us know.
TamarillasPress@outlook.com
Belle Henderson

Belle Henderson

Belle Henderson loves to read and write. She lives with her family and her rambunctious beagle in Wiltshire. She absolutely loves hearing from readers so please feel free to connect with her via email or on social media.

Email: **bellehendersonauthor@gmail.com**
Instagram: Instagram.com/bellehendersonauthor/
Facebook: facebook.com/bellehendersonauthor/
Goodreads:https://www.goodreads.com/author/show/189996 02.Belle_Henderson
Tiktok: https://vm.tiktok/ZMesW9RQA

What happens when you find yourself
homeless and relationshipless?

YOU
GROW
GIRL

BELLE HENDERSON

Tilly has her invite but he's. . .

NOT The *plus* One

BELLE HENDERSON

BELLE HENDERSON

What's
eating
FELICITY
FROST?

A quirky tale of love, forgiveness
and finding your people

BELLE HENDERSON

Livin' La Vida Lockdown

Life got hard but then love got interesting

BELLE HENDERSON
& CJ MORROW

We can Work it out

Two people,
one
opportunity

Printed in Great Britain
by Amazon